THE WILL

Rebecca Reid

PENGUIN BOOKS

TRANSWORLD PUBLISHERS
Penguin Random House, One Embassy Gardens,
8 Viaduct Gardens, London SW11 7BW
www.penguin.co.uk

Transworld is part of the Penguin Random House group of companies
whose addresses can be found at global.penguinrandomhouse.com

Penguin
Random House
UK

First published in Great Britain in 2022 by Penguin Books
an imprint of Transworld Publishers

A CIP catalogue record for this book
is available from the British Library.

ISBN
9780552177399

Typeset in 12 / 14.5pt Dante MT Std by Jouve (UK), Milton Keynes.
Printed and bound in Great Britain by Clays Ltd, Elcograf S.p.A.

The authorized representative in the EEA is Penguin Random House Ireland,
Morrison Chambers, 32 Nassau Street, Dublin D02 YH68.

Penguin Random House is committed to a sustainable
future for our business, our readers and our planet. This book
is made from Forest Stewardship Council® certified paper.

Rebecca Reid is the author of the novels *Perfect Liars*, *Truth Hurts* and *Two Wrongs*, and the non-fiction book *The Power of Rude*. She is a freelance journalist and columnist for the *Telegraph*'s women's section and a regular contributor to *Telegraph Culture*. She is the former digital editor of *Grazia* magazine and has previously written for *Stylist*, the *Independent*, the *Guardian*, *The Times*, *Marie Claire*, the *New Statesman* and *Glamour* magazine. She regularly contributes to *Good Morning Britain*, *Sky News* and various BBC radio programmes. She holds an MA in Creative Writing from Royal Holloway.

www.penguin.co.uk

Also by Rebecca Reid

PERFECT LIARS
TRUTH HURTS
TWO WRONGS

For Pom

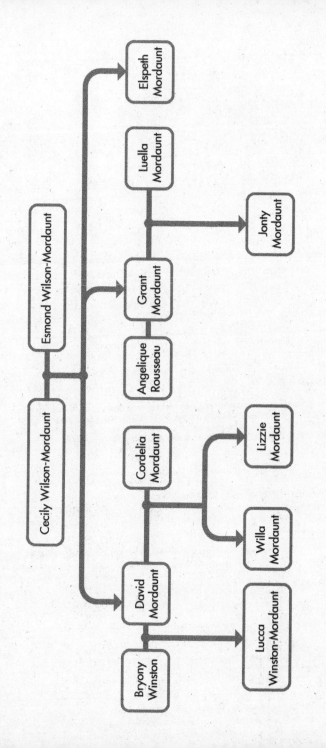

Roxborough Hall is an enormous house. Too big, really. Every person who has lived there in the last two hundred years has claimed that they'll be the last, that no one could possibly want to be saddled with this place. Fifteen bedrooms. Servants' quarters. A library, two kitchens, a small sitting room, a large sitting room, a drawing room, a dining room – the list goes on. Running Roxborough is no joke. It's a full-time job. A burden. A millstone. Inheriting it means tying one's entire life to the place.

And yet, they all want it.

No one is entirely sure when Roxborough Hall was gifted to the Mordaunt family. Some claim it was Henry VIII; others that it was Elizabeth I. It doesn't particularly matter. What matters is that, unlike most of these houses, crushed by death duties or destroyed by requisition, Roxborough still stands. There's a strange sort of pattern with the house, that whoever inherits it seems to live a surprisingly long and fruitful life. Of course, no one in the family is foolish enough to think that the house is magic. But it can't be denied that, in every generation, the owner has died peacefully in their own bed.

The far stranger thing about Roxborough is how it is inherited. Its first owner, William Mordaunt, was a surprisingly modern man. Or perhaps he just didn't like his sons. For whatever reason, William decided to do away with primogeniture. Instead, he left the house to his beloved niece. She left it to her second son, allegedly a far kinder and gentler man than his elder brother. At some point before their death, the current owner of the house would select a member of the family they deemed most worthy, or perhaps most in need, and leave the house to them.

Sometime in the eighteenth century, when a particularly dramatic Mordaunt had pierced the veil, a dinner was held on the night of her funeral. Each member of the family was given a letter explaining why they had or had not been left the house. And while there was something undeniably cathartic about the evening, it also solved any feeling of ill will. Anyone who felt they should inherit the house but had not was able to understand why. And so the tradition went on. The Victorians, with their love of death, adored the ceremony of it, and while the modern Mordaunts might profess to find the whole thing bizarre, it's in their blood.

Besides which, while none of them will admit it, they are all desperately hoping that the house is going to be theirs.

1958

The preparation for 'the family' to arrive had taken weeks. Miss Cecily was going to be twenty-one, and her aunt and uncle had decided that she should have her birthday party at Roxborough. She and her parents and her brother were going to stay a week, and then, on the 21 December – Cecily's birthday – all the great and grand from London and from the local area would be invited for a party. Violet couldn't imagine what two hundred people would look like when they were all in one room, but she had been told that the ballroom, which hadn't been used for two years, was going to be opened.

'Are you busy?' Mrs Hanson asked Violet, who was sitting in the back kitchen a week before the party, reading a magazine. Violet jumped up. 'No need to look so guilty,' Mrs Hanson said with a smile. 'I was just wondering if you wanted an extra job? I remembered that you'd trained at that smart place in London where they taught you how to do hair.'

Violet felt a little bead of excitement in her stomach.

She'd taken a two-day course in hair and make-up, and since she'd been at Roxborough (admittedly only a couple of weeks), she'd had absolutely no chance to use her newly acquired skills. Mrs Mordaunt was kind, but she mostly liked her horses and dogs. She viewed the Queen Mother as the height of sophistication and didn't like to be 'mucked about with'.

Violet was on her feet in a moment. 'I'd like that,' she said.

'Lovely. Miss Cecily is in the Orange Room.'

The Orange Room wasn't orange, but it had wallpaper with little orange blossoms on it. Violet had quite quickly realized that the names of the rooms rarely had anything to do with what they actually looked like.

Violet knocked on the door. 'I'm naked, but you can come in!' Cecily shouted from inside. Violet froze, not sure what she was supposed to do with that information. She waited a moment, and then opened the door. To her relief, the girl who was sitting on the enormous four-poster bed was not naked at all. 'Sorry.' She smiled. 'Old joke. We used to say it at finishing school.'

'Mrs Hanson said you might want help with your hair.'

'Yes, please,' Cecily said, jumping to her feet. 'In London I just go to the hairdresser whenever I have to look presentable, but I don't think that would be a good idea around here unless I wanted a blue rinse.'

Violet giggled. 'No. What would you like?'

They shared ideas and eventually Violet concocted a

surprisingly sophisticated updo. It made Cecily's neck look even longer than it was. 'Gosh,' Cecily said, looking in the mirror. 'You are clever. I look marvellous. Oh no, don't look like that. I know you're not supposed to say that sort of thing about yourself, but you know what I mean. I look nice. Nicer than I was expecting. I'm not vain, you know. I used to get teased at school for being vain but, actually, I'm just aware of my own shortcomings. I'm not very pretty naturally so I have to work jolly hard to look half decent.'

Violet wanted to disagree. Cecily *was* pretty. Extremely pretty. She had a ski-jump nose and a short top lip, huge eyes and unfairly generous lashes. She looked like she should be in the pictures. But it seemed wrong to argue. 'I'm glad you like it,' Violet said shyly.

'Will you do it for my party at the end of the week?'

'Oh, you'll want to have someone professional do it, won't you?'

'No,' Cecily said resolutely. 'I want you to do it. Just like this, or maybe even bigger. We've got to knock Esmond's socks off.'

'Who's Esmond?'

'I'm going to marry him.'

'You're engaged?'

'No. We've only met twice. But he's coming to the party and he's going to propose once he gets to know me. Do you want some?' She offered Violet a glass of the champagne she had been drinking. Her pink lipstick had stained the side of the glass. Violet took it and sipped, unsure whether or not she was allowed to. But then, when else was she going to get to drink champagne and talk about romantic prospects with someone so grand and wealthy as Cecily?

They chatted about Esmond and how the wedding would be until the dressing gong went and Violet jumped to her feet. 'I've got to go and help with supper,' she said. 'There's only five of us downstairs so we have to do lots of different things.'

Cecily kissed Violet on the cheek. 'You're an angel,' she said. Violet drank in the scent of roses and gardenias. She tried to remember what it smelled like all evening.

Cecily adopted Violet as her new best friend for the week. She would come down to the kitchen whenever Violet was peeling something or washing up, sit on the table or the counter and talk to her about life in London and films she'd seen and boys she would marry if Esmond didn't marry her. On the morning of her party, she came downstairs holding a pearl necklace. It was long and at the back there was a diamond clip in the shape of two 'C's. 'It's actually for Chanel,' she said. 'But I'm pretending that it's "C" for Cecily. I've got to wear it tonight because my parents gave it to me for my birthday. Will you wear it for me today?'

Violet was confused. 'Why?'

'Pearls get prettier if they've been worn. They like the oils from your skin or something, and they're nicer when they're warm. Anyway, I've got to go riding and then have a long, long bath. So, will you wear them for me to get them ready?'

Violet laughed. 'All right.' And so, she went about the rest of the day preparing for the party with Cecily's Chanel diamonds and pearls around her neck, under her dress. Later that evening, when she had put the finishing touches to Cecily's eyeliner – a perfect angular black wing along her lids, brushing her thick black eyelashes – she handed the necklace back.

'Do I look all right?' Cecily asked. The dress was a shocking fuchsia pink with a huge silk tulle skirt and no straps. Violet wondered what it was like not to wear a bra in front of other people but didn't like to ask.

'You look wonderful,' she said honestly.

'Thank you,' Cecily said. Then clipped the necklace on, checked her lipstick and disappeared downstairs.

Violet didn't want to watch the party from the sidelines; it seemed rather sad. So, she stayed downstairs, helping with anything that was needed. The Mordaunts had hired a team of party planners to do most of it, so it was largely out of their hands. She couldn't quite understand why she felt so morose. She had liked doing things for Cecily, it was true. But they had only been friends for a week. There was absolutely no reason to be so disappointed at the idea that she might not see Cecily again.

The next morning, she watched Cecily and her family leave in a fleet of black cars, standing at her bedroom window and feeling terribly dramatic. She scolded herself as she felt tears pricking in her eyes. Was she going to form this kind of attachment to everyone who came to the house? Of course not. She was just being silly.

Six months later, Violet got a letter on thick cream paper with pale blue edges. She tore it open, knowing instinctively who it would be from.

Violet [it read, in enormous loopy handwriting] *Esmond DID propose, just like I said he would. We're going to get married in three months (no, not for THAT reason, we just think it would be nice to be married soon). Then we're going to live at his house in Chelsea, which is a bit poky, but I think it could be very nice if he lets me redecorate it, which he will. Anyway, I'm writing because I've asked my aunt and uncle and they've said it's all right, so now I can ask you. Will you come and live with us and help me? I don't know what job it would be or how much I would pay you, but it'll be LOTS more than you get at the moment because I've got no idea how you run a house or do anything really and you'll have to teach me. Will you come as soon as we're back from honeymoon? PLEASE SAY YES.*

Violet folded the paper and pretended to herself that she needed to think about it, but there was not even the tiniest shadow of a doubt in her mind that of course she was going to say yes.

1
2022

It was a funny business, helping someone else die. Violet had spent weeks waiting for Cecily to leave her, arranging everything down to the finest detail. She had come to feel comfortable with the strange feeling in the house. Her own mother, long dead, had once said that when someone was dying it 'unsettled the spirits'. Violet had thought that nonsense, but while Cecily lay in the twilight between life and death, she realized that her mother had been right. After Cecily died – with as much dignity as was possible, and in her own bed, as she had always intended – Violet opened a window, as if to let something out, and then lit a candle. She held Cecily's cool hand and called the undertaker. She even watched her body being carried away in the rude black bag without a flicker of discomfort. And then, finally, it was time to do what she had been dreading the most: summon Cecily's family.

Grant first. The most-loved, younger son, now an ageing playboy with a taste for beautiful younger women. Then Grant's son, Jonty, a vet, and the only one of the family who lived near Roxborough. David, Cecily's dutiful, pompous elder son, who would have his even more pompous wife Bryony in tow, and their son Lucca, who would presumably rather be anywhere else. Willa and Lizzie, David's daughters from his first marriage, Cecily's adored granddaughters. Finally, Elspeth, who didn't pick up the call, or acknowledge it at all. And now they were all on their way to shatter the quiet, delicate bubble of grief in which Violet had lived for the last few weeks. Descending from their various homes, coming to see who was going to be the next owner of Roxborough.

David flicked the indicator and glanced over his left shoulder. Pointless, because the suitcases were piled so high in the back he couldn't see anything. His son, Lucca, resplendent in a booster seat, which David wasn't really sure he still needed at the age of nine, was flanked by enormous bags either side of him. Still, the car was the only 'screen time' he was allowed, so David sensed he wouldn't be complaining.

'Where are you going?' Bryony asked. 'It's straight on.'

Quashing the desire to reply, *It's my parents' house, I bloody well know how to get there*, David put on a smile. 'I'm turning off for the station.'

'The station? Why?'

Bryony was talking over the radio play that David had been enjoying and he sensed that this was going to develop into an argument, which would mean missing out on the denouement. 'To pick up the girls.'

'Why on earth are we doing that?'

Was it this next turn? Or the one after? Four decades of doing this drive and he never could remember. 'Because they need a lift to the house.'

Bryony reached over and flicked the indicator on the far side. 'That's ridiculous. It'll add forty-five minutes at least to go into the centre of town and back out. They can get a cab.' Bryony was dialling on her mobile before David could say anything. And he supposed she was probably right. It had already been a monstrous journey. His left foot was cramping on the clutch. It would be quicker and easier for the girls to get a cab and meet them at the house. They were, after all, about to spend ages together.

Willa's voice came over the car speaker. 'Hello?'

'Willa, it's Bryony.'

'I know.'

'Your father and I have had a terrible journey. You don't mind getting a taxi, do you?'

A brief pause told David that Willa did mind, very much. 'Not at all,' she said.

'Lovely. Your father will pay you back.'

'That's really OK.' Willa sounded almost amused. Given that she was a lawyer at a top firm in the city, David sensed she probably wouldn't mind turning Bryony's offer down.

'And liaise with Lizzie?'

'Of course.'

'There,' said Bryony as they rejoined the motorway. 'Much easier. Honestly, what would you do without me?'

'I hope I never have to find out,' David replied, putting his hand on Bryony's toned thigh. The detective with the silly French accent in the radio play was about to make an accusation. Bryony pushed the off button. 'Do you mind, darling? I'm getting a bit of a headache.'

'Of course not.' David smiled, eyes on the road.

In a dirtier car a few miles behind David and Bryony, there was another couple making the same journey. Only Grant and Angelique were having an enormous row.

'Why the fuck did you ask me to come?' said Angelique, twisting in her seat, reaching into the back of the car to find her handbag. 'Just let me out on the side of the road and I'll find my own way back to London.'

'Don't be so fucking stupid. You'd be killed.'

'Perhaps that would be better than spending a week with you in the middle of nowhere in some freezing house with terrible wine and terrible food.'

'You didn't have to come!'

Grant swerved into the fast lane and put his foot down as hard as he could. The old car couldn't do much to get a shift on, but Angelique still took a sharp intake of breath. 'I would be safer on the side of the road than with you, you shit!'

When they'd first met, Grant had marvelled at how much better English swear words sounded in Angelique's French accent. And it had transpired to be lucky that he liked them because he heard an awful lot of them. She was going through her handbag, throwing out old bits of plastic, receipts, lighters, hair ties, paperback books, all over the car. 'Do you have to be so French all the bloody time?' Grant said, swerving back into the middle lane, cutting up a neat navy SUV. The driver of the navy car smartly tooted his horn and Grant, without thinking about it, sounded his back. Only once he'd taken his hand off the horn did he turn to look at the car and realize that it was being driven by a man whose profile he would recognize anywhere. 'Oh Jesus,' he groaned.

Angelique followed his gaze. 'David?'

'And Bryony. And their kid.'

Angelique smiled. 'I should be sweet to you.'

'Why's that?'

'A weekend with your brother is going to be punishment enough.'

Grant smiled back. 'You're going to have to be very, very nice to me.' He stole a glance across the car to Angelique's long, tanned legs in cut-off denim shorts. There was a tiny band of tanned flesh between the waistband and the white T-shirt she was wearing. 'Still.' Grant smiled. 'David is going to be monstrously jealous. He was so proud of his "much younger wife". But Bryony's got nothing on you.'

'I didn't realize she was so much younger than him.'

'Eight years.'

Angelique raised one eyebrow in a moment of perfect judgement, without needing to say anything. She had spent enough family gatherings with Bryony to know that they were never going to be friends. And

Bryony was cruel enough to her stepdaughters that Angelique didn't feel the need to be kind. 'Perhaps it's looking after all those schoolgirls.' She smiled. 'It must be ageing.'

'We should count ourselves lucky that he's shacked up with Bryony.'

'Oh?'

'My mother couldn't stand her.'

'And that's a good thing?'

Grant saw the turning for Roxborough village and indicated, sliding across the lanes. 'A very good thing. Mum adored his first wife. If she hadn't died, Cordelia and David would have been a shoo-in to get the house. But she didn't want Bryony getting her hands on it, understandably.'

'So, you think it's going to be you?' Angelique studied Grant's profile, his perfect Roman nose, his salt-and-pepper hair. His linen shirt was unbuttoned and his skin tanned from their summer of lying in the garden, drinking rosé and reading. How strange this English family was, tangling the sadness of losing a parent with the competition for who inherits the house they all inexplicably loved so much. What would their life look like, she wondered, if Grant did inherit it?

'I don't know,' Grant replied after a moment of consideration. 'Mum was unpredictable. It could be any of us.'

'Apart from David?'

'Apart from David.'

★

14

Willa pulled her cardigan around her, not that it made any difference. When she'd dressed back at the flat that morning it had been stifling. But here at the train station the wind rushed along the tracks, stripping the warmth from the air. She watched yet another train pull into the platform and scanned the people getting off, praying that her sister would be one of them. Eventually, she felt hands on her waist, trying to tickle her. She jumped sideways. 'Jesus, Lizzie,' she muttered.

'Just looking for your sense of humour,' Lizzie said with a smile. Her hair, always chest-length and gloriously blonde, had got even longer. She was dressed even less appropriately than Willa herself, her arms and legs mostly bare under a patterned silk dress.

'You could have told me which train you were getting. I've been waiting here for half an hour.'

Lizzie linked her arm through Willa's. 'My battery died.'

'It's going to say "my battery died" on your tombstone,' Willa replied, without thinking. 'Sorry,' she added.

'Don't be. Granny would have thought that was hilarious. Where's Dad?'

'Bryony called. They need us to get a taxi.'

'Of course they do.'

'Can we go to Roxborough, please?' Willa asked the taxi driver.

He rolled the window down a bit further. 'Roxborough? What bit?'

15

Willa had had this exchange before and always found it faintly embarrassing. 'Roxborough Hall. On Roxborough Lane.' The taxi driver raised one eyebrow but gestured for her to get in.

Lizzie tugged open the boot, getting dirt all over her hands. She wiped them on her dress, shoving her bags in. 'I don't know how you pack so little,' she told Willa, who was standing with a neat little suitcase.

'I don't think we're going to need much. Jeans and T-shirts for the week, a black dress for the funeral.'

'Oh, fuck.'

Willa got into the taxi and put her seatbelt on. 'You're not going to say that you forgot to bring a black dress?'

Lizzie smiled guiltily. 'I know, I know, I'm the worst.'

'We'll have to go into Norwich one afternoon. I'll drive you, if Dad will lend us the car.'

'I think we both know Bryony wouldn't let that happen.'

'Well, we'll have to do something. You can't go to the funeral wearing a kaftan.'

Lizzie laughed. 'It's not a kaftan, it's a dress. And I can borrow something of Granny's.'

'You can't steal her clothes!'

'Why not? She doesn't need them any more. Don't look like that – you know she wouldn't have minded.'

Lizzie was probably right. Granny wouldn't have denied Lizzie anything. They'd been closer than close since Lizzie was a little girl.

Both girls looked out of their respective windows, watching the concrete give way to greenness. Willa opened the window and smelled the sweet air, always the same smell, always so different and infinitely better than London.

'It's going to be so weird. Getting there and Granny not being there.'

'I know,' Lizzie replied.

The girls had visited at least once a month throughout their childhood. Every time they arrived, Cecily would bustle to the kitchen door – no one ever used the front door – and gather them into her arms. Cecily had been a glorious grandmother, indulgent and exciting. When they were little, taking them to see fireflies in the garden or frogspawn in the pond. When they were older, regaling them with wild stories about her own youth and teaching them how to choose wine.

'I wish we'd known she was ill,' said Lizzie.

'That wasn't how she did things,' Willa replied. 'You know that. Anyway, who else is coming tonight?'

'Dad and Bryony are on their way,' Lizzie said. 'Grant and his girlfriend.'

'Sofie?'

'No, Sofie was ages ago. Angelique. She came for, like, half an hour last Christmas.'

Willa had missed Christmas. It was still something of a sore spot. But then she couldn't really blame her sister for being annoyed about it. She'd fobbed Lizzie off with a half-hearted excuse about work, unable to face telling her the truth. 'Is she nice?' she asked, trying to get away from Christmas.

'Yes. She can't stand Bryony. Are you going to come next Christmas? Or is it just a thing that you skip now?'

Willa had spent Christmas as a voluntary in-patient at the Crawford Centre. Most years, she managed to hold out until the summer and then spent her two-week summer holiday recovering, getting herself well enough that she could last another year. But last year, after it seemed like all of her best friends had got married or pregnant or bought houses with their boyfriends, and work was hideous, and Lizzie chaotic, she knew she would never make it through a Christmas surrounded by heaving tables and suffocating plates. So, she had made her excuses. Packed a small suitcase, devoid of the contraband that so many other patients always brought, and checked herself in. They gave her the same bedroom each time she visited – the same one she had slept in since her first visit, over a decade ago. The doctors knew her, and if they were disappointed in her for needing to come back, they didn't show it. It didn't really matter that it cost almost a thousand pounds a week, draining her entire savings account. 'Of course I'll be there at Christmas,' she said, hoping it was true.

'Good.'

'I'm pretty sure Elspeth isn't coming for the funeral, by the way.'

'Obviously.'

'And Jonty isn't arriving until tomorrow morning, but I'm sure you knew that.'

'No. Why would I?'

'I thought you talked.'

'Not especially.' Lizzie took out a pouch of tobacco and started rolling a cigarette. 'How long have you got off work?'

'They've been nice. Said I could take a week to start with, more if I need to. Most of the cases I'm working on aren't terribly urgent. How about you?'

Lizzie stretched out her long brown legs and reached her arms to the roof of the car, knowing that what she was about to say would go down badly. 'They wouldn't give me any time off, so I jacked it in.' She had been working as a teaching assistant at a fancy London prep school for the last year. It was a ridiculous place where the children were called things like Rudolph and Caspian, but the staff were nice, the parents gave insanely generous presents at the end of every term, and she liked the grave, serious children she looked after.

'Oh, Lizzie.'

'Don't do that voice,' Lizzie snapped. Willa had an extraordinary ability to express disappointment without actually having to say anything. God, it was such a cliché: the hard-working, type-A older sister lecturing the free spirit. And, realistically, which of them was happier? Willa had more money and more stability, but Lizzie had been able to feel every rib when she'd hugged her earlier, and there was a hollow between her torso and her arms. Willa was clearly as bad again as she ever had been. So, the impressive job, the neatly maintained friendships and the beautiful flat clearly weren't everything she needed them to be.

'I thought you liked it there?' said Willa.

'I did.'

'You've never stayed anywhere that long.'

'So?'

'And one of the mums gave you a Chanel wallet at Christmas.'

'Yeah, I know, but I don't know what I'm going to be doing or where I'm going to be from now on. So, I had to quit. OK?'

Willa looked out of the window, watching the sun set over the wide, flat fields. So that was it. Lizzie had given up her job because she 'didn't know where she was going to be' in the future.

Which meant she thought she was getting the house.

2

Violet had been ready for them hours ago, each bedroom complete with clean sheets, dusted and hoovered by the cleaner who came in from the village, the bathrooms polished until they gleamed. Cecily had been determined that she wouldn't become 'one of those old women who can't see dirt'. Thousands and thousands of pounds a year went on keeping the entire place spotless, even though most of the bedrooms were empty from one month to another. In the winter, she and Cecily created a house within the house, eating in here – the little back kitchen – and watching television in the snug next door. That was the key to huge houses, Violet had learned, after travelling around with Cecily for decades. You had to make them into lots of smaller houses.

She lifted the heavy hotplate of the Aga and moved the kettle on to it, wondering when she had started needing both hands to manoeuvre the huge thing. It was half past six, so they wouldn't want tea. Wine, all of them. But it was easier to be prepared, and putting the tea things out gave her something to do with her hands. There was a crunch of gravel and the dogs – all four of them – began barking. *And so it begins*, she thought. Who would be first? She hoped it would be the girls.

'Hello?' a voice called from the front hallway. Of course, it had to be David.

She went up the stairs that led to the main hallway and saw that David had come in through the front door, almost never used. *Already playing lord of the manor*, Violet thought.

'Are we first here?' he asked, dragging bags from the back of his enormous car and bringing them into the hall.

'Yes,' Violet said. 'Haven't you got the girls?'

'They're getting a taxi,' said Bryony brightly. Violet smiled at her; awful woman. Cecily had taken against people easily and Violet had spent many evenings throughout their life together putting Cecily's clothes away while trying to persuade her to be a little more generous in her judgements. But when it came to Bryony, she had to admit that Cecily had been right.

'Is there anyone else here who can help?' David asked, looking Violet up and down. She somehow seemed to have aged a decade since he'd seen her last Christmas. There was no way she could cart bags up and down the enormous staircase.

'Tom will take the bags up.'

'Who's Tom?'

'A boy from the village. He does anything your mother and I can't. Couldn't.'

Dear God, thought David. *How many people are going to have to be given the axe once the house is handed over?* His mother had an enormous propensity to hire people from the local area and then claim it was some sort of charitable service, when in fact it was born from a desire to fill the house with people all the time. She had a long spiel about the house having 'responsibility' to provide employment, as if she had inherited the house in 1800, not in 1961.

'Leave the bags there and I'll get Tom to take them up. You're in the Blue Room, as usual, and Lucca has the Flower Room next door.'

'I hate flowers,' Lucca said, looking up from his iPad.

'He's tired from the journey.' Bryony smiled. 'Shall we go through?'

Violet fixed an expression of neutrality on her face and led the way back to the kitchen. 'Tea?' she asked. She saw David glance at the clock on the wall, trying to work out if he could claim it was too late for tea and thus be offered a glass of wine. Apparently not.

'Yes,' he replied. 'Black for me. Bryony likes one sugar.'

Violet had started to pour the milk when the dogs went off again. She put the jug down and went to the hall to find Grant chucking bags through the side door. He wrapped his arms around Violet. 'How are you, Vi?' he asked, his hands on her forearms. It seemed like he meant the question, which Violet found increasingly unusual.

'Carrying on.' She smiled. 'Your mother wouldn't have wanted a fuss.'

'Oh, I don't know. She could be quite the diva when she wanted to be.'

Violet laughed. 'You're quite right. And you've brought?' she asked, looking at the tall, olive-skinned woman behind Grant, trying desperately to remember if it was the same woman he had brought for a flying visit at Christmas. Grant had a type. They all rather blurred into one.

'Angelique,' she said. Her eyes were long and narrow, dark green-brown. Another beautiful girl for Grant to toy with. Or rather, to convince himself was 'the one' until he got another flight of fancy.

'Of course,' she said. 'We didn't meet properly at Christmas because you had to head off. I'm Violet, I am – I was . . .' She trailed off. She and Cecily had never quite found the right expression for it. When she had first come to the house, in 1958, she had been appointed as a lady's maid. She'd had an interview at a dark house on Eaton Square and then been given her train ticket a week later. She had arrived at the house with her suitcase, been picked up by what was then the chauffeur, and thrown into the middle of it all. Even in the sixties, having a maid was rather an anachronism. They had tried out different words over the years. In the eighties, when Cecily had watched *Dynasty* on the black-and-white telly in the snug, she had taken to calling Violet her 'assistant'. 'PA' had been the more modern choice, decades later. And recently, as Cecily's illness swept through her body, doctors and medical professionals who visited the house had assigned her yet another word: *carer*.

'She looked after Mum for practically her whole life,' Grant said, before Violet could choose a description. 'Mum was brilliant at lots of things but utterly useless at organizing her life. Vi practically ran everything. Shall we go and have a drink?'

Grant came back from the wine cellar with a bottle of expensive-looking red. When Esmond was alive, when he and Cecily were the co-heads of the family, there had been a blotter by the wine cellar. Whenever anyone took a bottle out, they were supposed to write down the date and a description of the wine. That had died with Esmond, years before Cecily had become frail. 'It's just old fruit juice,' she would say, yanking the cork from it.

'Who's thirsty?' Grant asked, looking around the room. David and Bryony were sitting together on the sofa, her hand proprietorially on his leg. Angelique was stroking one of the dogs, presumably to give her something to focus on. Violet was making a salad, at ease, unlike the rest of them.

'I'm certainly ready for a drink,' said David, pompous as ever. 'Like to see you've raided the cellar before you've so much as sat down.'

Grant took his brother's hand and shook it. 'Good to see you,' he said. 'Bryony,' he added, bumping his cheek against hers. 'You remember Angelique.'

'Lovely to see you again,' said Bryony. 'Welcome to Roxborough.'

Grant caught Violet's eye from across the room, both

equally nauseated by Bryony's presumption to welcome Angelique, who had about as much connection to the house as Bryony did. 'Where's Lucca?' he asked.

'Oh, he's reading in his bedroom,' Bryony said. 'We try to get him to stop, but he's just such a literature addict. He's only nine and he's determined to plough through another Dickens.'

'How nice,' said Angelique, sounding like she didn't mean it at all. Bryony found that this happened often, that people weren't excited or enthusiastic about all of Lucca's amazing abilities. Perhaps it was jealousy on Angelique's part. She didn't have any children of her own, which must be dreadfully lonely. David had claimed that she was quite successful in her own right, but Bryony knew that, like all women, Angelique would only be fulfilled if she had children. And she was wasting her time with Grant, two decades her senior and perpetually lurching from one scheme to another. She should settle down, find someone who would give her some stability.

Grant took five glasses from the cabinet and put them on the scrubbed wooden table, which had sat in the centre of this room for his entire life. Longer than that, actually.

'Five?' asked David.

'One, two, three, four, five.' Grant counted the people in the room.

'Oh, Violet, are you . . . ?' asked David.

Violet smiled. God, David was a pompous arse. She had eaten every meal of every day for the last two decades with his mother.

'You're not serious?' Grant snorted. 'Should she go and sit in the servants' quarters upstairs?'

'I didn't mean it like that. Violet, you know I didn't, I just wasn't sure if you would want to be with us all evening. You've got your own life . . .' His neck was turning red. 'I wasn't trying to—'

'You're very kind, David,' Violet said, crossing the room to take a wine glass. 'But I'm very glad to spend the evening with you all. It's been lonely since your mother passed.'

An uncomfortable silence fell over the room. 'I think I'll just go and check a couple of work emails before I start drinking,' Bryony announced. 'David, let's unpack while we're up there. It is a little early for a drink, after all.'

David followed Bryony into the dark hallway, up the first flight of stairs. It wasn't until they closed the bedroom door behind them that Bryony's face changed. 'I hate this room,' she said.

'I could ask to move.'

'For God's sake, don't do that. You'll upset her even more.'

'Who?'

'Violet.'

'Vi? She doesn't get upset.'

'Of course she does. She was furious, all that business with the wine glasses. Do you want her to think that you're an enormous snob?'

'I don't much care what she thinks of me.'

'You bloody should.'

'Why? She was my mother's maid.'

'She spent every single day of her life with your mother. She was the only person who knew Cecily was ill. You think she doesn't have an influence?'

'How could she have influence? Mum's dead. There's nothing to be done. It's all decided. This hideous dinner party after the funeral is a tradition, a formality.'

Bryony looked arch, standing in front of the huge window. The green of the garden behind them, with the lake in the distance, made her skin even more luminously pale. Her eyes, always blue, were especially sharp today. She was one of those rare women who truly seemed to become more beautiful with age. 'We can't afford to take any risks. You know how much we need this.' She wound her hands around David, under his shirt, feeling the warmth of his back. She pressed her body into his, enjoying, as she always did, the feeling of power that she got from his enjoyment of her body. And why shouldn't she? She worked hard for this body, an hour in the school gym every single morning before the girls were even awake, and never so much as looking at a dessert.

'All right. I'm sorry,' said David. 'I don't think it will make the blindest bit of difference, but I will be more careful. I love you.'

Bryony presented a cheek to be kissed. 'I really do have to send an email. The predicted GCSE grades for the upper fifth are dismal and all the parents are calling to blame us. Oil on troubled water and all that. You go down and I'll be there in a few minutes.'

*

David could already hear laughter from the back passage. When he opened the kitchen door, he was greeted by the sight of Lizzie sloshing wine into everyone's glasses. Willa was sitting cross-legged under the window, a cushion clasped over her torso. Her arms were thinner than ever, he noticed with dismay. *You need to talk to her*, said the voice in his head that sounded like his late wife, the one he was usually so good at quashing. It was infuriating that his conscience had to sound like her. And of course it was true. He should talk to Willa. Offer to pay for her to go back to the rehab she'd spent her teens coming in and out of. But it cost a fortune and, besides, it hadn't worked so far, so why would it work now? And, if he was being really honest, he wasn't sure he would be able to convince Bryony to release the funds.

At least she looked happy. 'What's all this then?' he said, coming into the kitchen. Violet and Grant were still giggling and even Angelique, usually so cool, looked amused.

'We were just talking about the time Granny decided she wanted to try drugs—' began Willa.

'And that policeman came for tea and found a load of spliffs in the cutlery drawer,' interrupted Lizzie.

'He made some silly noises about it and your mother told him not to be so utterly ridiculous and gave him another piece of Victoria sponge,' added Violet. Her dark eyes were brimming with tears. For some reason, this made David feel terribly embarrassed. He dropped his gaze away from her face; her tears reminded him quite how stupid he had been to ask whether she was joining them for drinks.

'She was quite something,' David said with a smile.

The door opened behind him. 'Good morning, Ms Winston,' chorused Willa and Lizzie. Grant almost spat out his wine, snorting.

'Very amusing, girls,' Bryony said, trying to make it sound at least a little bit true, despite not being amused at all. Lizzie and Willa had been saying 'Good morning, Ms Winston' every time she entered a room since she had taken up with their father. And David, uncharacteristically, had refused to put a stop to it. 'They're only playing,' David had said, the last time she had asked him to intercede. 'And you must accept, it's odd for them. Imagine if one of your parents had ended up married to your headteacher.'

This would have been impossible for Bryony because she had gone to an enormous comprehensive managed by a grey old man who she couldn't recollect ever having heard speak. Most unlike St Catherine's, the bijou but impressive boarding school she had been running for the last fifteen years. She had been the youngest headmistress the school had ever seen – the youngest headmistress any of the surrounding schools had ever seen, in fact. And she had taken great pride in how the various fathers seemed to pay attention when she spoke at Speech Day.

Of course, she had never intended to marry one of them. Staying single had, at least initially, been her intention. Far less complicated that way. But then David – poor, sweet, widowed David – had been called in for a meeting about Lizzie's behaviour. Smoking, drinking, giving teachers lip. Not that any of the teachers seemed to mind much. She was 'adorable', according to her house mistress, who had let her get away with murder. Willa, too, had become a cause for concern, despite having been far less problematic than her sister.

Bryony had merely intended to ask David to read Lizzie the riot act and up whatever medication Willa was on until she passed her A levels and departed for Oxford. But it had turned into hours of talking, David's handsome face drawing her in and making her feel an unfamiliar sort of sympathy for his plight. Before she'd realized what she was doing, she had invited him to supper. The girls had been childish about it then, and they were still childish about it now. Even when Lucca was born – finally giving them a brother – they had been unable to be gracious about the match.

'They do that whenever they see me,' Bryony said, picking up an empty glass and lifting it in Angelique's direction.

Grant tried to look as if he weren't amused, as did Violet.

'Hello, Dad,' Willa said, crossing the room to hug her father.

'Hi, Daddy,' called Lizzie, who was rolling a cigarette.

'You're getting tobacco on Violet's nice clean floor,' said David indulgently.

'I don't mind,' said Violet.

'You shouldn't be smoking at all,' Bryony added, trying to join in.

'Are you going to give me detention?' Lizzie replied. 'Or should I run around the playing fields before breakfast?'

Everyone laughed again.

'Maybe I'll have you put in isolation,' Bryony retorted. No one laughed. She looked around, trying to work out why the room had gone silent.

'Supper will be ready for eight thirty,' Violet said, after what felt like an age. 'I didn't know when you'd want it, so I've stuck to Cecily's timetable.' Cecily had liked to eat then, after a solid hour and a half of drinks.

'It's a bit late for Lucca,' said Bryony.

'I can put some fish fingers in for him now, if you like? Cecily had me keep all sorts of frozen bits in the deep freeze in case people brought their children over.'

'Oh no, it's quite all right. He can eat with us this evening and then we'll just move dinner to six thirty for the rest of the week.'

'Like small children,' said Angelique.

'Perhaps eight o'clock, as a compromise?' ventured Willa, feeling panicked by the change in arrangements around mealtimes.

'What a good idea,' said Violet. She picked up a tray, as if she were going to fetch something from another room. It was too early in the week to be refereeing arguments between the extended Mordaunt family.

'When's Elspeth arriving?' asked David.

'You didn't know?' said Grant.

'You're not seriously telling me she's not coming?'

'Aunt Elspeth never comes to anything,' Lizzie said, lighting her cigarette. 'Why would she come now?'

'Shouldn't you go outside?' asked Willa.

'Granny always let me smoke in here.'

'I know, but—'

Violet returned to the kitchen with the silver napkin rings from the dining room. She opened the window behind Lizzie a little wider, and Lizzie climbed up on to the windowsill, exhaling smoke out of the window. 'Violet,' Lizzie asked, 'why does Elspeth hate Granny so much? Granny wouldn't ever explain.'

'It was complicated,' Violet said, putting the napkins into their rings, considering her answer. It was hard to know how much discretion she owed Cecily now that she was dead.

'Elspeth was always difficult,' David said, distracted, looking at his phone. 'They never got on.'

'Is it true that if she isn't coming that means she definitely can't get the house?' Willa asked, looking at Grant.

He nodded. 'But she wouldn't want it. She hated it here. Couldn't wait to leave as soon as she was old enough.'

'I mean, it's not like there's any chance Granny would leave it to her,' Lizzie said. 'Why waste the money on a flight?'

It was the first time since their arrival that any of them had acknowledged the reason they were here. It was strange that it wasn't the absence of Cecily that made this feel so different from every Christmas, Easter and August bank holiday, when all of them would gather together and sit in these exact same positions in the exact same room. It was the acknowledgement that, by the end of the week, the house would well and truly no longer belong to Cecily. It would belong to one of them.

'I suppose, seeing as it's come up, we might as well talk about Friday,' said Violet. She picked up the wine bottle and moved around the room, refilling each glass.

'I always forget,' said Grant. 'You've been to a bequest before.'

Grant was right. Violet had been to a bequest before. She was the only one of them who had. Cecily had been twenty-three when she'd been given the house by her uncle. Violet, two years into her life with Cecily but still rather overwhelmed by the strangeness of these people and their world, had taken it in her stride. It wasn't until years later that she had realized, even in the world of old, wealthy families, this was an eccentricity of extremes.

'So, what will actually happen?' asked Lizzie, closing the window but apparently now comfortable sitting on the sill with her long brown legs tangled underneath her. 'At the behest.'

'Bequest,' Willa corrected.

For the first time since they had arrived, everyone was quiet. Everyone was listening.

'Friday will be the funeral, of course,' Violet said. It had been quick to arrange because Cecily had been uncharacteristically organized about it. They had received her diagnosis in a small, plasticky room at the local hospital. The doctor had started to talk about chemotherapy and radiotherapy and other 'experimental' treatments, but Cecily had dismissed that straight away. 'I'm eighty-four,' she'd said. 'That's quite enough. Just make sure there's plenty of pain relief, and I'll be on my way.' Two weeks later, she had presented Violet with an envelope of funeral plans. The church, the vicar, the hymns, the readings. Who was to read what, who was to carry the coffin, even what to serve at the wake. She had paid the expenses up front. Violet had smiled to Cecily's face then allowed herself a short, aching weep in the larder.

'And then on Friday evening there's a dinner.' Cecily had left instructions for that, too. Violet swallowed, trying to decide how she felt about being in charge of all of this. 'Then, well, you all know how it goes. She left you each a letter, explaining why whoever will have the house is going to have it. Then there's a lunch on Saturday to celebrate, and on Monday most of you will go home, but whoever inherits the house will have legal appointments in town.'

'Do you know who's getting it?' asked Lizzie lightly.

Violet laughed. 'I can honestly say that I don't.'

'But if you get it – you just drop everything?' Angelique asked. She was sitting on one of the kitchen chairs, her posture perfectly straight. All of the Mordaunts turned to look at her.

'Yes,' said David. 'That's exactly what happens.'

'And you have to take care of this place? I thought all English people with large houses complained about how impossible they are to keep warm and the holes in the roof.'

'Grant hasn't explained terribly well, then,' said David.

'Roxborough comes with an income,' Violet said. 'Enough to ensure that living here is comfortable and that it can be kept in the family.'

'How much is the income?' asked Bryony, in a voice that was clearly supposed to be casual.

'That, I am afraid I do know,' Violet said, getting to her feet. 'But I'm not allowed to disclose the amount. I'm going to check on supper.'

Supper that evening passed pleasantly enough, food passed from serving dish to plate, wine glasses filled and refilled. Eventually, once the plates were empty, Bryony started to clear.

'It's quite all right,' said Violet.

'Don't be silly, we can't leave you to clean up on your own.'

'I wouldn't, don't worry. We still have two girls come in from the village each day to keep on top of the cleaning.'

Bryony looked surprised. 'What a lot of staff Cecily had.'

'It's a big house,' said Grant. 'When we were kids there were ten people living in.'

'Remember Mrs Haunch?' David laughed. He looked relaxed after a fourth glass of wine, his shirtsleeves rolled up, blue eyes sparkling.

'My God, I'd forgotten about her.'

'I don't suppose you'd forgotten about Emily.'

They both laughed now. 'Emily?' asked Bryony.

'She was one of the maids,' Grant said, looking smug. 'David had an enormous crush on her.'

'She wasn't exactly touched by the ugly stick, it's true.'

'He used to follow her around like a whippet.' Violet smiled. 'It was very sweet. But when we stopped having live-in staff it was rather simpler. Not so many worries about bedhopping when we had guests.'

Bryony looked rather shocked.

'We'd have had to watch Jonty like a hawk if we still had nubile young women sleeping in the servants' quarters,' said Grant. Privately, most of the family thought this was an odd and entirely inaccurate comment. Jonty really wasn't the playboy that Grant seemed to want to pretend that he was.

'Where is Jonty?' asked David.

Grant looked down at his hands. 'Good question, actually. I'll text him and ask.'

'He'll be here tomorrow,' said Violet. 'He called earlier. One of his clients has a mare in labour and the foal looked like it might be in difficulty so he's gone to help. He was very good to let me know, given what a rush it all was.'

'I'm going to go up,' said Lizzie, gathering the things she'd strewn across the room. She had an astonishing skill for mess, managing to trail her belongings as quickly as she breathed. One of her shoes had gone under the table; she cast around to find it, and then gave up.

'I'll come too,' said Willa. 'Don't want to wake you up.'

'Surely there's enough space for you to have your own rooms?' said Angelique.

'Oh, there is,' Violet replied. 'But they prefer to share, don't you, girls?'

They both nodded. Since they had been tiny children, the old nursery had always been their room. It was a long, low-ceilinged room right in the middle of the house, with a huge fireplace and an astonishing view. There were twin beds and a wardrobe filled with dressing-up clothes – mostly Cecily's party dresses from over the years and things that had been collected by the house. A Victorian riding habit, someone's ancient wedding dress, various furs. They'd spent hours playing with them as children and then borrowed them for parties as teen-agers. The bedroom was far less grand than some of the others, but it was the only place either of them had any real history with and, as such, the idea of moving into a 'grown-up' room was desperately unappealing.

As the girls were about to head towards bed, a sharp ring echoed throughout the house. Everyone looked up towards the door, behind which there was a hallway lead-ing to the front entrance.

'Who on earth is that?' asked David.

Violet got to her feet.

'You stay here,' said Grant, more quickly than her. 'I'll go and check.'

David took stock of the room. The only person who wasn't here who should be was Jonty. It was too late for any of his mother's friends to be paying their respects. Too late for anyone to be coming to check a meter, install or deliver anything. A cold, sickly feeling spread throughout his body. He tried to reassure himself that things hadn't reached that stage yet. He had moved some money around, temporarily. That wasn't a crime. Not really. He would put it back before anyone knew.

The door opened and David realized he had been holding his breath as Grant returned, followed by a man in a suit. Dark skin, dark hair, dark eyes. Who on earth was this? Why was he here?

'This is Rihan,' Grant said, his face impassive. 'Elspeth sent him.' For a moment, no one said anything. Then everyone started talking.

'Why has Elspeth sent anyone?' asked Bryony.

'It's a stipulation for the will to be read that everyone who is named as a potential inheritor either be here or send someone in their stead if they want any of the cash settlement,' said Violet faintly. Privately, Violet thought it unspeakably poor that Elspeth hadn't spoken to her mother in decades but had sent a lawyer to make sure that she got whatever cash was to be handed out. She had privately hoped that if she intended to take the money, Elspeth might have had the good grace to bother booking a flight. 'The law firm that deals with Roxborough offered her a representative, and she accepted.'

David, overwhelmed with relief that he had been foolish, that his fears had merely been stupid anxieties, held his hand out to Rihan. 'Hello,' he said. 'We're the family.

I assure you, we're not quite as monstrous as this whole situation might lead you to believe.'

Rihan didn't smile. 'I assure you, I have no opinion of the family at all.'

No sense of humour, then, David decided.

Violet tried to pull back some control over the situation. 'Please, sit down,' she said. 'Can I get you a glass of wine?'

'No, thank you.'

'You'll probably need it,' said Lizzie. 'Honestly, if you're going to be hanging out with this lot for the next few days.'

Again, no smile.

'Were you planning to stay here?' asked Violet, assuming that he would say no.

'Ms Mordaunt said that would be best,' he replied. 'If that isn't a problem.'

Everyone looked rather stunned. It wasn't a problem; there were more bedrooms than Mordaunts and the house liked to be full. But there was something rather invasive about this solemn, handsome man sitting among them.

'Of course it is,' said Grant, draining his glass. 'You'll keep us all on best behaviour. Violet, is there a room he can have?'

Violet nodded. 'Follow me upstairs. I'll show you where and get you some towels.'

They waited all of a second after Rihan followed Violet into the hall and then they were on their feet.

'What on earth does she think she's playing at?'

'She's sent someone to come to her own mother's funeral.'

'Granny would absolutely hate this.'

'Mum wouldn't have been surprised. Elspeth's always been a piece of work. This is exactly like her. Not turn up and then lumber us with some suit, to make things as awkward as possible. What's the point? It's not as if she's getting the house,' said Grant.

'I guess it's not impossible,' said Willa.

Grant fixed her with a stare. 'Not impossible,' he agreed. 'But it's not bloody likely.'

Willa regretted saying anything.

'Well, she certainly can't have it now,' said Bryony, who sounded rather smug. 'You have to be at the dinner to get your letter. David told me that ages ago. It's a simple rule.'

Grant sighed. 'Not quite.'

'I think there's supposed to be a precedent for proxy,' Willa said shyly. 'Someone inherited it, but she was in labour when the letter was read, so she sent a servant for her, and she still got it.'

'Well, that's different, obviously,' Bryony snapped. 'Elspeth isn't in labour. She doesn't even have children, for God's sake. She just refuses to come to the funeral because she's . . .' She hesitated. 'Difficult.'

Bryony had never felt especially welcomed by any of the Mordaunts. Cecily had been coolly kind, the girls never stopped taking the piss out of her, and Grant barely spoke to her. But Elspeth had been worst of all.

The first time Bryony had met Elspeth had been in New York. Bryony had been speaking at an education conference and David had accompanied her. She had applied four years in a row to be on a panel and, finally, because someone else had dropped out at the last minute, she had been asked. She'd bought three new suits for the occasion and had her hair done. It was the most excited she had been since Lucca had first been tested for being gifted and talented (which of course he was).

The evening after the conference, which had been a triumph, with Bryony answering pretty much every question the host asked, they had met with Elspeth. She had asked Bryony nothing about the conference, and basically talked only to David, going on and on about their mother and father and their childhood. In the end, Bryony had had to claim a headache and tell David to take her back to the hotel before they'd had pudding because the whole thing was so unbearable.

'Look, we'll deal with the details when we know what's in the letters,' Grant said. 'Chances of Mum leaving Elspeth as much as a postage stamp are somewhere between zero and fuck all. So, there's no point getting upset.'

Everyone seemed mollified by this, and a mutual agreement was made that they'd sunk quite enough of the wine and it was time to go to bed.

Lizzie and Willa tramped up the long staircase, listening to the silence. There were funny tricks to this house when it came to sound. In some places, even the most whispered conversation could be heard; in others, like on the stairs, it felt as if the entire house were empty even if a raucous party was raging downstairs. And by God, had there been parties in the past. Cecily had never seemed able to allow the house to be empty for more than a fortnight. Whenever the girls spent their summer holidays at Roxborough there would be a procession of fascinating people. Musicians travelling to give concerts, lecturers doing stints at Cambridge. Old friends of the family, sometimes very dull but often desperately interesting. They would arrive with strange presents – like the man who brought champagne bottles of North Sea saltwater, insisting that it was the best thing for the constitution if taken every morning before breakfast; or the opera singer who'd lost her flat in Paris to a messy divorce and taken up residence in the Pink Room for three months, waking them up by singing scales each morning and sunbathing on the croquet lawn with her enormous breasts on full display.

Lying in the dark, in the same beds they'd slept in since childhood, both girls looked at the ceiling.

'Are you awake?' asked Willa.

'No,' said Lizzie.

They both giggled, even though it wasn't especially funny.

'Who do you think will get it?' Willa asked eventually.

'I don't know.'

'No one knows. Guess.'

Lizzie thought about it for a moment. She knew who she wanted to get it. But was it likely? After everything that had happened the last time she had seen her grand-mother? Probably not.

'I think Grant,' she said eventually.

'Why?'

'Because you said I had to guess someone.'

'So why did you guess Grant?'

'Granny loved him. He's nicer than Dad.'

'True. But then he does burn through money, she always said.'

'And he has about nine girlfriends a year.'

'Maybe it'll be you then,' Willa said. It was somehow easier in the dark.

'I don't think so,' Lizzie replied after a while.

'Would you like it, if it was you?'

'Of course I would,' said Lizzie, honestly. 'Would you?'

Willa considered the question for a little while. 'I don't know,' she said. 'I couldn't stay working for the firm.'

'I don't think it'll be us. It'd make the grown-ups too cross.'

'Just as long as it's not Bryony.'

'Maybe it'll be Lucca.' They both laughed at the idea of their grandmother leaving the house to their obnox-ious half-brother, who had barely spoken two words to his grandmother. Cecily had once told Lizzie that while, on the whole, she did not approve of hitting children, for Lucca she would have seriously considered making an exception.

Willa picked up her pillow and squashed it, trying to make it into the right shape for her head. 'Maybe it'll be

Jonty.' She stared into the fuzzy navy darkness, trying to make out a reaction from Lizzie. But she was silent. Either asleep, or pretending to be.

Bryony was on her second cleanse when David came up to bed. There was a little sink in the corner of their bedroom with a mirrored cabinet above it. She opened the cabinet, looking inside. Little perfume samples. The kind of washbag you get free on an aeroplane, labelled 'British Airways, first class'. Some painkillers, a lipstick that smelled powdery and sweet. Presumably a collection of things that David had left here over the years. Or that Cordelia had left here, over her years.

Cordelia and David had married when they were twenty-one, and she had died when she was forty-five. So, plenty of time to leave her mark all over this enormous, groaning great house. There was a small part of Bryony, one of which she was not especially fond nor proud, that quite relished the idea of transforming the house and erasing the last vestiges of Cordelia that were left here. She had insisted on moving when she married David because she couldn't live in another woman's shadow, and it was only on the seemingly endless trips to this house that she was unable to escape it. A book with her name on the flyleaf, a pair of wellies by the back door, the photographs in silver frames on the mantelpiece. Small but undeniably real reminders that David's parents had adored Cordelia, that no one who came second would ever come close.

But it wasn't just that. There was another note there too. Something akin to snobbery, a sense that Bryony wasn't who they would have chosen for David, that she wasn't quite 'it'. David had always claimed that she was imagining it, but she knew deep down he must realize she was right. It was why they had visited so little once they were married. The girls came for all their university holidays, spending endless weeks here. But she had convinced David that four days for Christmas and Easter, and a long weekend for any significant birthdays, was reasonable. She knew it made her sound like a harpy, but she wasn't entirely sure that she cared. She had her own life back in Sussex. Lucca had football every Saturday morning, birthday parties with friends, homework and tutoring. He needed stability – the kind of stability that Willa and Lizzie had been denied, spending half their free time here.

'I've already checked on Lucca,' she said, before David had closed the door. 'So you needn't bother.'

David had no intention of checking on Lucca, who was nine rather than nine months and was perfectly capable of brushing his own teeth and getting into bed. 'Thanks for doing that,' he said, dropping a kiss on Bryony's neck.

She wrinkled her nose. 'Did you smoke?'

'No, I just stood next to Grant while he was. For old times' sake.'

'You smell terrible.'

'Thank you, darling.'

Bryony got into bed. 'Sorry. I didn't mean to be . . . I just don't like the idea of you smoking. You worked so hard to stop.'

David softened. 'I'm sorry.'

He brushed his teeth and stripped off, folding his clothes on the velvet armchair that had always sat underneath the window. He drew Bryony to him, his arms wrapped around her torso. 'You're cold,' he said, rubbing her arms.

'Freezing. I always am when we're here.'

David considered the back of her neck. She smelled wonderful. 'I'm sorry. I know you hate it here.'

'I don't hate it.'

'I know it isn't easy, then.'

'No. It certainly isn't that.'

'But things will be different, when it's our house.'

Bryony's body relaxed. 'It won't even really be a house by then.'

David made a non-committal noise. They lay in companionable silence until the calm was interrupted by David's phone vibrating. 'Who's calling you at this time of night?' asked Bryony.

David turned the phone on to silent. 'One of those "did you have an accident that wasn't your fault" numbers, probably. Let's get some sleep. It's going to be a long week.'

Angelique and Grant were walking through the grounds of the house, the legs of the white dungarees she had put on for dinner rolled up to mid-calf, feet in the damp grass, enjoying the lingering warmth in the air. She had a joint in her left hand and was exhaling clouds of smoke. She offered it to Grant, who shook his head. 'I don't any more,' he said. 'Enjoyed it too much back in the day. Besides, I need my wits about me with that nest of vipers inside.'

'I didn't think they seemed so bad,' Angelique said. 'What's over there?'

'The lake.'

He followed as Angelique made her way towards the water. 'It's so beautiful,' she said, taking it in. It was lit by lamps that Cecily's uncle had had installed at great expense. It was regarded as a folly at the time, but now, with the orange light glinting off the water, it seemed to Grant that it was the most sensible thing he could possibly have done.

He watched as Angelique picked her way up on to the wooden jetty that jutted over the lake and climbed on to the diving board. His mother had been strict about it: no real diving allowed, only jumping. The water was plenty deep enough, but she'd read some story about a back being broken in deep water and never allowed any of them to forget it. Elspeth, always the rebel, had ignored it, taking long swan dives off the board whenever she had the chance, her body piercing the water and barely making a splash. Grant had wanted to copy her, but he'd never really been able to shake off the dire warnings about broken spines and wheelchairs.

Angelique was beautiful, standing on the diving board,

all in white, her long hair streaming down her back. He knew it was a cliché, to be dating someone so much younger, someone so beautiful. But he didn't much care. She was brilliant. Aggressively alive, unburdened by the things that all of his friends seemed so transfixed by.

'What will you do with it? If it's yours?' she asked.

'I don't know,' he replied.

'Liar.'

'OK,' he admitted, climbing up on to the diving board. 'I have a few ideas about what I would do if I had to.'

'Like what?'

'Secrets. Probably very half-baked ones at that.'

'Couldn't you just sell it?'

Grant shook his head. 'That would be sacrilege.'

Angelique undid her white dungarees and peeled them off, throwing them back on to the jetty. She peeled off her T-shirt, now naked but for a pair of knickers. 'Can I jump?' she asked.

Grant tried to shake off the sense of disappointment that she wasn't going to push him on his ideas, that she didn't care enough to try to convince him. But, he thought, wasn't that what was so remarkable about her, perhaps?

'You can,' he said. 'But the water is freezing. You'll get cold.'

'Come in with me.'

'No bloody way.'

'You'll enjoy it.'

'I assure you I won't.'

She held her arms out to him, and he went to her, wrapping his body around hers. His hands were in her hair, their lips on each other's. He led her down from the diving board, on to the jetty, pulling her on to his lap, undoing his fly, her legs wrapped around his waist. She wasn't the first woman he had brought here, or fucked here. There had been dozens before, in the sunshine, in twilight, in this darkness. But perhaps, he thought, as she whimpered into his ear, she might be the last.

1987

'I can't believe you still get nervous when we come down here.' Grant laughed. He took his hand off the steering wheel to place it on Luella's long, pale thigh. She had the longest legs he had ever seen on a person. All of her limbs were slightly too long, actually, and covered in freckles. Those kinds of fake imperfections that weren't imperfections at all but made her more interesting to look at than the average beautiful girl. When he had first seen her from across the bar, he'd been shocked that other men weren't literally forming a line to talk to her. Apparently, other people were blind to the complete perfection that existed in every atom of Luella's body.

'I'm not nervous,' Luella said.

'Liar.'

'All right, I am. Last time we were here I told your parents that I don't vote Tory and that I believe in the legalization of cannabis.'

'They loved you.'

'Now who's lying?'

'OK, Dad loved you. And Mum will love you. She just takes a while to come around to new people. She's protective.'

'Are you sure they're going to take this well?' Luella held her hand out again, the stone on her left ring finger glinting in the sun.

'Of course they will,' Grant said. 'You're perfect. They'll be delighted.'

'I wish you'd told them before we got in the car.'

'And ruin the surprise? Anyway, they know something's up – Dad came back from London to be here. It's not going to be a big surprise.'

'We've only been together six months.'

'Seven and a half.'

'Oh yes, wildly different.'

'Far better to get married now – then we can have decades and decades together. And we can move to Roxborough and have parties every weekend. It'll be perfect.'

Luella laughed. 'I thought David was going to live at Roxborough.'

Grant made a face. 'Only because Mum and Dad are obsessed with Cordelia. They've been together since they were thirteen. But they'll be more obsessed with you.'

'Are you marrying me to get the house?' Luella laughed.

'Obviously,' Grant said. He fumbled to light a cigarette, taking one hand off the wheel. Luella took it from him and lit it, even though she hated the taste of smoke.

'Be careful,' she said. 'I refuse to die in a car crash in Norfolk.'

Grant was wrong about the surprise. Neither of his parents had expected that Grant was bringing the very beautiful, very young Luella to Roxborough in order to announce an engagement. They barely knew anything about her, other than the fact that Grant, who had taken the oat-sowing part of being a young man extremely seriously, had seemingly settled down. He'd never so much as mentioned a girl before, let alone brought one home. But for the last six months, in every phone call he had made to his parents the conversation had been about Luella, her work as an interior designer, the shared house she lived in in Parsons Green, the museum she had shown him, the dinner party she had thrown. Grant sent postcards from little holidays all around the UK and posted them a Polaroid of himself with his arm around Luella, both knee-deep in the water on a beach in Wales. He had gone from a bona fide party boy who spent every night at Tramp and Annabel's talking about the businesses he was going to start, to something all the more solid, all the more understandable. So, Luella was wrong to think that Grant's parents would mind the speed of their engagement. Their only worry about the relationship had been that it might not last.

Cecily threw her arms around her new daughter-in-law, delighted with the idea of another woman in the family. 'Will you have the wedding here?' was the first thing she demanded.

'Mum!' Grant chastised her.

'You'll have the wedding wherever you want it,' Esmond said, giving his wife a look. 'And your mother won't pressure you into anything.'

'I can't think of anywhere I'd like better.' Luella smiled as Violet handed her a glass of champagne.

'Thank God for that.' Esmond laughed. 'You'd never have heard the end of it if you had the wedding somewhere else.'

'Congratulations.' Violet smiled, clinking a glass against hers. 'What wonderful news.'

'We should talk about plans,' Cecily said, taking Luella by the arm. 'A marquee on the croquet lawn, I think. So that means summer. Next summer, or the end of this one? We could pull it together for September, I think . . .'

They had a raucous, drunken dinner, laughing and hearing stories about Esmond and Cecily's wedding. Luella noticed that Violet looked a little sad at times. Grant had explained that there was a rather unusual, unspoken arrangement in the house and that Luella should ignore anything that passed between the three elders. Privately, Luella didn't approve of this sort of thing. Her own family, far less grand and far more normal than this lot, made a point of discussing everything and anything. The idea of allowing some sort of complicated relationship to exist while everyone pretended it didn't was anathema to her. But there would be time for all of that. Eventually they would be her family, just as they were Grant's.

After more drinks, pudding, cheese and port, Esmond and Cecily called it a night, and Violet did the same a few moments later.

'Can we go for a walk?' Luella asked Grant.

'Of course,' he said.

It was only just dark at ten o'clock and the gardens at Roxborough were always well lit, even the wild parts. Apparently, some rather depraved uncle who had owned the house previously enjoyed the idea of guests being able to wander al fresco any time, day or night. Grant and Luella wandered along the river, which eventually fed into the lake, both gently drunk, Luella warm under Grant's coat. 'I need to tell you something,' Luella said.

'All right,' Grant said. 'What's that?'

'I went to the doctor a few weeks ago.'

Grant started to panic but forced himself not to interrupt Luella, one of his least appealing habits. 'Why?' he asked.

'I was worried that I hadn't had my period for a while.'

Grant's heart leapt with excitement. 'You're not pregnant?'

'No,' Luella said.

Grant tried to hide his disappointment. 'That's good,' he said, because it seemed like the right thing to say.

'Actually, I might never be pregnant.'

Grant tried to keep his voice light. 'Oh?'

'They did some tests and things, and they found that there are some things wrong with me. Inside. They said

55

it's not impossible, but it's very, very unlikely that I'll ever get pregnant. And that if I ever did, it might be quite dangerous.' Her voice caught. 'I was going to tell you, and then you proposed. I just wanted a week or so to think about it. Please don't be cross that I kept it a secret.'

Grant stopped and pulled Luella into his arms. She was almost six feet tall, but somehow she still felt tiny to him. 'Please don't, darling,' he said, as she cried into his shirt. 'It couldn't matter less. We'll have far more money and far more fun without babies. And we can always adopt when we're older if we want to. I'm marrying you, not a load of hypothetical children. There's really nothing to be upset about.' Everything he said sounded stupid, but Luella stopped crying, wiped her face and gave him a half-smile, which made him feel ten thousand feet tall. 'You know, if you don't want to get married, I'll understand. We've hardly told anyone. It wouldn't be embarrassing.'

Grant smiled. He took the ring off Luella's finger and got down on one knee. 'Luella Kingdon, who may or may not have children, you are the single best thing that has ever happened to this world. I want to marry you more than anything. Will you marry me?'

She half sobbed, half laughed. 'Get up, you daft bugger. The ground's wet, your trousers will be soaking, we're already engaged!'

'Don't care. Say you'll marry me.'

'I already said I would!'

'Say it again.'

'Yes, I'll marry you.'

Grant got to his feet. 'There,' he said. 'That wasn't so hard, was it?'

They found their way back along the path to the lake. Luella pulled off her dress. 'Come on,' she said. 'Let's swim.' Grant watched her dive perfectly into the water and then followed her in. They swam to the middle of the lake and then held on to the side of the dock, looking up at the stars. 'Is this where you brought all your girlfriends, growing up?' she said with a smile.

'Yes,' Grant admitted. 'It was occasionally part of the seduction routine.'

'I can't believe I didn't get seduced here.'

'You didn't need to be seduced.'

Luella splashed him. 'Rude.'

'But you will be the last person I bring here,' Grant said quietly. 'Which is rather a nice thought.'

'Yes,' Luella agreed, gently swimming backwards. 'It is.'

3

Jonty was woken partially by the early-morning sun and partially by the incredibly uncomfortable position he had fallen asleep in. He sat up and wound the passenger seat back into an upright position, then stretched. He looked around the car for a discarded bottle of water and realized there wasn't one. His mouth was dry, and his head ached. He hadn't been drunk when he fell asleep – he wasn't quite that irresponsible – but he'd been attending to the very expensive racehorse for eight hours by the time her foal arrived, unscathed. Before that, he had been at a rather smart afternoon of racing, wearing a morning coat. An hour or two later, halfway to Roxborough, he had been overcome with extraordinary exhaustion and decided that he wasn't driving to the house. He had pulled over to the side of the road and been out like a light within moments. It had seemed enormously sensible, but now, as he flicked his indicator on and rejoined the quiet country lane, the rationale was rather less clear.

The crunching of gravel always announced visitors to

Roxborough, and then a chorus of barking dogs. Jonty tried to creep down the drive, keeping the car as quiet as possible, aware that it wasn't seven o'clock yet and that the rest of the family might not be pleased to have their morning disturbed. Plus, there was something faintly embarrassing about arriving wearing a morning coat.

He lined his car up between Uncle David's enormous SUV and his father's pretty Alfa. The door opened and, for a moment, he expected Cecily to emerge, carrying a bowl of scraps for the hens.

'Jonty!' called Violet. 'Aren't you a sight for sore eyes?'

'I'm sorry I wasn't here last night,' he said, honestly. He kissed Violet on each cheek. 'How are you? I'm so sorry. I know you and Granny were practically the same person.'

'I'm all right.'

'Really?'

'Well, no, not really. But you know how your grandmother felt about grumbling.'

'She was old-fashioned. There's nothing wrong with grieving. Everyone tried for years to get her to see someone after Grandpa died.'

Violet laughed. 'I would feel for any therapist charged with getting your grandmother to talk about her feelings. Come and feed the hens with me?'

Jonty took the bowl from Violet and linked arms with her as they crossed the driveway to the field furthest from the house where the chickens were. 'How many have you got?' he asked.

'Ten,' Violet replied. 'It was twelve, but the bastard fox got them. Cecily kept threatening to take a shotgun to bed with her and watch for him.'

Jonty laughed. There'd never been any point negotiating with his grandmother about animal rights. The day he'd announced he was a vegetarian was possibly the only time he had been aware that she disapproved of him.

He and Violet scattered the scraps and the feed for the hens, then wandered back to the house. Violet's hip was hurting, not that she liked to mention it. The last thing anyone needed was to worry about her, and she had a horrible feeling Jonty, Grant and Lizzie might get together and offer to pay for it to be replaced, which would be shaming, especially as she had no intention of having surgery at her age.

'How have they been?' Jonty asked as he opened the gate.

'It's only been one night. The girls keep teasing their stepmother.'

'She *is* bloody awful.'

'No comment.'

'And Dad?'

'He seems happy.'

'How's the latest girlfriend behaving herself?'

'She seems nice enough. You don't know her then?'

Jonty shook his head. 'We've met briefly. We've got an agreement now. So many lunches getting to know women only to have him chuck them the next week. I don't spend much time with them until it's absolutely serious. Present circumstances excepted, of course.' Jonty registered the disapproval on Violet's face and reminded himself that there was nothing to gain by complaining. He was an adult; he didn't need Grant to play the father. Violet was protective of them, still saw them as a band of motherless children who needed to be looked after. 'But I liked her at Christmas. She makes Dad happy.'

Violet pursed her lips. 'I'm going to feed the horses. I'll be in in a moment to make some coffee.'

Jonty pushed open the door to the kitchen. Standing in front of the Aga in orange silk pyjamas, her hair piled on top of her head, was Lizzie. She was tanned, her hair lighter than it had been last time he saw her.

He smiled. 'Hello.'

'Oh, you're here,' Lizzie replied.

Jonty went to kiss her.

'Don't,' Lizzie said, holding her arms out. 'I haven't had a shower yet, I probably stink.'

'Not keen to brave the children's bathroom?'

Lizzie laughed. The children's bathroom was the one in between the nursery, where she and Willa slept, and the Yellow Room, where Jonty always slept. It famously didn't have hot water because some previous Mordaunt had claimed warm water was bad for children, made them soft or something. Everyone else said it was because he was too tight to put in hot water all over the house. Cecily hadn't had any such Victorian ideas, but it had become a game when they were children, to try to have a bath or a shower in the icy bathroom, all three of them putting on their swimming things and competing to see who could get in the freezing water with the least fuss. 'I think I'll use Granny's bathroom,' Lizzie said. 'She wouldn't mind.'

'No,' agreed Jonty. 'She wouldn't.'

Lizzie poured herself an enormous cup of coffee in one of the outdoor mugs reserved for people doing things in the garden.

'How are you?' Jonty asked, looking at the stone floor.

'Fine.'

'I'm glad.'

'Are you?'

'Yes, of course I am.'

'I'm surprised you care.'

Jonty wasn't sure what to say, so he said nothing. Lizzie drained her cup and put it on the table.

'Right. I'm going to go up then.'

'Right.'

'See you later.'

'Yes. Later.'

She closed the kitchen door behind her and paused for a moment in the dark passage, the stone cold under her feet. She took a deep breath and tried to compose herself, telling herself to stop being so stupid. Trying not to think about everything she wanted to say to Jonty. Everything that she hadn't said.

Lizzie wasn't sure who she should ask about using Cecily's bathroom. She'd always used it when she stayed before. So had Willa. But at Cecily's invitation. Should she ask

Violet? She decided not. She pushed the bedroom door open, feeling it drag against the high pile of the carpet. The room was quiet, so filled with beautiful soft things that sound went dead. She breathed in her grandmother's scent, which wasn't at all like the sort of smell you associate with old or ill people. Not powdery or sweet, or stuffy or chemical. Granny had worn an old Penhaligon's scent her entire life, sharp and citrussy, and it hung in the air here. The huge bed sat at one end of the room, facing the window. Her grandmother had never closed her curtains, preferring to wake up with the light, but they were slightly drawn now. Lizzie pulled them open properly, as if she were somehow doing Granny a favour.

The bathroom was a carpeted en suite with a bath on a plinth in the middle of the room, facing out over the wide green fields. When she was a child, Lizzie had assumed this was what being a grown-up meant – having a very large and very glamorous bathroom entirely to herself. She put her grandmother's old radio on and filled the bath, then added a generous splurt of bath oil. Then she stripped off her pyjamas, leaving them lying in a silk puddle on the floor, and lay up to her neck in the scented water.

It was hard to believe that, when she came out from the bathroom, wrapped in one of the enormous navy towels, her grandmother wouldn't be standing in the bedroom brushing her short hair with a silver-backed brush at the dressing table. Everyone always said that was the strange thing about grief – that you couldn't quite believe someone was dead. It hadn't been like that with Lizzie's mother. David had stripped out everything Cordelia owned within hours of her death, putting anything valuable into their safe, and anything enormously sentimental into storage. He'd taken the photographs off the mantelpiece and thrown away all her make-up and shampoo. He had made it so that she was truly gone in every imaginable sense from the moment she had died. No 'she's still with me in spirit' or 'I can feel her every day'. But it was different with Granny. The house was still just the same as it always had been. Lizzie liked it that way. If she had the choice, she would try to keep it like this. Like the last time she had seen her grandmother. Or rather, given that the last time had been the worst time, the time before last.

'Do you have any cereal?' asked Lucca. His blond ringlets brushed his shoulders and Violet wanted to feel it was fine but couldn't help her sense that his mother should take him for a haircut. A couple of years ago, Cecily had called Lucca 'she' and Bryony had started bandying the word 'dementia' around. She and Violet had laughed until their stomachs hurt, once they were safely out of earshot.

Violet looked up from the recipe book she was perusing. 'We do. Lots, actually. I got some in case you wanted it. Go into the larder and choose what you like.'

Lucca came back with a miniature box of Frosties and another of Coco Pops. 'Can I mix these two together?'

'Would your mother let you?'

'Yes. We do it all the time at home.'

'All right then. You know where the bowls are. The milk is in the jug.'

Lucca beamed as he made his cereal into a chocolatey sludge, and shovelled it into his mouth. When he had slurped his way noisily through most of a bowl, the door opened. His face fell when he realized that it was his mother.

'What on earth is that?' asked Bryony.

Lucca looked down at his feet. 'Cereal.'

'What type of cereal?'

'Just cereal.'

Bryony knelt down, her eyes level with Lucca's. 'I need you to be honest with me, Lucca. What sort of cereal are you eating?'

'Frosties.'

'Frosties?'

'And Coco Pops.'

Bryony picked up the bowl and dropped what little remained into the bin. 'Why would you eat those cereals when you know that you're not allowed them?'

Lucca looked his mother in the eye, his blond eyebrows raised and his pink lips pouty. 'Violet said that was what I should eat.'

Violet put her recipe book down, no longer pretending not to hear the conversation. 'I'm not sure that's quite true, is it, Lucca?'

'It is,' he said. *The little monster,* thought Violet.

'Please, don't encourage my son to eat refined sugars,' Bryony said, with the kind of voice that belonged to the survivor of some terrible disaster. 'It's not kind. His behaviour issues are triggered by sugar.'

Violet looked at Lucca and realized that he was worried. 'I'm sorry,' she said. 'I should have offered him the Alpen.'

'Yes. You should.'

Bryony left the room, presumably to find a lemon on which she could suck. Lucca dropped his gaze.

When Lizzie went back to her bedroom, her skin pink from the hot bath, the last of her mascara sitting underneath her eyes, she found Willa sitting cross-legged on her bed. The gap between her sister's upper arms and her torso was even wider than usual. Lizzie tried to push away the sense of guilt. There was nothing she could do. She'd tried for years. If anything, trying to help made it worse.

'What time do you want to go?' she asked her sister.

Willa looked up from her laptop. 'What?'

'To Norwich. What time do you want to go? I thought we could get some lunch after we find me a black dress.'

'I thought you were going to borrow something of Granny's.'

'I went through her wardrobe and I didn't recognize any of her stuff. She must have had a massive clear-out. It was proper old-lady clothes, nothing like how she used to dress. So, I have to buy something. We can go to the cute place by the market after for food.'

'I can't.'

'Why not?'

'I have to work – I didn't get a chance to hand over properly and there's all this stuff they need for the case. If I don't do a proper handover now, then they'll be set back days, and then they'll be furious.'

'You said you'd drive me.'

'Why don't you drive?'

'Fine,' Lizzie said, pulling a pair of jeans and a T-shirt from her bag, leaving the rest of her clothes strewn over the floor. Willa hated mess. But Willa had reneged on her promise and was refusing to hang out, so Lizzie decided she no longer cared.

Her father was drinking a cup of coffee in the kitchen, looking like the lord of the manor, when Lizzie got down. She hunted under the kitchen sofa for her shoe, finding a pair of her grandmother's instead. They were dusty, must have been under there for years. Brown leather sandals.

'Are those Cecily's?' asked Violet, coming in carrying a vase of flowers.

'I think so. They were under the sofa.'

'She was furious when she lost them, years ago. Got them in a Greek market with your grandfather, said they were her favourites.'

'Can I borrow them?'

Violet smiled. 'Have them.'

'We should probably keep a list of what you've given away, Violet,' said David.

Both women turned to look at him. 'It's a pair of shoes Granny lost twenty years ago,' Lizzie said in a sneering voice, which made David angrier than he'd like to admit. 'It's not as if she's been giving away the artwork.'

'I haven't given away anything,' Violet added, keeping her voice light and even. 'I'll start a list, if you like.' She took a piece of paper and wrote 'Greek sandals' on it. David started to feel rather foolish. He hadn't meant to suggest that Violet was giving things away willy-nilly, just that the legals of this house were particularly compli- cated because the owner wasn't allowed to leave any special items to anyone; they had to stay in the house, listed and witnessed, to avoid the person who inherited it feeling as if the house had been raided. He wanted to explain himself, but sixty years of people taking what he said badly had shown him that he wasn't the sort of per- son who could explain himself. He might as well allow them to think he was being tight.

'Can I borrow the car?' Lizzie asked.

'I don't think so,' David replied.

'I need to go into Norwich to buy a black dress.'

'You didn't bring anything for the funeral?' Her father sounded more shocked than he had any right to. He had known her her entire life; he surely couldn't be surprised that she was a little scatty.

Jonty came through the kitchen door, sleeves rolled up to his elbows. He had changed out of his morning coat as soon as humanly possible – in case anyone thought he was showing off – drunk two cups of coffee and had a blisteringly hot shower.

'Jonty, will you take Lizzie into Norwich?' asked David.

Bloody hell, Jonty thought. How was he supposed to get out of that? 'I can . . .' he said, haltingly. He couldn't think of a good reason not to.

'It's fine,' Lizzie said, buckling up the sandals. 'I can get the bus.'

'That'll take hours,' Violet replied. 'I can take you later. I've got rather a lot to do before the funeral, but I'm sure I could make some phone calls from the car—'

'It's fine,' Jonty said, unable to bear it any longer. 'I'm happy to go. When do you want to leave?'

'Whenever.'

'Well, then, let's go now. We can be back in time for lunch that way.'

'Shall we have the top down?' Jonty asked, looking across the car at Lizzie, who was practically curling inside herself.

'I don't care.'

Jonty pulled the canvas top back and, eventually, once it was tucked away, turned the engine over. 'Get in, then.'

'I would have been perfectly happy on the bus.'

Jonty turned the car smoothly in the drive and pulled out on to the long sweep of grey road that carried them away from the house. 'When have you ever been on a bus?'

'All the time in London!'

'That's different – the buses actually work in London. And that's bollocks. You're addicted to taxis. Your father goes on about it.'

'Yes, because everything David says about me is so measured and true.'

They didn't speak for a while, and Lizzie was grateful for the lack of a roof because it gave her something to look at. Jonty shifted between gears and glanced across at Lizzie's tanned ankles, trying to convince himself not to look.

'Why are you being weird with me?' Lizzie asked eventually.

'That's rich. You've been off with me since I arrived.'

'You've been off with me since last year.'

'You know I wasn't being off with you. I was trying to give you space.'

'What made you think I wanted space?'

'I assumed we both did.' Another silence. Then, unable to bear it, Jonty said, 'I used all the hot water this morning. After your bath.'

'Why?'

'I heard Bryony telling your father she had a meeting and that she would shower afterwards. So, I used it all. I'm almost certainly going to hell.'

Lizzie laughed, something she didn't do often or easily. She smiled a lot. Sniggered or snorted. But real laughter was unusual. Anything that spited Bryony was likely to elicit it, though.

'She so thinks she's getting the house,' Lizzie confided, drawing her legs up to her chest.

'How could she possibly think that?'

'She keeps saying how Granny adored Lucca, how they were closer than anyone realized. Which is mad. Granny thought he was a complete brat. She just hoped he might come around eventually if he got to spend some time away from her.'

'Would they even want it? She bloody loves that job in Sussex.'

'I think everyone wants it,' Lizzie said, tracing her finger along the ridge in the door that the car window disappeared into. 'Don't they?'

Jonty shrugged. 'I don't think I do.'

'What would you do if you got it?'

'Stupid question. I won't. They'll want it to stay in the family—' He cut across Lizzie before she could speak. 'Blood family, I mean. Adopted grandson isn't much of a claim really. I sort of hope Dad gets it.'

'Why?' Lizzie privately thought that the last thing Grant deserved was any sort of reward. He was an even worse father than David.

'I know he wants it. I think maybe it's the only thing he's ever actually wanted.'

Lizzie didn't know how to respond to that. The silence seemed rather loud, so Jonty asked, 'What would you do? Sell it, and spend the rest of your life travelling the world?'

'Take lots and lots of lovers, live in the penthouse of a grand hotel. That sort of thing.' Lizzie smiled. They both knew it was a complete lie. Lizzie would die before she sold Roxborough, if it were hers.

They couldn't find a parking space in Norwich. Eventually, after driving round and round, Jonty getting more frustrated with every passing minute, Lizzie jumped out, climbing over the closed door of the car. 'Go around the block twice and then meet me back here. OK?' She turned on her heel and disappeared into an ancient-looking department store. What on earth was someone so young and full of life going to find in there, where they probably sold the dresses with the mothballs included? But, after only fifteen minutes, when Jonty had expected to be hovering by the side of the kerb much longer, making himself unpopular with the locals, there she was, standing on the side of the road looking smug and holding a bag.

'I can't believe you went in there,' he said. 'You must have been the youngest customer by about a decade.'

It was true. Lizzie and her grandmother had been into Wilton & Harris years ago, when Cecily had wanted some tights. 'Try not to breathe,' she had said as they went through the revolving doors. 'These places suck the life out of you.' But, ever since they'd arrived, Lizzie had been filled with a strange need to stand in the places she had stood with Cecily. She was struggling to make herself understand that her grandmother really was dead, that she wasn't going to pop up at supper making excuses

THE WILL

about being late, blaming some boring garden show or needy local friend. Wilton & Harris hadn't done it, of course. But still, it had felt like the right place to buy something for a funeral. All the shops she normally went to, for clothes to have fun in, seemed flippant and silly. She'd found a black shift dress on a hanger and bought it without trying it on. And then, when she was watching the shop assistant ring it up on the ancient till, with buttons that beeped, she had felt like crying.

'Ready?' Jonty asked her.

'Ready.'

2007

Lizzie threw her rucksack down on her bed, pulled off her school jumper and started to unbutton her shirt. She heard a knock at the door as she started to unfasten her kilt. 'Come in!' she shouted. The bedroom door opened behind her.

'Shit, sorry,' Jonty said, taking in Lizzie's tanned shoulders and her bright green bra. One of the straps was twisted. Why was he looking at her bra straps? He was the one who was twisted. He focused intensely on the floor. 'I heard the car and I thought you'd be back. Where's Willa?'

Lizzie didn't seem bothered by her toplessness. She reached for a pink T-shirt and pulled it on, then put a pair of shorts on underneath her kilt and peeled it off, dropping it on the floor triumphantly. 'No uniform for nine whole weeks,' she said proudly. 'I can't believe it's finally summer. When did you get here?'

'Dad dropped me yesterday.'

'Is he here?'

''Course not. He'll be picking up someone my age to spend the summer shacked up with.'

'Classic.' Lizzie laughed. 'Willa isn't coming until next week. She's doing an elective summer-school thing at Oxford.'

'Good for her.'

'She's such a loser.'

'She'll be far more successful than either of us.'

'Speak for yourself. I'm going to marry incredibly rich and never have to work. That's the most successful thing you can do.'

Jonty laughed. 'Granny's out with Violet, so we've got the house to ourselves. What shall we do?'

'I'm in the mood to celebrate,' Lizzie said. 'Let's make cocktails.'

'It's barely five o'clock.'

Her eyes glittered. 'Come on. You have to do what I say now. I'm a member of the Dead Mum Club.' Her voice cracked slightly.

Jonty wanted to wrap his arms around her. Luella. Grandpa. Now Cordelia. No wonder Lizzie had developed a sort of halo of sadness around her. 'All right,' he said. 'Let's make cocktails.'

They covered the drawing room with bottles taken from the drinks cabinet, bowls of ice forming puddles on various surfaces, mint leaves strewn across the floor. Lizzie had made them a painfully strong set of Mojitos, something she claimed was a Martini, and she was now attempting something involving champagne. 'Should we open that?' Jonty asked weakly as she popped the top from a 1992 bottle of champagne that wasn't even cold.

'If you don't drink it, then it's just a waste,' Lizzie said brightly. 'Do you have any cigarettes?'

Jonty shook his head. 'I don't smoke any more.'

'Why?'

'Because it's bad for you.'

Lizzie slopped champagne over the glasses. 'Because of Mum?'

'No.'

'Liar.'

'All right. A bit because of her.'

'She didn't smoke.'

'No. I know.'

'It was just "bad luck".'

'Yes.'

'It's quite impressively bad luck, isn't it? Both of our mothers dying.'

'Yes,' Jonty said. 'Very impressive.'

'I wish she wasn't dead.'

'Cordelia?'

'And your mum. I liked your mum.'

'So did I.'

'When does it stop hurting?'

Jonty considered lying to her but decided it would be unfair. 'I'll let you know,' he said.

Lizzie looked disappointed. 'I thought maybe it would just be a few months or maybe a year.'

'I don't think so.' Jonty shook his head. 'At least not for me.'

'Dad's already getting ready to move on.'

'Really?'

Lizzie was sitting on the sofa, very close to him. She'd draped her legs over his lap, and he was trying very hard to keep his hands in a position that looked entirely natural without touching her. There were tiny, blonde hairs on her knees, and her skin was very soft and tanned. He could smell her, the sugary, fruity body spray she used, her coconut shampoo. It was all so artificially sweet and tropical. He shouldn't like it. But he did.

'Dad's got women sniffing around him everywhere,' she said. There was a hint of a slur in her voice. 'All these divorcees from school, they keep coming over to tell him how brave he is. Even our headmistress fancies him.

Jonty laughed. 'Imagine if he shags your headmistress.'

Lizzie stuck both fingers in her mouth and made a puking noise, then laughed. 'I like it here when it's just the two of us.' She rested her hand on his face. If Lizzie were a normal girl, he would know what to do now. Not that he was madly experienced. But he'd slept with a few girls; enough to know that when they draped their legs over you and touched your face, you were allowed to try to kiss them. But this was obviously completely different. Lizzie wasn't a girl. Not really. She was his cousin. And there was no way that she could want him to kiss her. He shouldn't be thinking about slipping his hand under her

T-shirt or running his hands through her shiny blonde hair.

'What are you thinking about?' she asked.

'Nothing.'

'Liar. No one thinks about nothing.'

'You say "nothing" when you don't want to tell the other person what you're thinking about. It's a very nosy question.'

'I'm very nosy.' She smiled. 'I think you were thinking about me.'

'What?'

'I think you were thinking about me.'

Jonty looked down. He could feel his blood getting prickly, and there was an uncomfortable pressure in his lower body, which was probably going to lead to a very embarrassing erection. 'What do you think I was thinking about you?'

'I think you were thinking that you'd like to kiss me.'

Jonty almost dropped his drink. Which would have been a relief because the cocktail Lizzie had made was absolutely disgusting. 'What if I *was* thinking that?' he asked gently.

'Then I'd say you should do it.'

Jonty looked at her lips. And thought about the fact that they didn't share any blood. That she wasn't really his cousin. That her lips were pink and full and that her teeth were white and that there was a freckle on the side of her nose. He leaned forwards and pressed his lips against hers. She opened her lips, and he tasted the sugar and fruit juice on her tongue. Then she was on his lap, unzipping his jeans, kissing him, pressing her body against him. 'Are you sure?' he breathed, willing himself to slow down, to act like an adult, not to take advantage. She was younger than him. She had been drinking. 'Are you totally sure?'

Lizzie paused. Her pupils were huge, her smile wide. 'I've never been surer of anything.'

They pulled her shorts off in a tangle of denim and legs, and she pulled her knickers to the side, wrapping her legs around his waist. Then he was inside her and it was like nothing he had ever experienced before, so sharp and so sweet. He kissed her hungrily and pushed against her. She whimpered, and he stopped, worried that he'd hurt her. 'What?' she said impatiently. 'Don't stop!' So he didn't. He moved against her and she pushed her body back. 'I'm going to come,' she whispered in his ear, and the words pushed him over the edge. He came inside her, his hands gripping her. Then they stayed, fixed, perfectly still. He wasn't sure how long it was before she untwined herself from him and picked up her shorts from the floor. Then the tidal wave arrived. Guilt. Shame. Abject horror at what he had just done.

'I should go,' he said, getting to his feet.

'Where?' Lizzie objected.

'Sh–shower,' he stammered. Then he was upstairs, yanking the metal handle on the shower, turning the water up as hot as he could bear.

He tried to tell himself that what had just happened

hadn't really happened, which was utterly ridiculous. Then, eventually, he got dressed, went downstairs and started to clean up the mess they had made. Lizzie was nowhere to be seen, which was a complete relief. He wiped down every sticky surface, put the bottles back on the cocktail table, and decided that it would be far too childish to top them up with water. His grandmother never begrudged them anything; she wouldn't mind that they had enjoyed some drinks to celebrate the end of school. He wanted to turn the sofa cushions over, but he knew that was entirely pointless. There wasn't a single trace of what they had done in this room. And they would be able to pretend that nothing had happened. That unspoken, sharp, sweet feeling that had sat between them for the last few months would be gone. They had acted on it. Done what needed to be done. Got it out of their system. Now they could move on and never, ever do it again.

That night, he was lying in bed with the windows open, enjoying the cool breeze from outside, when he heard the door open. Lizzie stood at the door, wearing nothing but pyjama shorts. Again, that unignorable feeling in his groin. Why did she have to be so beautiful? Why did she have to be so painfully attractive?

'Can I come in?' she asked.

Jonty nodded.

'Can I get into bed with you?'

He nodded again. She lay down next to him, her body cool, his warm. Then she ran her hand down his bare stomach, into the waistband of his pyjamas. 'We shouldn't,' he whispered.

'Why not?'

'You know why not.'

'It's already done.'

'We can stop. If we don't do it again, then . . .' He trailed off.

'Then what?'

'Then it's like it never happened.'

'But it did happen,' she said, kissing his shoulder. 'And we both know it's going to happen again.'

'We shouldn't.'

'Why not?'

'I'm your cousin.'

'Not by blood.'

'No,' Jonty said. 'But what would everyone think if they found out?'

'They're not going to find out. It'll be a secret.'

Jonty turned over to face her. 'You can't tell anyone.'

'Cross my heart and hope to die.'

'Not even Willa.'

'Obviously, I don't tell Willa about my sex life.'

'And it's only for this summer. Never again. Just while we're here. Temporary.'

'Temporary,' Lizzie said, moving her body against his. Her skin was so soft. 'Very, very temporary.'

'OK then,' he said, kissing her.

4

The morning of the funeral dawned suitably grey, cooler than the days that had preceded it. David woke, grateful for it. His father's funeral had had the backdrop of blazing sunshine. It had felt incongruous. He tried not to think about that day, about what a balm it had been to have Cordelia next to him, her cool hand in his.

One of the things David had always liked best about Roxborough was its ability to remain quiet. Even with a houseful of people – and throughout his childhood Cecily really had filled the house – there was a blissful kind of silence to be found if you only closed your bedroom door and took a moment away from the party.

He closed the bedroom door behind him now and took a long breath. The room smelled like it always had. He had noticed it the first time he came home from boarding school, that the house had a smell. He supposed it always must have done, and that he was only noticing it because he had been away. It had made him sad. Not that being away was such a horror. School had been reasonably nice.

Nothing compared to the place where the girls had gone, where Bryony was head. They had a riding school, yoga classes, an on-site therapist. It was a hotel with lessons, rather than a school. And now Bryony had her sights set on expansion.

He had four missed calls on his mobile. Couldn't they leave him alone for a week? He had been perfectly clear that he had come to Norfolk for his mother's funeral. His clients were all fussing about their money, as if ringing him over and over again was going to make any difference. There were emails, too.

> David, I'm concerned that I can't get hold of you. I need to release some capital this week as my daughter has found a flat she wants to buy. The estate agents have been clear that if we don't start moving quickly, someone else will buy it. Please call me tomorrow.

He'd chosen a job as a financial adviser because he was good with numbers, not because he was good with people. And back in the old days, he'd been able to deal exclusively with the former and never with the latter. But he had had to let his secretary go a few months ago, and the previous year his partner had left to go out on his own. So now there was no one to shield him from these hungry, demanding people. The daughter buying the flat would inevitably be another complaining millennial, in a desperate rush to own something she probably wouldn't value.

David knew he was being unfair. She was probably a perfectly nice girl. He was just panicked because he didn't have the funds to release. They were currently being used to prop up someone else's investment, which had been plundered to pay his mortgage. And he was jealous of his client, swanning around buying homes for his children. Not something he would ever be able to do for his girls. Or for Lucca. God, would he even be alive when Lucca was old enough to need a house? Bryony went on and on about going to the gym, cutting all the sugar and fat out of their diets, 'so you'll be around for Lucca'. He'd started to privately wonder if seeing Lucca graduate would be worth a life without eating or drinking anything that tasted of something.

A knock at the door pulled him from his moping.

It was Grant, carrying a glass of whiskey. 'Angelique's drying her hair and I was wandering around the house feeling like a knob,' he said. 'Thought you might be up for some company.' He was dressed in black trousers and a white shirt; he was almost wearing a suit.

'Bloody hell,' David said. 'I didn't think you owned anything like that.'

'I don't.' Grant laughed, coming in and sitting on the desk in the corner where David had slaved over his extra essays ahead of his Oxbridge exams. 'It's Dad's. Look, it's got sort of velvet stripes up the side, from the seventies. It's got moth holes, too. God knows what Mum was doing, holding on to it.'

'You can't wear that for the funeral.'

'It's fine. No one will notice.'

David took a garment bag from the wardrobe. 'You can borrow this. I brought a spare.'

Grant smiled. 'You must be the only man in the world who travels with two black suits.'

'I don't like to be caught off guard.' He swallowed. 'Dad always did.'

Neither of them said anything. The ticking of the alarm clock on the bedside table rang around the room. 'How are you?' Grant asked, after a while.

'Fine,' said David quickly. 'Sad, obviously. But this is the worst part, isn't it, the funeral? Get that over and done with and then we can start to move on.'

Grant shrugged. 'I think conventional wisdom is that it's worse after the funeral. Life begins again. We have to go back to our real lives.'

'Well. Not all of us.'

'True.'

Another silence. Both of them knew what the other would be thinking. They had talked about the house before, many times. In the car back to school on a Sunday night. Lying awake in the nursery as kids. When Grant's wife had died and then, unbelievably, when David's first wife had died months later, and they had sat up together, drinking and not saying anything because they had absolutely no idea what they were supposed to say. Two young, widowed men, searching for answers. After that, David had married Bryony and Grant had dated younger and younger women, and the idea of spending time together had become unappealing, but this conversation had always been a safe place. What would you do with the house? How would you change it? What would you stamp all over it so that everyone remembered your tenure? It was like discussing what you'd do if you won the lottery. Only now, it wasn't hypothetical at all. It was very, very real. And only one of them – or neither of them – was going to get it.

'Do you think it'll be one of us?' David asked, feeling safe at least in that question.

Grant nodded. 'I suppose so. It usually goes to one of the kids.'

'Maybe it'll be Elspeth.' They both laughed.

'What on earth did she think she was doing, sending that lawyer? She thinks Mum would have left her cash, after all of that?'

'She's not going to get the house. It doesn't matter. She's just being awkward from the other side of the Atlantic, that's all. Do you ever wonder why she is so difficult?' David asked.

Grant considered him. But it wasn't the moment to explain. 'She was always difficult,' he said. He picked up a picture of the three of them from the mantelpiece. It must have been taken forty years ago, when they were in their late teens and early twenties. They were sitting in a row on the jetty over the lake. Elspeth in tennis whites, holding a racquet. She was a terrible player but always liked the outfits. David bookish with little glasses, a paperback self-consciously held in his hand. Grant, topless and tanned. He had spent that summer putting up marquees for smart parties, getting tanned and strong. It was the summer he had told his parents that he wasn't going to go to university. They'd been disappointed but, he sensed, not surprised.

The clock was terribly loud again. 'I should change,' Grant said, picking up the carrier. 'Cheers for this.'

'You're welcome,' David responded, finding almost to his surprise that he meant it. It felt rather reassuring to be able to do something for someone else. A nice break from feeling so fundamentally useless all the time.

Bryony and Grant crossed in the hallway and exchanged an awkward half-hello.

'What did Grant have in that bag?' she asked as she went into the bedroom. David looked handsome, if a little pale, looking through the huge window out to the garden.

'He borrowed a suit.'

'What on earth is wrong with your family? Lizzie didn't bring a dress, Grant didn't bring a suit. Honestly, you're the only one of them who can be trusted to get anything right.'

He wanted to defend them, to tell Bryony that Grant and Lizzie were chaotic but that they always found a way to solve the problem, that they never let anyone down. But she wouldn't change her mind, and there was no point. She was heating up her hair straighteners, ready to iron her sheet of silky dark hair. 'Shall I leave you to it?' he asked.

'Probably best.' Bryony smiled. 'Why don't you go and make sure Violet has everything in order? We've got to leave in half an hour. Also, Peter Wilkins called me – he's on the board of governors. He said he's been trying to get through to you about some transaction. I know today isn't ideal, but I said you'd give him a very quick bell this afternoon, after the funeral. All right?'

'Of course.' David smiled, closing the bedroom door behind him. *Fuck*, he thought. *Fucking, fucking, fuck.*

The cars drew up outside the house. Four neat black ones. Cecily had left instructions for those, too. David, Elspeth and Grant were supposed to travel in the first one, behind the hearse. Their partners in the next, with Lucca, and the grandchildren with Violet in the last. Violet tried to explain this to the family as they lined up outside the front door. It was the first time she had seen them all stand next to each other in years, perhaps decades, not running or rushing or gathering in groups like they did at Christmas and Easter. The Mordaunts weren't ones for big, posed family photographs. It was quite extraordinary how much Willa and Lizzie looked like Cecily, and how smart they all were in their black.

'Cecily suggested that David, Elspeth and Grant were to go in the first car—' Violet started.

'Well, Elspeth isn't here, which will have thrown everything off,' announced Bryony. 'David, Lucca, and the girls will come with me in one, Jonty can go with Grant and Angelique in another, and you and Rihan can go in the last one.' David nodded, so everyone else followed suit.

Jonty paused for a moment, looking back at Violet. 'Do you want to come with us, V?'

'We really need to get going,' Bryony called to Jonty.

'It's fine.' Violet smiled at Jonty. 'You go.' She watched the rest of them slide into the cars. Willa and Lizzie threw her sympathetic, apologetic looks. Then she opened the car door to sit next to Rihan. Both the 'staff' travelling together.

1969

It had been the hottest summer Cecily could remember at Roxborough. Even the hallways, usually so dark and cool, were stifling. Entertaining was the last thing she felt like doing. The only bearable activities were swimming in the lake or sitting in the little rowing boat with one hand trailing in the cool water. But Esmond had invited various work colleagues for dinner, and Cecily had diligently spent the week preparing. There was a cold poached salmon in the larder, salads had been made (though not dressed, as wilted leaves were unforgivable) and any moment now she was going to get up off the bed and go to have a lukewarm bath. Drying her hair would be hellish, but she'd found a silk dress in the back of her wardrobe that was almost a dressing gown and would be mercifully cool. From downstairs she heard the phone ring, the shrill sound bouncing off the hall walls.

'Violet,' she called. 'I'm going to have a bath. Could you answer it?'

*

Lying in the scented water, Cecily looked at her body. She would be thirty-two this year, and things weren't nearly so bad as they might be, especially considering all the children. Her breasts had always been on the smaller side. She'd cursed them when she and her friends had measured their busts obsessively at boarding school to see who was the sexiest, but it had turned out to be rather a blessing, because they hadn't dropped so much after the children. Her limbs were brown because she'd been sunbathing naked on the roof, and her waist was still reasonably small. All in all, she felt that her thirties were passing with some dignity. She had a few years left of being able to argue that she was young, but the idea of being older wasn't so bad.

A knock at the door distracted her from her self-indulgence. 'Yes?' she asked.

'It's me,' Violet said.

'What's wrong?' Cecily asked. She got out of the bath and wrapped herself in one of the peach-coloured towels that Esmond had insisted were fashionable. 'Who was on the phone?'

'It was Esmond.'

'Are the children all right?'

'Yes, no, nothing like that. It's just that he says it's far too hot to ask people to travel out here, so he's told everyone they can just go to an air-conditioned restaurant in London. It'll go on late, so he's going to stay at a hotel. He won't be back until tomorrow. Are you dreadfully disappointed?'

Cecily laughed. 'Not at all. We've got far too much food, but we'll manage that. We'll have the house to ourselves, without having to make conversation with all of his dreadful friends from the office. And now you won't have to do my hair.'

Violet smiled. 'I like doing your hair.'

When Violet had first come to help Cecily, having a maid had been almost normal. Cecily had been almost twenty-two and newly married. She'd needed Violet because, unlike Cecily, she knew how to do things. Violet had been to some sort of school where they taught you how to manage a house. Of course, it would have been more sensible, Cecily thought, if she herself had been to the school, and then she wouldn't have needed to employ Violet. But she had been glad of her advice. People now seemed increasingly surprised that Cecily had a lady's maid, and of course it was an anachronism, but she couldn't imagine how she would go on without Violet. It had never occurred to her, though, that Violet liked doing these things for her.

'Really?' she asked. 'How extraordinary.' Violet was blushing and, not wanting to embarrass her, Cecily said, 'Well, then, why don't you? That would be nice.'

When her hair was dry and Violet had set it into fat blonde curls, Cecily put on make-up, painting her lashes a sooty black and her lips a pale chalky pink, just as everyone seemed to be doing in the magazines. She wasn't sure why, but it seemed like fun. 'We'll pretend that you're Esmond for the evening,' she announced. 'And we'll eat in the dining room.'

And so, they did. They ate the food, painstakingly prepared by the cook, in the dining room, from salad to profiteroles, drinking glass after glass of champagne. And then, almost without thinking about it, when they were drunk and Violet had smoked two of Cecily's cigarettes, Cecily put her hand in Violet's and asked, 'Would you like to come upstairs?'

Violet nodded, her eyes, almost as purple as they were blue, enormous. They had walked slowly up the huge staircase, to Cecily's room, and undressed each other with the kind of reverence that can only exist the first time two people make love to each other. There had been a sort of inevitability about it. When they kissed it was new, but not a surprise. Perhaps they had always known that, one day, they would find themselves tangled in bed together, kissing each other's breasts, hands between each other's legs. Esmond was perfectly good in bed, nothing to complain about, and Violet was inexperienced. And yet, somehow, this was a kind of painfully delicious ecstasy that Cecily had never previously known.

After what might have been hours or minutes, they lay together naked, the bedsheets everywhere. Cecily got up and started to close the curtains.

'Oh, don't,' Violet said. 'I'd far rather sleep with them open. I love that view.'

When Cecily woke the next morning, she realized that there would only ever be one person with whom she wanted to share her bed, for the rest of her days.

Violet had started to creep from the room the moment

she awoke, hoping that she could slip back to her bedroom and that this wouldn't cast some embarrassing shadow over what had been such a happy working relationship for the previous decade.

'Where are you going?' Cecily asked sleepily.

Violet flushed at being caught. 'Back to my room.'

'Why?'

It was impossible to answer that. Cecily didn't wait long. 'Come back to bed,' she said. In years to come, Violet would wonder what might have happened if she had said no, whether she might eventually have been happier for it. But it was impossible to deny Cecily anything. And she would have been just as much denying herself. So, she did as she was told and climbed back into bed with Cecily, marvelling at the idea that she was allowed to touch her.

5

Everyone kept saying that the funeral service had been lovely. Violet couldn't decide what she was supposed to say to that. It hadn't been lovely to watch the people who loved Cecily weep for her. Or to hear words she wasn't sure Cecily had believed. Or to watch Cecily's body being lowered into the ground. She knew that the 'lovely' comments were supposed to be a compliment, an acknowledgement that she had done a good job of putting the thing together. But it felt like something else, like she was being patted on the head. Patronized.

It had been a perfectly decent funeral in the sense that nothing had gone wrong. David had done a reading from the Bible. Grant had read a poem. The three grandchildren had carried the offerings for the Mass to the altar. Everyone who had wanted to be included was included. There was a part of Violet that had expected Elspeth to arrive at the last moment and sit tight-lipped at the back. But she hadn't come. Would she regret it, eventually? Violet wondered. It wasn't as if she could change it. If you missed your own mother's funeral, you missed it.

Violet hung back in the church, watching David and Bryony lead the charge towards the wake, Bryony furtively passing Lucca an iPad, presumably to assure good behaviour. Lizzie and Willa, tightly grasping each other's hands. Willa's green eyes bloodshot, her cheekbones razor sharp. She looked perfect in a neat black dress, black high heels, a black jacket; Lizzie an utter contrast, her hair wild. The 1960s-style shift dress she wore was strange, and the hem was fraying where she had cut it, but she was undeniably lovely. Jonty followed behind them. Grant and Angelique, and then, hanging back as if he knew his presence was rather odd, Rihan.

The wake was exactly as it should be. Held in the music room, which was long and low-ceilinged and at the back of the house, looking out over the gardens. It had been Cecily's favourite room. Every few months, she would invite some young musical star who was living off bread and water while training at the Royal College of Music. She would pay them an extraordinary sum to visit and then invite all of her friends. The room would be filled with little chairs and, afterwards, she'd ply everyone with wine. Violet often suggested buying boxed wine from the local Oddbins because no one would know the difference, but Cecily had scoffed. 'I'm not going to leave the cellar untouched for whoever gets it next,' she had said.

Violet had never asked Cecily who was to have the house next. It wasn't so much that she couldn't ask, or even that she respected the sanctity of the arrangement, more that it felt like crossing some invisible border. The relationship between them as employer and employee had dissolved years and years ago, but the house somehow seemed to re-suggest it, to press the strangeness of their situation back upon the conversation. And besides which, Violet didn't want to know. The event of the house passing to someone else would mean that the person she loved most in the world was no longer here. The idea was too horrible to bear.

The only good thing about the wake was that she was busy. While the family stood around receiving visitors, listening to anecdotes about Cecily, smiling politely through their sadness, Violet was free to refill the wine glasses and top up the urns of hot water for tea. Being known to be a member of the staff was like a sort of superpower. It made her invisible. And while there had been times that the invisibility had hurt her, today it suited her entirely.

She slipped out of the side door carrying a bottle of wine, more as a prop than anything else.

Standing, with his back against the ivy-covered wall, was Grant. He was staring out across the garden, down to the lake. The noise of the door jolted him. 'Jesus,' he said. 'You made me jump.'

'I'm sorry,' Violet said, moving to go back inside.

'Don't go.'

She froze, unsure what to do next.

'I miss her,' Grant said.

'Me too.'

The birds were singing. Cecily had always loved birdsong. More than most people – everyone likes birdsong, but Cecily had loved it. Slept with the windows open even when it was freezing so that she might hear the dawn chorus of early spring.

'You know, she was the only person I know who had money and didn't send her children to boarding school. I mean we went, but she didn't send us. She waited until we were old enough to know what we wanted, and then when we asked, she said yes. No one at Dunam Hall could believe I'd never boarded until I was thirteen.'

Violet smiled. 'She was a forward-thinker in lots of ways.'

'True. But desperately backwards in others. Remember when recycling came in?'

Violet laughed. She did remember. It had been an impressively enormous battle, Cecily following the rules to a T, carefully rinsing every tin and jar before throwing them away, but harumphing about it. 'So where do the bloody milk-bottle lids go now?' she would shout every morning when the milk was delivered.

'How long do you think it'll be before that lot clear off?'

'I'm not sure. Another hour?'

'Christ alive.' Grant exhaled. He realized, though he would never breathe a word of his revelation, that he wanted to know that his mother had left him the house. That she had judged him the best custodian for this place that she had loved so much. And, he

supposed, all of the associated implications that his sus-
picion was right. That she had loved him best. He took
a long slug from his drink, trying to rid himself of the
unpleasant, petty thought.

The door opened and Angelique, beautiful in a black
silk dress with cap sleeves, picked her way out. She wound
her arms around Grant, and Violet took this as her cue to
leave. 'Don't worry, *mon chéri*,' she heard Angelique say. 'It
will be over soon. And I am sure it will be you.'

It seemed to Willa that people were very slow to leave the
wake. Of course, most of them knew the house and the
family and because of that they knew what was going to
happen next. Generally, they were too polite to actually
acknowledge it, but she caught snippets of conversations
as she moved from group to group and she could feel the
sense of electricity in the room.

She supposed that they probably had favourites among
the family, preferences about who would take over the
house. Which made sense. Whoever ran the house would
be a pillar of the local community. Willa wasn't entirely
sure what a pillar of a local community was, but she'd
heard people say it often enough to believe that it was
important. Everyone here was about to inherit a new
neighbour and, depending on who it was, that might
mean parties and village fetes in the gardens. Or it could
mean the land being sold to build piles of new houses.

They almost certainly hoped for Lizzie, who right
now was holding court, sitting on a leather sofa with her

legs pulled up to her chest, telling a loud story about Cecily while people laughed. If they did all hope that Lizzie was the heir apparent, Willa couldn't blame them. Her beautiful, glittering sister would be just the right person to breathe life back into this house. Their father would be the least exciting, without a doubt. He stood in the far corner of the room, looking rather grey, gravely nodding while an older man with extraordinary eyebrows talked. Bryony was clamped to his side, which was hopefully a comfort to him because it certainly wasn't to anyone else. He was the obvious one to inherit, of course. No one would be upset, exactly. But Willa had a feeling that her grandmother, so sharp and perspicacious, wouldn't risk the house falling into Bryony's hands.

Willa picked up some empty glasses, placed them on a tray and was taking them back to the kitchen when she found Lucca, sitting on the main stairs, holding an iPad and playing some sort of war game with the volume turned up.

Lucca had been 'entertaining himself', as Bryony called it, all day. Willa had heard her father telling Lucca that this was going to be 'a fun trip' after the funeral was over, and that they would go to the safari park. Privately, Willa had thought this unlikely, and Lucca seemed unimpressed that, so far, there had been no safari park. Just endless adult conversations. How miserable it must be, trying to find a way to entertain yourself here, without any siblings to play with.

'Are you OK?' Willa asked, reminding herself to be friendly to her brother. The word 'brother' still seemed so unlikely after three decades of a sister and yet only a few years of him.

'Fine,' said Lucca, without looking up. Then he seemed to realize what he'd said. 'I mean, sad.'

Willa sat down on the step, not exactly next to him – she didn't particularly like to sit close to anyone – but close enough.

'It's OK if you don't feel sad, you know.'

This seemed to surprise Lucca enough that he put the iPad down. 'Is it?'

Willa nodded. 'Sometimes it takes ages to realize that you feel sad. The feelings might not have caught up with you yet.' She sensed that this wasn't quite what Lucca had hoped to hear. 'And sometimes,' she added, 'when someone is very old, and you didn't know them very well, you don't feel sad because you know it was their time to leave.'

Lucca looked enormously relieved. 'Mummy said I should show everyone that I feel sad, so they don't think I don't care.'

Willa had never had quite the same level of antipathy towards her stepmother that Lizzie did – probably because, long before meeting their father, Bryony had given Lizzie two weeks of detention, which involved scraping chewing gum off the bottom of the dining-room tables, because she'd been caught smoking. But occasionally she heard David or Lucca repeat Bryony's words and she was struck all over again by how stagger-ingly awful the woman was.

'You don't have to prove anything to anyone,' she said to Lucca, getting to her feet and reclaiming the tray. 'And there's no one in the little telly room where the Play-Station is.'

Lucca grinned and was on his feet almost instantly.

Standing at the kitchen sink, apparently washing up cut-lery, was Violet. Willa put the tray down quietly and tried to escape unnoticed, but Violet's hearing was still perfect. She whipped around, wiping away tears. 'I'm sorry,' Willa said.

'No, no, I'm being silly. We're not even supposed to wash the cutlery before the caterers pack it up. I just feel like such a spare part. No one quite seems to know what to say to me.'

'I don't know what to say to anyone,' Willa admitted. 'Lizzie and Jonty and Grant are all brilliant at it. They know exactly what to say to make everyone else feel bet-ter. Even Dad seems to be doing a decent job. I just keep trying to top up everyone's drinks. And I can't stop think-ing that we've got a whole bloody dinner to get through tonight.' It was strangely nice to be able to admit dread-ing a meal, for once. Dinners were always such nice things for everyone else. She had already asked Violet four times what was going to be served tonight, carefully planning out which parts were safe to eat and which parts would have to be avoided.

Violet nodded. 'It's an extraordinary system.'

Willa sat down on the windowsill. 'I think I always knew there would be one in my lifetime, but it felt so unlikely. Like a family fairy tale.'

Violet nodded. 'Your grandmother said the same thing. You know, she talked about cancelling the whole thing.'

'Really?'

'Oh yes, all the time. Said it was a stupid, archaic idea, that she should just choose who to give the house to, pass it on and let everyone else ask her questions while she was still alive. She said it was cowardice to hide behind death and not tell people why they'd been found lacking. She said she hated her one.'

'I don't think I ever heard her talk about hers.'

Violet got to her feet. 'We should go back through.'

There was no point in trying to drag anything further from Violet, so Willa followed her back to the music room, and passed around drinks and canapés until, eventually, the last of the last of the last hangers-on departed.

The room was littered with coffee cups, wine glasses, water glasses and side plates. Lizzie and Jonty sat on one sofa, David and Bryony on another. Angelique's head was resting on Grant's shoulder, Violet was instructing the caterers quietly in the corner and Willa was trying to be discreet about the fact that she was checking her email.

'Right,' Violet said. 'Cecily's instructions ask that we meet in the drawing room at seven thirty, ahead of dinner at nine. So, I suppose we had all better go and get ready.'

★

The drawing room was beautiful, furnished with antique furniture and silk wallpaper, but it was draughty and difficult to keep warm, and so usually avoided. Gusts of cold air ran along the floor, freezing your feet, which in turn made it difficult to relax. Cecily had famously used it for social occasions she wanted to get over and done with. Christening parties for the grandchildren had been held in here, as had meetings for the parish council. Anyone who knew Cecily would know to neck a quick glass or cup of whatever was being served and then be on their way if they were invited into the drawing room. But this was, as all the Mordaunts knew, where the drinks were supposed to be held before an entailment.

Looking at the portraits that lined the walls – gloomy men and mysterious women – Jonty thought about all the other Mordaunts who must have gathered here hundreds of years before, similarly tightly wound and wondering whether they were going to inherit the house.

He was always acutely aware that he'd been adopted into this illustrious family, but usually it didn't bother him. This weekend, though, it was weighing more heavily than it ever had before. It was ironic, probably, that a ceremony formulated on the idea that houses shouldn't be passed down a bloodline was making him more self-conscious than ever before that he didn't share a drop of blood with these people. They all looked so much more related than he had ever previously registered: the same full bottom lip partnered by a narrower top one, the characteristic hair that was neither blonde nor brown and yet couldn't be described as mouse. All things that he seemed to share at first glance, but didn't really – not if you really studied them.

As a child, he had worn his adoption lightly, accepting that it made him rather more interesting than other children. And later, it had been easier that he wasn't a real Mordaunt, because it meant that he and Lizzie shared no genetic reason not to give in to their urges. In adulthood, he liked the cachet too. It allowed him, he told people, to be dispassionate about the nature/nurture debate. It was quite extraordinary how often people would ask him deeply personal questions about his adoption, apparently assuming that, because he was open about it, he wanted to be interrogated. The popularity of those misery memoirs in bookshops – with titles such as 'Don't Hurt Me, Daddy' and 'Please No' had never surprised him. Other people's misery was, he knew, irresistible to anyone who had enjoyed an easy, drama-free life. It was distasteful, but not worth going to war over. So, he would add with a laugh at parties if people asked him about it, he had landed on his feet with the Mordaunts. Life had been cushy: boarding school, university, a job he loved. How could he complain about that?

'You're early,' said Lizzie, taking a glass of champagne from the tray on a little table by the door.

'So are you.'

They faced each other for a moment, neither of them really sure what to say.

'This is weird.'

'Yes.'

Another long silence, broken by Lizzie asking, 'You still don't think it will be you?'

Jonty laughed. 'Of course not.'

'Why not?'

'I'm not a proper Mordaunt.'

'Doesn't work like that,' Lizzie said, kicking off her shoes and sitting cross-legged in a velvet armchair. It was a relief, somehow, to see her unable to sustain the strangely adult composure she had worn for all of five minutes. 'Granny always said it didn't need to be blood. Sometime in the 1800s, someone left it to a gamekeeper, remember?'

'And they tried to overturn that decision – there's a whole book about it in the library upstairs. Plus, he married the youngest daughter, so they ended up with Mordaunts in residence anyway.'

'Everyone loved him eventually. He made the land work better and hired local people. Don't look so surprised. I read.'

Jonty hadn't meant to look incredulous. He wasn't taken aback by Lizzie's smarts, but research wasn't really her forte. Lizzie liked to start books and then leave them splayed with a broken spine because she was reading something else instead. Perhaps her uncharacteristic attention to detail demonstrated just how much she wanted this place.

Unlike most people, Lizzie had never pretended otherwise. She had loved the house since she was a child and she had told anyone who would listen that she wanted to live here, that she had plans for the house. She would throw huge parties in the gardens, invite creative people without much money to stay and write for free. And eventually she would throw herself an enormous white wedding by the lake and give herself away. She had asked her grandmother many times as a child if she could have the house, and Cecily had always smiled, unperturbed by the question but refusing to be drawn on it. Of course, as Lizzie had got older, she had stopped asking; even she wasn't quite that ballsy. But her grandmother knew that this was Lizzie's real home, the only place she'd ever really been happy. And Lizzie knew, somehow, that this house was meant to be hers. She was the only one of the Mordaunts who would breathe life into this place in the same way that her grandmother had. It was supposed to be hers.

The door opened again; this time it was Bryony. All three of them realized their mistake. Bryony couldn't retreat back upstairs without the embarrassing admission that she didn't want to stay and talk to Lizzie and Jonty, and Lizzie and Jonty weren't quite awful enough to turn on their heels and ignore her.

'Where's Lucca?' Lizzie asked, knowing that Lucca was their safest subject. When her father forced Lizzie to speak to Bryony on the phone, Lizzie would ask about Lucca, put the phone down and wander off for five minutes, knowing that her stepmother would still be going when she came back.

'He's reading upstairs,' Bryony responded. 'He's not sixteen.'

Jonty and Lizzie nodded at this statement of the obvious. They both knew that the house couldn't be left to someone under the age of sixteen, but from Bryony's expression, akin to that of someone who's just discovered sick on their new carpet, it seemed that perhaps she had only recently learned it herself.

'He's been so good,' Willa said, coming in. 'It must be a pretty boring trip for him.'

Bryony's face looked pinched. 'He doesn't get bored. He's an extremely creative child.'

'That must be nice for him.' Willa smiled. 'I wish I was so creative that I didn't get bored during long meetings.'

Bryony didn't reply.

'Drink?' Jonty asked, handing Bryony a glass of champagne from the tray.

'Thank you,' Bryony said, taking it rather gratefully. Jonty wondered what it was that she had to look quite so nervous about.

'How are you feeling about the A-level results?' Jonty asked Bryony politely. Lizzie rolled her eyes at him.

Violet arrived and shortly afterwards came Grant and Angelique, then David. David looked at them in turn, hating himself for sizing them all up. His daughters both looked so adult, something he had assumed he would stop noticing as they approached thirty, but in fact seemed to strike him time and time again. He tried not to think about what would happen if his mother had left the house to one of the girls. Better it was Jonty, if his mother hadn't done the decent thing and left it to him. At least he could resent Jonty quietly and just see him once a year at Christmas. Refilling his glass, he noticed that Angelique's hair was slightly roughened at the back, and that Grant looked happier than he had any right to. Had his brother really managed to find time to screw his girlfriend between the funeral and now? How tasteless.

When his father had been alive, drinks had always been held in the drawing room on Christmas Day, before the enormous lunch, and then, finally, presents handed out from under the tree that dominated the hall, opened in the snug. After his death, Cecily had streamlined the system, allowing the grandchildren to open their presents before lunch and doing the whole thing in the warmer and more comfortable parts of the house. But for David, this room was always tinged with a sense of anticipation, with the feeling that he might be about to get a new bike.

Violet cleared her throat and stood up from the chair she had been inhabiting in the corner of the room while the rest of the Mordaunts filtered in. Her feet were tired. Actually, her entire body was tired. Cecily had always praised her for being so fit, so able to run up and down the stairs, but the unavoidable truth is that age, which she had watched sand the edges of Cecily's sharpness, was now coming for her.

'I won't go on,' she said, as the family looked at her expectantly. 'In a moment, we'll go through to the dining room. The letters are on the table by your seats. We'll read them, and then have supper. The terms of the entail state that you're in no way obliged to share the contents of your letter with anyone else, though whoever has been left the house will need to make themselves known. That person will then go with me on Monday to the solicitor's office to deal with all the paperwork. The death duties on the house are being held in an account and will be paid immediately, after which the house will legally belong to one of you. This, you remember' – she gestured to the man in the dark suit – 'is Rihan. You met before. He's here for Elspeth, so she doesn't have to forgo any bequests. And he's from the firm that has worked with the family since the Ark, so he's familiar with how all of this works. He's here to oversee things, and he can answer any questions you might have later. Two birds with one stone.'

She finished, but nobody said anything. 'Shall we go through?'

Most of the glasses were half full – not finishing a glass of champagne was very out of character for almost all of them, but no one could bring themselves to tarry in the drawing room when their fates were sitting on the dining-room table.

Willa took a long, slow breath. It wasn't going to be her. She knew that. So why was she so nervous? Did she really care whether it went to her sister or her uncle? Her father, she noticed, was paler than usual. His shoulders were higher too. He so clearly wanted it to be him. Willa wondered how he was going to handle it when he discovered that the house wasn't going to be his. Would Bryony break the habit of a lifetime and discover some selfless resource to support him? Willa suspected not.

The dining room had been decorated according to a very specific set of instructions left by a nineteenth-century Mordaunt with a love of ceremony. The room was lit with an enormous number of candles, presumably an essential when the instructions were written, so that everyone could reliably read their letters before the advent of electricity. The long mahogany table gleamed in the warm light, covered with highly polished silver-ware and garlands of green flowers. There was a seating plan, each name written in a curling italic script. And at each place setting, between all the silver cutlery and the linen napkins, was an envelope with their name on it.

Everyone stood in a cluster by the door, no one willing to be the first to sit down. Eventually, Grant laughed. 'Well, we might as well get on with it then.' He took his seat, between Bryony's and Willa's. One of the discreet staff members brought in from the village, a woman in her twenties who had helped in the house since her teens, picked up a bottle of white wine, its cool glass sweating in the warm room, and began to fill glasses. Violet took a breath and took her place, waiting to see whether the family would register that she was taking a place at the table, that she herself had a letter. She caught Jonty's eye. He nodded at her with a half-smile; he at least was apparently not going to be angry with her.

Bryony had noticed too. So, Lucca was too young to be

included, despite being a member of the family, but Violet, who was a member of the family's staff, had been. *Oh God*, she thought. *Does that mean she's been left the house?* It seemed so obvious now. She had spent the entire week worrying that Grant might have charmed the house from his mother, or that Cecily might have done something foolish like leave it to one of the grandchildren, that she hadn't stopped to worry that it would be Violet. If that happened, who would Violet leave it to in turn? She had no children of her own and her closest friend had been the woman she had worked for for decades. The entire system would fall apart.

'Well,' David said when all the glasses had been filled and the waitress had made a tactful exit. 'Shall we?'

There was a long silence, which was probably not long at all, and then they each lifted their heavy cream parchment envelopes, waiting to see who would be the first person to open theirs.

Lizzie slid one long finger under the flap, feeling the glue give way easily. She hadn't ever been one to worry about exam results, working on the basis that she would pass or not pass, and that either way it would probably be fine, but she assumed this must be how other people felt about finding out how they had done in their A levels or whether they had got into university. All the old clichés: her heart was absolutely thumping, she felt somehow both hot and cold at the same time, everything around her felt overwhelmingly loud and sharp. She caught her breath then pulled a piece of paper from the envelope, telling herself that it could be her, that it might be her, that if it wasn't her there would be a good reason for it. She opened the piece of paper and stared down at it, willing herself to understand what it said. But the paper looked blank. She blinked, trying to focus on it, trying to wrestle the paper into something that made sense. Then she looked up across the table, to where Willa sat, and realized that in fact she wasn't being stupid; her eyes weren't failing to work. The piece of paper she was holding was blank.

Everyone had now opened their envelopes; Grant was turning his letter over again and again, as if some writing were going to magically appear on one side. It didn't. So, it wasn't really a letter. It was a piece of completely worthless paper.

'What's happening?' David demanded.

'Is everyone else's . . . ?' Willa asked.

'Blank,' Lizzie finished. 'I think so.'

One by one they held up their pieces of paper, showing each other that every single one of them had opened their letter in this ornate, archaic tradition, to find that it was completely and utterly blank.

6

For a few minutes, almost everyone spoke, but no one listened to anyone; it was just noise. The only silent ones were Jonty, who was watching dispassionately, and David, who was drinking his glass of wine, willing this to be some kind of mass hallucination that could be remedied neatly straight away. Eventually, the noise gave way to quiet, and everyone looked to the top left of the table where Violet sat, neat as ever in her navy dress.

Silently, Lizzie rose to her feet and left the room. Willa and Jonty both got up to follow her. 'I'll go,' Jonty said. Willa knew she should disagree, that she should insist it was she who went. But she couldn't face it, so she sank back into her chair, staring at the naked piece of paper in front of her.

'Mum must have got confused,' David was saying now. 'She must have put blank paper in our envelopes and put the real letters somewhere else. They must be in the house somewhere.'

Grant shrugged. 'Maybe.'

'She was elderly,' Bryony added. 'I've seen it happen to lots of people. She will have just been muddled.'

'She wasn't confused,' Violet said sharply. 'She wasn't confused at all.'

'What does this mean?' Grant asked.

Violet wished she knew what to say. 'I'm afraid I have no idea,' she ventured.

'So, who has the house?' Bryony asked.

Violet shook her head. 'I don't know.'

'You must know who she was leaving it to,' David countered. 'You were with her every minute of every bloody day.'

'I don't,' Violet insisted. 'Truly.'

They all looked to the corner of the room where Rihan sat, looking faintly horrified. 'But you know, don't you?' Bryony asked him.

'I am afraid I do not,' said Rihan. He looked at the floor. 'I will have to let Mrs Mordaunt's daughter know that this has happened.'

'Excuse me,' said David, getting to his feet. He took his glass of wine and left the room.

Bryony watched him, trying to decide whether he would be better off alone. She felt the weight of the others' eyes on her and stood. 'I'll be back in a moment,' she said.

He had gone back to their bedroom and was standing in front of the window, swaying slightly. 'Are you all right?' she asked, wrong-footed by his haunted expression. 'What's wrong?'

115

'Nothing.'

'That's not true.'

'I'm fine.'

'You're grey and you're shaking. Tell me what's going on.'

She tried not to use her teacher voice with David, but occasionally it was unavoidable and, in this case, it seemed to work. 'She didn't leave me the house,' he said.

'Why are you saying that? All the letters were blank. You don't know it wasn't left to you.'

David laughed an oddly unhappy laugh. 'Yes, I do. If she was going to do the sensible thing and leave it to me – like she should have – there'd have been a letter. She's done this on purpose. She always had to be different. It'll be some kind of game. You know, most people get married and have children and begin acting like adults, start putting their children first all of the time. That's what I did, that's what Cordelia did. But not my mother. She always had to be a character, always wanted to be the centre of attention, being clever and witty and brilliant. This is just the last in a long line of things she screwed up because she couldn't stop being so bloody selfish.'

Bryony raised her eyebrows as much as the minuscule amounts of Botox she had in the summer and Christmas holidays would allow. She had never heard David speak about his mother in anything other than hushed reverential tones, just like everyone else. Cecily was so brilliant, Cecily was such a star, such a beauty, everyone adored her, so funny, so clever. Bryony hadn't ever seen it herself. She'd only ever observed a privileged older woman who saw her children as an extension of her social life.

'It doesn't matter,' Bryony said, putting her hand on David's shoulder. 'If we don't have the house, we'll wait until we raise the funds and we'll buy somewhere else to put the new school.'

David did the same laugh again; it made Bryony uneasy. 'You think I'm upset because I wanted to turn this place into a school?'

'That's what we always talked about.'

'I didn't think you were serious.'

Bryony felt stung. She had been more serious about converting Roxborough into a school than she was about anything else in the world – other than Lucca's future. It was the perfect place for a bijou girl's school. She'd drawn the uniforms in her head, planned how the morning room would become her study, how it would become a beacon of excellence for female education.

'No,' Bryony said. 'Of course not.'

David turned to face her. She was so beautiful when she wasn't wearing her severe headmistress garb of a suit and a tight updo. He knew she had to try to look older so that parents weren't put off by her age, but he found the whole thing rather disturbing. The first time they'd had a dinner date, when he was still living in a fog of grief, he had almost talked himself out of the whole mad idea. And then, when he'd got to the restaurant, he'd waited for her to arrive, planning how to tell her that he'd had a moment of madness and that he wasn't at all ready to go out with anyone, least of all the headmistress of his daughters' school. But then she had arrived and her dark hair had been softly curled around her face, her shoulders tanned, peeking out from under a pale pink top, and he had melted.

'We're broke,' he said finally.

Bryony's face contracted. 'What?'

'Well, I suppose it would be more accurate to say that I am broke.'

'I'm sorry?'

'The house is mortgaged and remortgaged. I'm at the bottom of my overdraft. I owe money to friends. There's a credit card – several credit cards, actually. A loan, some-where, I think.'

'How?'

'Oh, the same way it always happens. Money was tight, I borrowed some at a ridiculous rate; it got tighter, I bor-rowed more. Our wedding, the girls' universities, helping with Lizzie's rent, Willa's therapy.' Bryony winced, remem-bering the conversation with David when she had fought tooth and nail, saying that Lizzie was spoilt and didn't need help with her rent, and that Willa, who was earning close to six figures at a law firm, certainly didn't need any help pay-ing her therapy bills. But he had ignored her. And kept all those bills and bits of paper away from her. Jesus, two weeks ago she had been at a Slug & Lettuce with her university friends, gloating about how David managed everything, how he would barely let her look at the statement for their joint account. How stupid had she been? For the thirty-seven years of her life before meeting David, she had been ruthlessly, painfully independent. She'd never had a joint account with a boyfriend lest he ruin her credit score. The majority of her savings were in a private account. Even opening a shared account with David had felt dangerous. She had never paid a bill late, never so much as stolen a library book. Her life had been run with a ruthless efficiency, which hadn't been fun. David had teased her for being tight, for gripping the reins so hard. And slowly, as she felt herself unfurling around him, she had relinquished them. That had been, she now saw, a catastrophic mistake.

'Say something,' David said quietly. 'Please.'

'How much?'

'I don't know exactly—'

'Yes, you do.'

He looked down at the floor. 'A shade under a million.'

It was worse than Bryony had thought it would be. But she controlled her face, making sure he didn't realize this.

'That was why you wanted the house so badly?'

David nodded.

'But the income with the house can't be enough to pay that off?'

'No. I don't think it is.'

'So, what, you were going to sell it?'

'No.' He sat down on the bed, slow and broken in his movements. 'I was going to sell two of the fields. They're out of the way so no one would mind much, and it would be easy to get planning permission. You could put fifteen, maybe twenty houses on them. I could get most of a million for it.'

Bryony sat next to him and, after a moment of wrestling with herself, put her hand on his thigh. 'Who else knows about this?'

'No one.'

'You're sure?'

'Absolutely sure.'

'Good.' She got up. 'We have to go downstairs.'

David's face was half lit by a low lamp, the only light in the room. He looked older. 'Why?' he asked.

'Because they're going to be talking about what to do next. And you're the eldest child. You should be leading that conversation.'

She was right. They were all back at the table, except for Lizzie and Jonty, who hadn't yet returned, and Grant, who was smoking out of the window. Angelique was smoking too, not even really out of the window.

Bryony was making ostentatious coughing noises despite the fact that the room was enormous and barely smelled of smoke. David found himself pacing backwards and forwards, something he had assumed that people only did in bad plays. Willa sat at the table, her long arms crossed, her body perfectly still. 'What happens now?' she asked no one in particular.

'You,' David said, rounding on Violet. 'You're the executor. What do we do?'

'I'm not the executor. I don't know who is. Mine was

blank too. The will isn't read until the house entail is given. Perhaps Rihan might have a better understanding of what should happen next . . . ?'

Everyone stared at Rihan. He realized they wanted him to explain further, so he got to his feet, and began slowly. 'Your mother's arrangement to pass on the house was extremely unusual. She would have written the letters, and then, in the usual run of things, she would have had a will, which would be witnessed. But if whoever gets the house isn't stipulated, then there isn't anyone who knows where she wanted the money to go, as far as I can tell.'

'So, who gets the house?'

'It's hard to tell. I suppose it would have to be sold.'

'And then?'

'The money would either be split between her children or, if anyone contested it, it could be argued that it's as much the right of one of you as any other, so it would be split between the family. Or perhaps between everyone who received a blank letter.'

Bryony started totting it up in her head. One for her and, arguably, one for Lucca, if all the rules had gone out of the window; after all, he was as much a blood relation to Cecily as any of the other grandchildren were, even if he hadn't had a letter in his own right. And one for David. The girls wouldn't want to share theirs; they weren't generous like that. But still, they would have three portions of the total cost. Would it be enough to pay off whoever he owed the most pressing loans to?

'Did she write letters?' Willa asked, looking at Violet.

Violet looked strained. 'Yes. At least I think so. She told me she had written them. I saw her writing them. But of course I never read them.'

'Well, if she told you she wrote them, she must have. So, we need to find them,' Willa said.

'Well, then, we should look for them,' Bryony said.

'Yes, obviously,' said Grant, rather more sharply than he had intended. He wondered if he should apologize, but Bryony had gloriously thick skin.

David looked rather grey, Angelique thought. 'Don't you think it's possible that perhaps she did not write letters?' she asked.

'No,' Grant said. 'Mum loved tradition. There's no way that she would have done it like this on purpose. She must have become confused towards the end and screwed it up somehow. We have to look for the letters.'

'What, as if the blank letters were an accident and the real ones are just hanging around the house?'

'Maybe she moved them before she died. Maybe she changed her mind. I don't know. But we can't just do nothing, can we?'

'You think she hid the letters? You think she wanted us to do some macabre treasure hunt after she was dead?'

Grant stubbed out his cigarette. 'I don't know what's going on, David. None of us do. But finding those letters is going to be the easiest way to finish this whole nightmare. What else can we do?'

David sighed. 'Would it actually help? If we found the letters?'

Rihan had been miles away, wondering about how long this might end up taking and whether he could reasonably expect overtime. 'Yes,' he agreed. 'It would certainly be easier – as long as we can be sure that they're the real letters, it would solve the problem.'

'Right then,' said David, getting to his feet. 'Let's look.'

David caught Grant's arm in the corridor. 'Look, I know how this is going to sound,' he said, hoping his brother wasn't going to make this any more uncomfortable than it had to be. 'I think we should look in Violet's room. For the letters. Just to rule it out – I'm not saying she took them, I'm just thinking – why are you laughing?'

Grant wasn't really laughing, more smirking. 'You're not serious?'

'I just think it might be better to be sure.'

'Where do you think Violet's room is?'

David was wrong-footed. 'Upstairs? It used to be upstairs.'

'Used to when?'

'I don't know, when we were kids.'

'David. You're not seriously telling me that you don't know?'

'Know what?'

'Violet sleeps in Mum's room.'

'What? Why would she sleep in Mum's room?' He had a feeling he knew where Grant was going with this, but it seemed so enormously unlikely he couldn't quite believe his brother could be driving at something like that. 'You're saying . . . ?' He trailed off.

'She and Mum were a couple. I'm sorry, I thought you knew. I think Mum thought you knew. They didn't ever try to hide it.'

'When did it start? After Dad died?'

Grant decided there would be no harm in allowing his brother to believe that his mother had a close companionship with Violet born of being a lonely widow. Of course, that couldn't be further from the truth. But David didn't need to know that. 'Sorry, mate,' Grant said.

'No, it's fine,' David replied, dazed. 'I should have . . . known. We should get on with looking, though. I'll see you later—' He was halfway up the stairs by the time he finished his sentence.

Grant had played hide-and-seek at Roxborough more times than he would ever be able to count. Games in the summer when the hallways felt cool in comparison to the hot air. Drunken games as a teenager, inviting dozens of friends over for parties, which ended with hiding in the seams of the house, which in turn inevitably ended in hands under party dresses and lipstick on each other's mouths. And now, here he was, once again, following a beautiful girl up the main stairs in the hallway, but for once, rather than looking for a dark hiding place to wait in and the tension of hearing someone looking for them being strangely panic-inducing and heady, they were hunting.

'Where are we even supposed to start?' asked Angelique.

'I don't know. David and Bryony are doing the study.

Willa is looking in her and Lizzie's bedroom. I suppose we might as well try the library. She worked in there occasionally.' 'Worked' was probably too strong a word. Cecily sat in the library when she wasn't planning a party, walking the dogs or looking after the horses. She wrote the occasional letter and, before the internet, made some phone calls.

The library was just as its name suggested: an enormous room lined with books. It smelled like old paper and dust, and there were long ladders to enable you to reach the higher shelves. Grant couldn't remember anyone in the family being much of a reader, other than Willa, who had always been consumed by what she had to read for school or university, never by reading for pleasure. So, the room had always been a slightly odd, pointless part of the house.

There was a tiny box television in one corner, opposite a squashy brown armchair. Sometimes, Grant had sat on it to watch *Crossroads* as a teenager and wondered if actually it might have been nicer to live in a normal house with a big telly, a corner sofa and one of those fridges that made ice. Years later, when the grandchildren felt the same way, they told Cecily and she cheerfully repurposed the snug as a teenage den. He wondered whether she would have done so for him and then felt stupid for resenting a group of teenagers, one of whom was ostensibly his son. He tried to correct himself, just as he always did when the truth of Jonty's parentage inserted itself into his mind in an unpleasant way. 'Son' wasn't about blood or birth. He was as much Jonty's father as anyone else was.

'I feel as if I'm trespassing,' said Angelique as she opened the desk. 'Should I just look?'

'Yes,' said Grant.

'You know, you don't have to be such a dick to me,' Angelique said lightly.

'I know. I'm sorry. I'm just . . .'

'You think it's yours.'

'It should be mine.'

'Why?' asked Angelique, pulling out each of the desk drawers in turn. It was sectioned into dozens of little compartments, all filled with things Cecily had clearly judged too important to throw away but had no real purpose for.

'You don't think it should be mine?' Grant felt his temper rising.

'I didn't say that. I asked why you think it should be.'

'I was the closest to Mum.'

'I thought the grandchildren were always here?'

'Closest of her children.'

'Oh.'

'What?'

'Well, I thought the idea of this crazy system was that she was allowed to leave it to whoever she thought needed it the most.'

'So?'

'You don't need it.'

'I don't?'

Angelique closed the desk. 'You have enough money. You like your apartment. You're a good fuck, still handsome. What have you got to feel so sad about?'

Grant snorted and wrapped his arms around Angelique. 'It's hard to explain. They scrapped the primogeniture thing because it was unfair. And I suppose it was. It must have been awful that the eldest got everything even if they were a feckless waste of space. But at least you knew. It's a bit like being royal. Like it or not, you're aware that the crown is coming your way from the moment you're born. But this way . . .' He paused. 'All three of us have spent our entire lives wondering. It's a bit like not knowing whether a delivery is coming on a certain day. You can't get on with things and go out in case you miss it. But then you get to the evening and you realize that you've spent the entire day killing time, wondering if it's going to turn up.'

Angelique reached up and kissed him. 'Did you ever consider telling her that you didn't want it?'

He smiled. 'No.'

'You could have done. Escaped the whole thing.'

'Yes,' he said. 'That's true. But the thing is, I did want it. I still do. I want us to live here. Maybe have more children. See if we can grow wine in the upper fields. Throw a festival in the woods. Have friends to stay for long weekends. That sort of thing.'

'Well, then, we had better look for these letters.'

1997

It was impossible to know where to bury Luella, because they had never discussed funerals. Why would they have? She had been so completely, utterly alive. Everyone always said that about people who died, but in Luella's case it had been true. And anyway, they were in their early thirties. They'd done the absolute bare minimum when it came to mortality. Life insurance when they bought the house, and a depressing letter about who would raise Jonty if they both copped it in a car accident. But that was it. Why would they need to know what kind of hymns should be at their funerals, or whether they wanted people to wear black?

In the end, he had left it to Cecily and to Luella's mother. And Luella's mother was so knocked out by grief that Cecily had taken over, which was probably for the better. If there was one skill Cecily truly had, it was an ability to put a party together. The flowers – fat, waxy, white roses – were beautiful. The music had been haunting and delicate. It had been as lovely as a funeral could be when the people being buried were a woman who was barely over thirty and the baby boy she had lost everything trying to deliver. William. His name, Grant kept reminding himself, was William. They'd wanted him to give it a name, even though it hadn't lived. Him. Not it. Grant kept forgetting how he was supposed to talk about the baby, as if it were his son. As if he didn't blame the baby for everything.

Luella's parents and Grant had agreed that they should be buried at the local church. There had been a short ceremony. The vicar hadn't tried to make it uplifting. There wasn't anything good to say. She was dead. Far, far too young. The baby was dead too. These things weren't supposed to happen any more, not in modern hospitals with doctors and nurses and all the machines and the drugs. It was so unlikely. Impossible, almost. Luella hadn't been religious, so there was no comfort to come from talking about how she was in heaven, and she hadn't been ill, so she wasn't 'finally at peace'. She was just dead.

She had been so excited to be pregnant. Never a single word of complaint about throwing up or having enormous feet. Just pure, unwavering joy in experiencing something she never thought could happen. Grant hadn't liked any of it. He thought there was probably a reason they hadn't managed to get pregnant before, that Luella's body wasn't designed for it, that it would be dangerous for her. And they had Jonty, who was as much their son as any child could be. Why knock their world off its axis with another baby? But Luella had been so delighted by the discovery that Grant hadn't been able to bring himself to question whether it was a good thing or not. Perhaps if he had done, she would still be alive now.

After the burial everyone trailed back to Roxborough and drank white wine or whiskey. David and Cordelia passed around trays of food. On the piano sat a bunch of roses from Elspeth, *in absentia*. Luella's parents sat on a sofa in their black clothes, hardly able to speak to each other. The children ran around outside. Jonty chased Lizzie, while Lizzie chased Willa, and Grant wondered how much Jonty would remember of his mother. He was six. Not young enough that this whole thing would be forgotten. Grant supposed he would probably be traumatized by it all; the memory of his mother going into hospital, glowing with excitement and pride over her baby bump, and then never coming back. How on earth was he supposed to raise Jonty on his own? Luella had been the one who was good at parenting. He could kick a football around, put a load of laundry on, read a story. But all the enormous infrastructure of having a family, he didn't know how you were supposed to achieve that. Were they a family now? Could two people constitute a family?

'You should eat something,' Cordelia said, nudging Grant with a tray. 'When did you last eat?'

'I don't know,' he said honestly. 'I'm not hungry.'

'I know.' Cordelia smiled. 'One stupid sandwich. For me.'

Grant smiled at her, thinking how like Luella she was. It was strange that he and David, two such different men, had found themselves loving and marrying two such similar women. If he were to visit a therapist, he imagined they would probably tell him that these women were different from his mother, and that was significant. Which was one of the many reasons he had no intention of doing so. He looked past Cordelia, out of the window, to where the children were playing.

'They're very sweet together,' Cordelia said. 'Lizzie wants Jonty to play kiss chase with her.'

Grant laughed. 'She's going to be a liability, that one.'

'Don't get me started. We're going to have fireworks by the time she's a teenager. At least Willa will be easy.'

'I don't know how Jonty will be—' Grant broke off and looked at the ground. 'I'm worried it's going to fuck him up. Losing his mum.'

Cordelia wrapped her arms around him. It was a level of physical contact he hadn't experienced since Luella died. His mother had patted his shoulder, his father had clapped him on the arm and said, 'Bad luck, old boy.' No one had actually held him in the three weeks since he had lost his wife. He let himself collapse into Cordelia and sob on to her black dress. When he eventually peeled away, he saw David standing next to her. His face was hollow, eyes red. He'd cried at the funeral. Grant hadn't seen him cry for decades.

'I'm so sorry,' he said. Grant could tell what his older brother was thinking. *Thank God it's you and not me.* Just as Grant couldn't help looking at Cordelia and thinking, *Why did it have to be my wife, instead of yours?*

'It's going to get easier,' Cordelia said, with her relia-
ble, head-girl energy. 'Eventually. I promise.'

'And Jonty can stay with us whenever he likes,' David
added. 'And we'll all come here every summer. So, we'll
be together.'

Grant nodded weakly. 'Thank you,' he said. 'Both of
you.'

On the way to the kitchen, he bumped into his mother.
'Come with me, darling,' she said, putting down the tray
of glasses she had been carrying. He followed her through
the kitchen, to the back kitchen. Cecily ran the kitchen
tap, as if she were trying to make sure that no one could
hear what she was saying.

'Darling,' she said. 'I am so sorry.'

'I know, Mum. And thank you. For doing all of this.'

'And I know that this is horrid timing. But I think we
must be very clear with each other.'

'About what?'

'About Jonty.'

Grant looked at his mother, trying to guess what she
was going to say next.

'I realize,' Cecily said carefully, 'that you might be considering telling him where he came from. And I want you
to know that I think that would be the most enormous
mistake. He's so young, and he must be so confused.
Luella was his mother, and he's always been so brave
about not knowing where he came from. If you start giving him more information now, that's only going to make

things more complex. Let him grieve for his mother. Don't make things any more complicated.'

Grant wanted to tell his mother that he hadn't even considered talking to Jonty about his birth parents, that he had barely been able to think about anything at all, other than constantly trying to recall Luella's voice inside his head so that he didn't forget what she sounded like. 'I'm not going to rock the boat, Mum,' he said quietly.

'I'm glad,' she said. She reached up and kissed him on the cheek. 'I really am so sorry, my darling. She was quite wonderful.'

'She was, wasn't she?'

They stood in companionable silence for a few moments, and then they straightened up. 'We should get back,' Cecily said.

'Yes. I've barely spoken to Luella's father. I should go and find something to say.'

Cecily watched her poor, broken son walk back towards the drawing room and wished, not for the first time in her life, that she knew how to make her children happy.

After the funeral, Grant left Jonty at Roxborough. David and Cordelia stayed with their girls, and Cecily promised to look after them all. He drove back to London and packed up the little house that he and Luella had lived in in Clapham. He threw away her glasses. The book on her side of the bed – barely started. Her hand cream, her toothbrush, everything too personal to give away. Then he bagged everything else up and left a message for her parents asking them to take anything they wanted. And finally, he had a shower, got dressed, locked the house and went to a bar in Leicester Square.

He bought a packet of Marlboro Red, despite having quit smoking years ago, when Luella was still hoping she might fall pregnant, and took up a seat at the bar in a trendy new place he hadn't heard of. It was less than half an hour before a girl in a black dress with straps so thin they were almost invisible came over to him. 'You look sad,' she said.

'I am sad,' Grant replied.

'Why?'

Grant considered it. 'My wife died,' he said.

The girl melted. 'That's so sad.'

'Yes,' Grant agreed. 'It is.' Then he ordered them both a drink and quizzed the girl about what she was doing in London, where she had come from, who she hoped to be. She was sweet. Not especially bright. New to London. Hungry for an adventure. And within less than an hour he knew that there would be enthusiasm and absolutely no resistance to the suggestion of going to a hotel with him.

He hated sleeping with her. But knowing that Luella was the last woman he had touched was too agonizing a thing to maintain. So, he undressed this girl. Kissed her. Told her that she was beautiful and perfect and all the things that he knew she would want to hear. Then he fucked her. He made her come as a point of pride. And then, when she was sleeping, he looked at her naked shoulder, studded with freckles, and felt slightly sick. So, he wrote a sweet note before slipping out, paying the bill and going home. 'I'm sorry,' he said stupidly to the sky as he walked home. 'I had to. I couldn't bear it any more.' And something told him that somehow, somewhere, Luella would understand.

7

Jonty pushed the barn door open, surprised by his own hesitance. The dark never usually frightened him. But something about the huge ceiling, the smell of oil and old stone, the cold air mixed with the indoor silence, brought to mind every horror film he'd felt obliged to watch at school. It was almost impressive that Lizzie was so totally unafraid, that running to this pitch-black place didn't frighten her. Shining the light from his phone, the light he'd used to attend so many unwell animals in light-less countryside locations, he scanned around.

'Lizzie?' he called.

He heard a sniff and realized that she was sitting on the rough wooden stairs that led to the upper level of the barn. Her skirt was hitched up, and even by the cold light of his phone he could tell that her mascara was streaming down her face. 'Go away,' she said.

'It's OK.'

She shook her head. 'Leave me alone.'

'Is that really what you want?'

She shook her head again. So, Jonty sat on a step, a few below Lizzie's perpetually bare feet.

'That light makes it creepy in here,' said Lizzie.

'It's an empty barn in the middle of nowhere. It's already about as creepy as anything can be.' But he turned it off. Eventually, he felt Lizzie's foot nudge his back. He reached upwards, putting his hand on the cold skin of her leg. They sat like that for a while, neither of them entirely sure how long. Eventually, Jonty shifted on the step.

'You think it means you haven't got the house?' he asked.

'Of course it does. If it were going to be me, she'd have done it properly so no one could argue about it. They'd all have been furious – she wouldn't have given them a chance to take it away.'

'Did you think it would be you?' Jonty couldn't help asking. The question hung in the dark.

'Yes,' Lizzie said eventually.

Neither of them said anything for a while. Then Lizzie asked the question Jonty had been desperately hoping she wouldn't ask. 'Do you think it was because of what happened?' Jonty stared out into the dark. His eyes had adjusted now. He could make out the shape of a load of chains hung over the back of the huge barn door. They were for pulling cars out of the mud when they got stuck, or when they mistook the sticky, sandy wetness left by the sea for safe ground. They looked menacing.

It was a good question. Was it because of what had happened?

They had been at Roxborough for Christmas, just as they were every year. Lizzie had been distraught because Willa had claimed to have too much work to do to be able to attend. Of course, Lizzie didn't tell anyone she was upset; that wasn't her style. Instead, she just drank too much and moved from room to room, complaining. Eventually, on Christmas Eve, Jonty had had enough of her. He knocked on the bedroom door of the nursery, where she and Willa had both slept ever since they had been children. 'Come downstairs,' he had said. He had led Lizzie down to the drawing room, where the fire was dying. They had sat by the hearth, just like when they were children and they'd put their letters in the flames to go up the chimney to Father Christmas. The room had been warm, the embers glowing, and Lizzie was so beautiful in her silk pyjamas and the firelight.

They had made a promise once they had both turned twenty-one that they would stop. That the furtive explorations of each other's bodies that they had initially blamed on being teenagers and then tried to pretend weren't really happening had to stop. For eight years, they had managed to ignore the extraordinary chemistry that existed between them. Whether it was Willa's absence, Lizzie's loneliness, or just too many years of denying themselves, the resolve disappeared. Jonty's hand had slipped under Lizzie's top. Their lips had met. Within moments, both raging with the frustration they'd pushed away for so long, they'd both been naked, their limbs tangled, his hands in her hair, her fingernails down his back, trying to drown in each other's skin.

Cecily had come downstairs at two o'clock in the morning and found Jonty and Lizzie having sex on the drawing-room floor. Jonty could still hear her calmly telling them to get dressed.

The moment they were decent, Jonty and Lizzie had followed their grandmother into the kitchen, both horrified by what they had done, by the expression on their grandmother's face. They hadn't discussed it since, but neither Jonty nor Lizzie had been able to rid themselves of the vision of Cecily, standing in the kitchen, looking frailer than either of them had ever seen her look, gripping on to the back of a chair. 'No more,' she had said. 'No more.'

Lizzie had wanted to explain, wanted to tell her grandmother that she had tried, that she had searched for other men who made her feel like Jonty did, that they had been fighting the desire to be together since they were teenagers. But Jonty had pulled her by the arm, walked behind her to bed, and then very briefly held her in the corridor outside their bedrooms. He had felt her tears seep into his chest before pulling away. 'Go to bed,' he had told her. And the next morning, before anyone woke up, he had taken the car and gone home. It was the last time that he had seen Cecily, and the last time until this week that he had seen Lizzie.

'I don't know,' he said now. 'It was pretty grim.'

'I still don't understand why she was so angry,' Lizzie

said. She leaned her head against the cold stone wall, allowing herself to articulate something she had thought for years but never allowed herself to say. 'She wasn't a prude. She was always telling me about all the men she'd had. And we're not related by blood. It's not that disgusting. Is it?'

Jonty moved up two steps, sitting next to Lizzie. 'It's not disgusting at all.'

'Ever since she saw us, I've felt so . . .' Lizzie paused. 'Dirty. Guilty. Bad.'

Jonty put his hand on her leg, willing himself not to feel the thudding of arousal that always accompanied being near Lizzie. 'You're none of those things.'

She leaned into his body. 'I wish we'd talked about it. I wish I knew why she was so cross.'

Jonty could feel his body stirring at being so close to her. It would be too easy to kiss her, to guide her on to his lap, to hold either side of her waist and briefly become one person, motivated only by pleasure. It wouldn't have to take long, and here in the darkness where no one ever went, it would be like it had never happened. But somehow, he knew that it would be completely, entirely wrong. 'We should go back,' he said. 'God knows what will be going on inside.'

Jonty dropped Lizzie's hand as they reached the dining-room door. 'You first,' he whispered. Then, a few moments later, he followed. Lizzie had slipped back into her seat and was sitting with her knees pulled up to her chest. There were mascara tracks on her cheeks, but otherwise she looked perfectly composed. The dining room was still lit by candlelight, but someone had turned on the electric lights too, which looked wrong. Willa had put a jumper on over her dress, and Angelique's hair was pulled up into a bun at the back of her head. The atmosphere so delicately created earlier had been punctured.

'What's been going on?' he asked, knowing the answer.

'Violet thinks Granny wrote letters. Real ones. We've been trying to find them.'

'Any luck?'

'No,' said his father, without looking up. 'Nothing.'

'And you looked everywhere?'

Grant shrugged. 'Probably not. It's late, dark. We've all been drinking. We should look properly again tomorrow.'

'Where's Violet?' Willa asked then. Everyone stopped and looked around stupidly, as if they were suddenly going to be able to see Violet if they looked hard enough.

'When did she go?'

'Probably when we all started looking. Maybe she's still looking.'

'I think Rihan needs to note down that she isn't here. That she wasn't with us when we were looking. Just in case this gets more . . . complicated,' David said. The feeling in the room was tighter now, as if they were plotting something. Grant looked at David and wished that he didn't agree with him. David was the stick-in-the-mud who didn't trust the staff. He didn't like to see himself that way at all. And yet, David did have a point. Violet had been here when the letters were written, had had access to Cecily the entire time she had been ill. She was the only one with Cecily at the end; she chose not to seek them out, not to tell them that their mother was dying.

'Maybe you're right,' he said, hating himself for it. 'We can't rule it out.'

David stood up. 'It's midnight and we've all been up since the crack of dawn. We should go to bed. Tomorrow morning, we'll look properly. Breakfast at eight, proper search at nine. No one goes looking until then, to keep things simple. All right?'

2008

'Violet!' Cecily called. 'Can you come here?'

Violet took the stairs two at a time, worried by what she heard in Cecily's voice. 'What?' She was standing in the nursery, presumably preparing the room for Willa and Lizzie, who were arriving the next day to stay for the Christmas holidays. She had opened a drawer in Lizzie's desk and found an envelope with 'Lizzie' written on it. She recognized the handwriting instantly as being Jonty's. His writing was far neater than that of any other boy she had ever known. Unable to stop herself, she had pulled the paper from the already open envelope. It had been ripped at the top, as if the person reading it had been too eager to drink in the contents to slowly remove it.

L–[it started]. I know, I feel the same. But it's not as if we're really related, and I can't help thinking that if we weren't supposed to do this, it wouldn't feel so . . . right. You were so beautiful yesterday. I keep thinking about the way you looked with your hair wet, coming out of the lake. I wish we could

*go away, just the two of us, and do all the things I would do
with any other girl. But then you're not like any other girl.
You're so different. I love you. J.*

Cecily felt sick.

It wasn't as if she had been unaware of the flirtation
between Jonty and Lizzie. It had always been there. Lizzie
had demanded that he play kiss chase with her, that he
was her husband when they played mummies and dad-
dies. She had told herself that they were being raised
together, that there was no way they would ever act upon
any strange, teenage, chemical, hormonal feelings that
existed between them. But she had been wrong. Jesus,
why hadn't she done something sooner? Why hadn't she
pointed out that being adopted cousins was just as real as
being any other kind of cousin? That this sort of behaviour was completely unacceptable? She handed the letter
to Violet, who read it twice and arrived at very much the
same conclusion.

'Let's take the dogs out,' Violet said after a few
moments. It was getting dark, only about four o'clock,
but the middle of winter. If they didn't go now, they'd
lose the light. The sky was already turning purple and
orange, like an old bruise.

They walked in silence for a while, just the sound of
their wellingtons on the muddy field. Then, eventually,
Violet broke the silence. 'What will you do?' she asked.

'I don't know. Perhaps I should do nothing.'

'Can you do nothing?'

Cecily stopped and called one of the dogs, which was hanging back, sniffing something in the grass that was dead. 'The last time I interfered in one of the children's lives, I lost Elspeth,' Cecily said. She tried to sound as if this were incidental. As if she didn't think about it every single day. 'I thought I was helping then, and look what happened.'

'This is different,' Violet argued. They'd taken the dogs for a walk because, when they came to a misunderstanding, it was the best way to avoid things getting out of hand. They could walk as they talked and focus their eyes on the horizon. 'They don't know what they're doing.'

'Is it really so awful?'

'You know the answer.'

'Yes. I'm afraid so.'

After supper, Cecily made herself a very large gin and tonic, then picked up the phone. It took Grant an age to answer. He was probably looking for the phone under a pile of women's clothing left at the bachelor pad where he spent most of his time. What kind of a place was that for Jonty to grow up? Eventually, Grant answered. 'Hello? Mum? Is everything OK?'

'Can't I call when things are fine?'

'You can, but you usually don't.'

'I suppose you're right. Listen, I'm sorry to do this, but I don't think Jonty should come and stay for the holidays.'

'What?'

'I think he should stay with you for the school holidays. You're welcome to come for Christmas Eve and Christmas Day, but I think that should be it.'

Grant could see his break to Paris with Lelani, his latest squeeze, disappearing. 'Why? What on earth has he done?'

'Nothing. I think you two need more time together, and I don't approve of the way you leave him with us for such a long time.'

'David does the same thing!'

'David is marrying Willa and Lizzie's headmistress; they need to get away from him.'

'He's going to be so hurt.'

'You'll make it up to him. You might even enjoy spending some time with him.'

'Mum, is there more to this than you're saying?'

Cecily looked at the clock on the wall. 'Yes.'

'Are you going to explain?'

'No.'

'All right,' Grant said. 'I'll tell him.'

That night, Jonty lay in bed, staring at the ceiling. His father had gone out with whoever he was currently seeing, leaving him a credit card and a full fridge. 'I think you should stay here for the holidays,' he'd said casually, earlier. 'So we can spend more time together. We'll go to Roxborough for Christmas itself, but otherwise let's stay in London.'

It was impossible to know who knew what. But Jonty

knew he and Lizzie were being separated. Punished. To his own abject embarrassment, he felt tears slipping from the corners of his eyes, on to his pillow. An entire month here, getting in the way of his dad bringing women home. No Violet, no Cecily, no Willa. Worst of all, no Lizzie.

'I miss you,' he wrote. Then he deleted it. Who knew who might find Lizzie's phone? It wasn't worth the risk.

8

Bryony woke to the smell of woodsmoke. She was used to the fact that this house was filled with smells – dogs in the library, garlic in the kitchen, wood polish on the stairs. David always talked warmly about this, and Bryony tried not to mind that he seemed to enjoy the olfactory profusion of this place, when she made sure that their house – a beautiful modern townhouse – always smelled like candles and fresh laundry. But even here, the smell of smoke wasn't entirely normal, or to be ignored.

She pulled on her dressing gown and put her glasses on, looking out of the window. It was the strange half-night that came just before morning arrived, blue light and pregnant sky. No fire outside their bedroom window. She got back into bed and then, unable to shake the feeling that something was wrong, she went out into the hallway. The smell was stronger here, unquestionably burning.

She shook her husband. 'David, there's a fire.'

'What?'

'Downstairs, there's a fire.'

'Someone's probably having one to keep warm.'

'It's 4 a.m., David.'

David sat up. He always looked older when he had just woken up. Bryony tried not to notice, because noticing his age brought up all sorts of inconvenient truths that she would prefer to ignore. 'Are you sure?'

'Can't you smell that?'

He could. Bustling with his own importance and secretly rather glad that he and Bryony had been the ones to discover it, he pulled on trousers and a jumper, jamming his feet into a pair of shoes and running down the corridor. He banged on Grant's door. 'There's a bloody fire downstairs!' he shouted.

He reached the back kitchen, where all the animal feed and bins were, and searched frantically for a bucket. He found one, full of chicken feed, and emptied it dramatically on to the floor. By the time he had filled the bucket, which took rather longer than he had anticipated, and reached the small sitting room, the fire had mostly gone out. There was a large, charred hole in the carpet in front of the fireplace, which was still smoking, and the floorboards underneath were also charred. He threw the bucket of water over it, extinguishing the embers, making sure it was really, truly out.

'What on earth are you doing?' asked Grant, appearing groggily in the doorway.

'I'm putting out a fire that might well have taken out half the house.'

149

Grant raised one eyebrow. 'Why was there a fire here in the first place?'

David looked at him, exasperated. 'I don't bloody know, do I?'

'Well, you're the one standing here next to it.'

'I was putting it out!'

Grant knelt down in front of the fireplace and reached into the pile of ashes. 'Someone has been burning things,' he said.

'Yes, I had rather worked that out myself,' David said, sounding rather pompous, knowing as soon as he said it that Grant would have a much cleverer and more exciting theory. 'The fireguard wasn't up properly. An ember must have fallen out and caught on the carpet. It was an accident.'

'I'm not worried about the fire,' said Grant. 'I want to know who was burning something. Look.'

Grant lifted out little fragments of paper. Like pieces of confetti, they seemed to be the remnants of documents, perhaps bills. One of them had his mother's name half charred at the top. He could make out the occasional word, but it was impossible to tell what any of them had actually said. 'Someone was burning papers.'

'Why on earth would they do that?'

Grant looked grave. 'I think perhaps we should call the police.'

'For a little fire? Mostly in the fireplace?'

'You were running around like Fireman Sam five minutes ago.'

'I was trying to get it under control. Which it now is. We should go back to bed and talk about it when everyone is up in the morning.'

'What if someone was burning the letters?'

David laughed. 'That's a conspiracy theory and a half.'

Grant gave him a look. 'It's the obvious option.'

'Why would anyone do that? If the letters were gone, then the house would be sold and no one would get it. None of us wants that.'

Grant didn't look as if he believed a word David was saying. He didn't regard his brother as dishonest, not really. But self-interested, certainly. The sort of man who was susceptible to influence, and Bryony really was the Lady Macbeth type. Who knew what David might do in order to please his grasping wife?

'It's got nothing to do with me, and I'm rather offended that you would suggest it did.'

Grant looked around at the house, huge and beautiful and the cause of everything that was wrong with his life. 'I'm sorry,' he said after a long while. 'I'm still half asleep. You're right. Let's go to bed. We can sort out all of this in the morning.'

They walked back up the stairs in silence, both internally enjoying the periwinkle of the early morning, and both assuming that the other knew far, far more about what had taken place than they were willing to let on.

'Where have you been?' asked Angelique sleepily as Grant closed the door behind him. He had tried to be quiet because he wasn't entirely sure how to answer a question like that.

'David woke me up,' he said.

'Why?'

'There was a fire. Downstairs.'

Most women – most people – would have reacted with some kind of interest, surprise or horror. But Angelique wasn't interested in the things other people found interesting. She rolled over, the sheet slipping down over her tanned back. There was a small star-and-moon tattoo on her right shoulder blade. He traced it with his finger. 'I've never asked where you got this.'

'Some disgusting tattoo parlour in Marseilles,' she said, her face in the pillow.

'How old were you?'

'Sixteen.'

The idea of a teenaged Angelique, with thick black eyeliner and a heavy fringe, smoking a cigarette and then telling some older boy to pay for her tattoo, made Grant feel something rather confusing. Protective. Lustful. A strange sort of feeling he decided it would be better not to focus on.

'Anyway, the fire is out. It looks like someone was trying to burn some documents.'

But Angelique was asleep again.

Lizzie was woken around nine – earlier than she liked to get up – by the dogs barking downstairs. They'd been subdued ever since everyone had arrived, presumably sad about Cecily's death. Lizzie had tried stroking and cuddling them, but they weren't really those sorts of dogs. People like Cecily didn't have animals because she loved them – even though she did love them. She had them because houses like this were supposed to have dogs and horses, and cats for catching mice. The attachment formed to them was almost incidental. But they were barking their heads off.

She pulled a jumper on over her bare chest and then, reflecting on the fact that there was quite so much of her family around, added a pair of denim shorts. She padded down the hallway, to the top of the big stairs, and watched as the front door opened. A woman pushed the door open and threw a large leather weekend bag on to the floor. She was pretty, in an old sort of way. Early fifties, Lizzie supposed. Thin. She wore expensive running leggings, trainers and what looked like a cashmere jumper. She was tanned and thin, with lots of delicate gold jewellery. She certainly wasn't a local from the village or someone who had come to offer their condolences on Cecily's death.

'Who are you?' asked Lizzie from her position at the top of the stairs. She couldn't help feeling that she might have had more authority if she'd put a bra on.

The woman looked back at her. 'Who are you?'

Lizzie laughed. 'I asked first.'

The woman didn't laugh back. 'You're Willa?'

She shook her head. 'Lizzie, the other one.' She realized that she was being stupid. 'You're Elspeth?'

'Yes,' she said. 'I'm Elspeth.'

'Bloody hell,' said David, who was carrying a tray with a cafetière and croissants on it. 'Elspeth?' He approached her at speed, as if he were going to throw his arms around her. But apparently something about her demeanour made him think better of it, and he stopped a few feet short of her. 'It's been years. What on earth are you doing here?'

Elspeth was looking in her large leather handbag for something – her phone. 'Rihan called. Apparently, he was obliged to. He told me that there was going to be endless complication with the will and that it was going to be easier if I was here. I told him I didn't want anything to do with any of it, but he wouldn't listen, and I couldn't face the idea of years of paperwork and probate. I thought it would be better to come.'

'Years?' asked David, feeling faintly horrified. 'It won't be years.'

'Well, I hope not. Where shall I put my things?'

'I'll ask Violet,' said Lizzie, hoping for something to do.

'No, God no,' said Elspeth. 'I don't need to be told what to do by Mum's number two. I'll sleep in my old room.' She picked up her bag with yoga-toned arms and started upstairs.

Elspeth had expected to feel some kind of sadness upon arrival. She had left the house over thirty years ago, admittedly under something of a cloud, and hadn't so much as seen a photograph of the place since. It hadn't changed in any significant way. Kept up to date – her mother was always terrified of the house looking or smelling as if an old person lived there – but otherwise, unremarkable.

Left at the top of the stairs, second door on the right, her bedroom. Not that anyone would have been able to tell. These weren't the kind of bedrooms that you were allowed to decorate with pictures of pop stars. Elspeth had longed to rip sheets out from *Rolling Stone* and plaster them around, but the wallpaper was from the eighteenth century and couldn't be disturbed. She was just about permitted to put some of her showjumping rosettes around the mirror in a half-hearted attempt at personalization. Though they were long gone now. This, like all of the other bedrooms at Roxborough, was a spare bedroom, primed to be used when an important guest or influential visitor came to stay.

It was wrong, she thought, as she pulled open drawers and put her clothes into each one, that any one person could inhabit this much space. How many families could fit in this house if the entire Mordaunt clan weren't so obsessed with keeping it as a single house? Passing it down from generation to generation based entirely on who would be most obsessed about preserving it further, so that it could become even more anachronistic for another generation.

Why had she come? She'd been asking herself the same question since she had booked the flight. All the way to the airport, all through the flight. When she landed at Heathrow she had seriously considered trying to move her return ticket to the same day and go straight back. And yet here she was.

She had told herself it was for the money, and because the house might be sold, and if it were sold, then she had a right to a portion of that money. She didn't need the money, not really. But it belonged to her, and she wasn't going to let the fight, which had been entirely her mother's fault, prevent her from having her inheritance. That was what she would tell them when they inevitably asked her why she had come. It was what she kept telling herself, too.

There was a knock at the door, so soft that she ignored it at first. Then, another. 'Yes?' she called. The door opened tentatively and behind it was another girl, like the one with the long legs who'd been standing on the stairs when she arrived. This girl was thinner than her sister – too thin, actually. Her eyes were huge in her head, the lollipop look that so many of her friends spent their lives at spin classes trying to emulate.

'Hi,' said the girl. 'I'm Willa.'

'Elspeth.' God it was strange, seeing a young woman with a face comprised of other people's. She looked like Cecily. And Esmond, and David.

'Nice to meet you.'

'We've met.' Elspeth was hanging dresses and blouses in the wardrobe now.

'I'm sorry, I don't remember.'

'You were two, I wouldn't expect you to.'

Willa smiled. 'We're having a meeting downstairs. We wondered if you wanted to join us.'

156

'Sounds terribly formal.'

'No, not really. It's to talk about what we're going to do about the letters. Everyone's still pretty upset.'

Elspeth snorted. 'No idea why. It might sound like a win but, trust me, inheriting this house is not what you want. Whoever gets it has lost. Not won. Honestly, selling it and splitting the money is the best possible outcome.'

Willa had absolutely no idea what she was supposed to say to that. Obviously, she disagreed. Having Roxborough would be the greatest possible outcome for anyone who loved it, and they all loved it. 'Well, if you want to come. We're going to be in the dining room, and they're going to try and come up with a plan.'

'Fine,' Elspeth said, pulling off her top and swapping it for another one, conscious that she had been in perpetual motion since she'd got on the plane from New York and badly needed a shower. 'Let's go.'

Violet had changed rather a lot in the decades since Elspeth had last been at Roxborough, and Elspeth felt rather pleased about it. She looked older, which was unsurprising, given that she *was* older. But time hadn't been especially kind to Violet. Which was very much what she deserved.

'Hello,' she said, from the other end of the table, smiling at Elspeth. So, they were going to pretend to be friends, it seemed.

'Hi,' Elspeth returned. 'Is that coffee?'

'Yes, the silver pot is coffee; the one with the lid is tea. Would you like some?'

Elspeth fought the desire to tell Violet that she wasn't just asking about the contents of the tea and coffee pots for something to say. She accepted a delicate cup of coffee and wished that her mother would have allowed them to use something so practical as an actual mug.

David caught Violet's eye as everyone began to file in. 'Violet, is it normal to have fires in the small drawing room?'

'Yes,' Violet said, bemused. 'Very normal.'

'In the summer?'

'No, not really in the summer.'

'Did you light one last night?'

Violet laughed. 'No, of course not. Why on earth do you ask?'

David looked at his feet. 'This morning Grant and I found a fire in the small sitting room. It had caught the rug; the room was about to go up.'

Violet looked horrified. 'What on earth—? Is anything damaged?'

'It was almost out when we got there. But it looked like someone had been burning documents.'

'How extraordinary. I'm afraid I don't know anything about that at all – I'll ask the staff whether they had anything to do with it. Shall we sit down?'

David tried to catch Grant's eye, to see whether he found this blasé reaction concerning. But he was piling his plate high with toast and buttering it far too thickly. 'What?' Grant asked, with his mouth full.

'Nothing,' David mumbled.

Eventually, everyone was settled around the dining table, which had been cleared of the previous night's pageantry. It looked somehow naked now, just bald wood. 'Right. Well,' said David. Elspeth wondered if a small part of her older brother might be rather enjoying having to take charge of this 'extremely difficult situation'. 'I'm sure everyone is feeling similarly confused about this whole thing. But we've all had some sleep, and we've got clear heads now. Rihan has done some research into our situation,' said David, 'and now I believe he is going to make it clear what is going to happen next.'

Rihan got to his feet and then immediately regretted it. Now he was going to have to stay standing for the entire duration. 'So,' he said. 'It's much as I thought. The first port of call is to make sure that the letters weren't misplaced. Ms Mackenzie confirms that she remembers seeing Mrs Mordaunt write the letters, and is confident that they did indeed exist, but that she doesn't know what the contents of those letters were. The first step will be to have the keys to Mrs Mordaunt's personal desk and filing cabinet released, where the letters may well be contained. If the letters are found, things are quite simple. If not, it is rather more complicated. It would be likely that the house would be sold and that the proceeds and remaining capital would be divided equally between Mrs Mordaunt's three children. However, there could be an argument that it should be divided between everyone who was given a letter, as the letters demonstrate that all those people were in consideration to inherit the house.' Rihan took a long breath. 'As such, I would suggest that we wait until the keys to the desk and filing cabinet have been released, and then we can—'

'When you said you looked everywhere last night,' said Elspeth, who sat at the far end of the table with her legs crossed, the cup of coffee in her hands, 'are you sure that you looked everywhere?'

'Yes,' said David. 'Obviously, we tried to look everywhere, but it's a big house, in case you've forgotten.'

'Have you got some bright idea you'd like us to try?' Grant asked, with rather more edge than he had intended.

'Yes,' Elspeth said, with a little half-smile. 'There's a stack of letters over there.'

And she was right. On the sideboard, in a neat stack, were eight envelopes.

'Those must be the empty ones,' Lizzie said.

'No.' Violet shook her head. 'We gave the empty ones to Rihan.'

'Have they been there the entire time?' asked Willa.

'Of course not – they can't have been,' said David.

'We would have noticed them,' added Grant.

They all turned to look at Rihan. 'What should we do?'

Rihan considered them for a moment. 'I suppose you should open them.' He took the envelopes from the side and passed them down the long, shiny table. They slipped over the surface towards each person, Lizzie taking hers with her bitten fingernails, Bryony with her French manicure. And then they sat, for a moment, completely still.

No one willing to make the first move. No one willing to be seen to be wanting it. Then someone – no one could quite say who – opened theirs, and the rest did the same. The room sat in a kind of suspended animation while everyone drank in the contents of their letters. Tears swam in front of Lizzie's eyes as she read hers. David's stomach twisted. Bryony read over her husband's shoulder and tried to remain calm.

'Well,' said Grant after he had read his letter twice. 'Anyone got anything to share?' He looked around the table. Lizzie looked heartbroken. He felt for her. Clearly, his mother had made the same judgements about both of them.

'Lovely letter,' Jonty said, with a wide smile. 'I'm glad to have it. But the house isn't mine.' Jonty would, in some ways, have been the obvious choice. He lived locally, he worked with animals. He would have made a good, sympathetic lord of the manor. Grant was a little ashamed of his relief not to have been passed over for his son. A nasty thought rose unbidden. A son who wasn't really his son.

'Or mine,' ground out David. Grant's sympathy for Lizzie paled in comparison to his sympathy for his brother. He was, in fact, surprised by how sad he felt at the appearance of his brother's waxy grey face. His last hope at getting the house had clearly been dashed and he wasn't taking it easily.

'You'll be shocked to hear that I didn't get it.' Elspeth smiled. 'Thankfully.'

'So, who did?' asked Lizzie.

Willa half raised her hand, like she was back at school and dreading the indignity of asking if she could go to the loo. 'I did,' she said, her voice tiny in the huge room. She wasn't entirely sure whether the looks of shock on the faces of her family were genuine, or if she was imagining them.

'You?' asked Lizzie, with apparent horror.

She nodded. 'Me.'

'Let me see,' said her sister, grabbing for the letter. Instinctively, Willa grabbed it back. 'Why can't I see?'

'The letters are private,' Jonty said. 'Leave it, Lizzie.'

'They're not private. If they were private, everyone could say the house was theirs.' She could hear her voice getting higher, and she didn't want to behave like this. It felt horrible to be this angry with her sister, to have completely lost control of herself, to let everyone see how miserable she felt about it. But she couldn't stop herself.

'It's fine,' said Willa, letting go of the letter. 'Lizzie's right. Everyone's got the right to read it.'

Lizzie scanned the paper, having a hard time forcing the words into sentences.

Darling Willa,

It is extraordinarily strange to think of you reading this letter when I am gone. I am simply furious to know all the things you will do that I won't be around to see. But that is my loss, and I must be sad about it. You, however, must not be sad. You will be far too busy for that.

I have left Roxborough to you. I realize this might be
something of a surprise, as you are so young, and we had
never discussed it. But I think you will be happy there,
happier perhaps than any of the others would be. And, most
of all, I think you will be an appropriate guardian for the
house. You'll make sure that it's still a home for all the
family, and that it safely reaches another generation of
Mordaunts.

I hope that the house will bring you as much joy as it
brought me.

All my love,
Granny

Lizzie blinked back tears. So it was true. Cecily really
had left the house to Willa.

Violet got up and put her arms around Willa. 'Congratulations, darling,' she said. 'I hope that you will be
very happy here.' Everyone seemed to realize that Violet
had done as was expected and followed suit, getting up,
hugging Willa, wishing her congratulations and good
luck, each of them in turn wondering how it could be
possible that Willa, the least exciting of them all, the one
who was followed by a strange ring of sadness, could be
the one who had inherited the house.

'There'll be lots and lots of legals to explain later,' Violet said. 'Rihan and I will go with you into town tomorrow
and you can meet the solicitor, and they will explain it all.
And then we'll need to talk about what you would like to

do – if you're going to move in, which bedroom you'd like, whether you'd like me to stay—'

'Of course I want you to stay!' Willa interrupted. That was the only thing she was sure about right now.

'Well, that's not something you need to decide now. We can talk about it later.'

'No, I've decided. I want you to stay.'

Violet smiled. 'Well. I will understand entirely if you change your mind. But in the meantime, shall I make something special for dinner this evening to celebrate?'

Guilt shifted in Willa's stomach. Her father looked ashen. Lizzie wasn't even managing to hold back her tears. Jonty had his arm around her, Grant looked like he was trying with superhuman strength to seem happy. Violet mistook Willa's expression. 'I can make something very light. Some fish, a salad—'

'It's not that,' Willa said, too quickly. 'I just think, under the circumstances, it might be a bit—'

Violet gently took her hand. 'It is traditional.'

'All right,' Willa said, already regretting it. 'OK.'

Jonty knocked on the nursery door, not entirely sure what he was hoping to find.

'What?' called Lizzie. She was sitting cross-legged on her bed, clearly trying very hard to look breezy. 'I thought you had work to do today?'

Jonty shook his head. 'It can wait. I wondered if you wanted to go out.'

Lizzie looked incredulous. 'Why?'

'Because you're upset—'

'I'm not upset.'

'Yes, you are.'

'I'm fine.'

'I've known you since before you pretended to be Sabrina the Teenage Witch. Come on. We need to clear our heads.'

Lizzie considered it. A day alone with Jonty was dangerous, obviously. They'd never been trustworthy together. But a day of wandering around the house trying to forget all of the plans she had made for it when it would be her home, that sounded much worse. Everyone seemed to have retired to their own bedrooms, presumably so that they could process the news that Willa – the person who no one for a moment had thought was going to get the house – was going to become the family matriarch.

'All right,' she said, getting up and pulling on a pair of Converse. Her legs were brown, but they needed shaving. Which shouldn't matter. 'Let's go.'

Jonty considered asking if she wanted to put anything else on – whether she might get cold in shorts and a top, through which he could see the heart-stoppingly sexy outline of her breasts. But she hated being told what to do, and he didn't much like sounding like some elderly relative. So instead, he grabbed a jumper from his own room on the way out.

In the driveway Lizzie made her way towards the car. 'No,' Jonty called. 'I've got a better idea.'

There were dozens of bikes in the shed, and someone in charge of keeping the garden running had clearly also made an effort to keep them in decent shape. Jonty slung a bag into the basket of one of them.

'Where on earth are we going to cycle to?' Lizzie said. She'd been just about convinced by the idea that Jonty would drive them into town, where she would be able to get drunk on white wine and pour her heart out to him.

'Follow me,' he said, getting on the bike.

'You're being very annoying,' she shouted at his back as he whipped down the drive. She got on one of the other bikes, caught the pedal with her foot and pushed down, enjoying the strange yet familiar sensation of moving through the air.

Jonty turned left at the top of the drive, down a slight incline. The bike flew underneath Lizzie's body without any need to pedal. 'See?' Jonty called from in front of her. 'Fun.'

It was. But the fact that she was having fun reminded her of why it was surprising to be having fun, and then she was sad all over again. She didn't want to be. Willa being happy was all Lizzie had ever really wanted. All through their childhood, the grey moods had descended on her sister and Willa would be unable to get out of bed, just working and working on homework and things school sent back, without going anywhere or seeing anyone. Lizzie had tried everything to cheer her up. Gossip, telly shows, sharing an iPod with one earbud each. Jokes, stories, imagining the future. None of it had worked.

Eventually Lizzie had realized that she just had to wait for her sister until she was better. And then Mum had died, and they'd both been miserable. Just sort of floating in a very cold sea, numb, letting themselves be carried by something else's movement.

Her sister had never really got better. Most people Lizzie had known at school who had problems with food had just sort of grown out of it. Not Willa. Lizzie was used to it, of course. But occasionally, if she hadn't seen her sister for a little while, she would notice the panic in her eyes if the restaurant they were in didn't have something she had prechosen from the menu, having looked up the calorie content online. And even when the food stuff wasn't so bad, when she'd spent time at that centre she seemed to think Lizzie didn't know about, there was still a sort of heaviness about Willa. She never seemed happy. At least, not in the way that other people did.

She had her flat, perfectly decorated and spotlessly clean, and her impressive, highly paid job. She had done a year's secondment in Singapore. Gym classes. Trips to galleries and museums at the weekend. But there hadn't ever been boyfriends or girlfriends or best friends. No complaining about spending all her money on hen dos, no Instagrams from holidays to Ibiza, or bottomless brunches. She went to the occasional wedding when an old school or university friend invited her, the odd dinner when someone was short of a single woman. But none of it stuck. She was solitary. Solemn. She worked, she saw her family, she turned up whenever Lizzie invited her to something, and she tried her best. She went on dates intermittently, because she felt she had to, and because it was something to talk about, but it never turned into anything of any significance. And Lizzie felt angry with her for being unable to just be normal, and then angry with herself for being so devoid of understanding.

If the house was going to make Willa happy, perhaps it was worth it. Lizzie just wished she hadn't had that stupid, stupid feeling that the house was going to be hers. Or she wished that, if she had to have the feeling, there was a way of talking to someone about it without seeming monstrously self-involved. It wasn't as if she thought she deserved Roxborough. No one deserved a house like that – it was a ridiculous thing for any one person to own. But she had thought – really, truly believed – that her grandmother wanted her to have it. All those summers when she would race back to Roxborough from school and run up the drive, throwing her bags down so that she could jump into the lake or visit the horses or feed the chickens. Evenings watering the gardens, watching her grandmother delicately prune and deadhead the flowers. Baking in the warm kitchen, eating on the terrace. She had thought that it was preparation for when this would be her home.

Ahead of her, Jonty pulled away into a little indent on the side of the road. She followed suit. They left the bikes lying next to each other against the bank of the road, poorly hidden by the branches of a tree.

'No one's going to nick them,' she said, watching Jonty look back over his shoulder.

'I hope not. It'll be a very long walk home.'

'Where are we going?'

'Down here.'

Jonty opened a gate on the side of the lane, a kissing gate. They both knew what it was called. Jonty blushed a little, Lizzie noticed, but said nothing. She followed him as the path sloped away from the lane, a beaten patch of ground between trees, worn by people walking there rather than by any deliberate effort. It had the kind of quiet you'd find in a room filled with soft furnishings, the trees and the grass deadening the sound. Not that they were talking. Just the pace of their feet on the ground, and the sound of the birds and her own breath. There was a canopy of green above their heads and a sweet, herbal smell of bluebells and wild garlic. The grass whipped her bare legs, but it was cool and fresh in here, better than being out in the sun. She thought of asking Jonty where they were supposed to end up but realized that she didn't much care. She just liked the feeling of being away from the house, away from everyone else.

It was hard to say how long they walked for, but eventually they came to a clearing where the little spit of a stream they had been following to their left opened into something far deeper. Jonty stopped and laid out a rug on the ground. He took the bottles of beer he had packed and placed them in the stream, digging them into the sediment.

'Clever,' Lizzie said.

He tried not to enjoy her praise too much. Instead, he handed her one, saying, 'There's a bottle opener in the bag.'

They sat on the rug, looking up at the canopy and drinking their beers.

'So,' Jonty said, after a long, comfortable pause. 'Willa.'

'Yes. Willa.'

'Exciting for her.'

'Absolutely.'

A long pause.

'I can't fucking believe it.'

Jonty laughed. 'I know, I know. I didn't see it coming. But I suppose, as long as she's happy, that's what matters.'

'Yes.'

He propped himself up on one elbow. 'You know, we'll still be able to come here. She'll want us to spend summers and holidays here.'

'I know.'

'It could have been far worse.'

'I know. I read Bryony's emails once, years ago, and she was telling Dad that "when" they inherited the house it would make a "marvellous" boutique girls' school. Can you imagine?'

'Jesus, that would have been terrible.'

'What would Grant have done?'

'I think he wanted to use the land as some sort of glamping venue.'

'That would have been fun.'

'Yes. I guess.' Jonty wasn't disloyal enough to say it, but it wouldn't have been fun. His father would have spent a fortune planning it, hired lots of friends to help out without a contract and probably given absolutely no thought to the clean-up that came afterwards. The idea of hundreds of strangers tramping over the neat gardens felt very wrong.

Even without comment, Lizzie could read him. 'You don't think so?'

'It would have been different. I think I'm being a bit wet about change.'

Lizzie raised her bottle. 'I'll drink to that.'

'But Willa's the best possible defence against change. She'll want it to be like it always was for us.'

'True.'

Lizzie rolled the beer bottle between her hands, listening to the water move. 'I just . . .' She tried to find the right words. 'I can't help feeling . . .' She stopped again.

'That it's harder that she left it to one of the three of us but that it wasn't you?'

'Yes. That's exactly it.'

Jonty considered her, her hair curling and light, a faint trace of old mascara under her eyes. 'I understand.' He wasn't sure whether what he was about to say was sensible or not. But he was so sick of guarding himself while he was around Lizzie that he decided he didn't care. 'If it helps, I really thought it was going to be you.'

'Do you think it's weird,' Lizzie asked, 'that the letters just turned up like that?'

'Weirder that Elspeth turned up, and then the letters did,' Jonty replied. 'The whole thing is pretty mad. Why? Have you thought about saying something?'

Lizzie shook her head. 'It'll look like I'm bitter that I didn't get the house. Like I'm trying to take it away from Willa.'

'I don't know if this is a good idea,' Willa said, sitting at the table, half-heartedly hulling strawberries and shelling broad beans. 'It feels like I'm rubbing everyone's nose in the fact that I got the house.'

'That's how it works,' Violet responded. 'You'd do it for any of them, wouldn't you?'

Willa nodded and tried to work out privately whether that was true. Would she have done it for any of them? Would she resent whoever had got the house if it hadn't been her? Would it matter who it was?

Later, when the potatoes were peeled and sitting in a huge pan of salty water, Willa let herself ask the question she had been wanting to voice ever since the letters had been read. 'What was it like when Granny inherited the house?'

Violet started making a sweet pastry for biscuits. She claimed they were a treat for Lucca, but really they were for all the 'children'. Lizzie would eat six in one sitting, just as she had as a child. What must it be like to be able to do that, thought Willa.

'Cecily's letter was a surprise,' Violet said.

'Like mine?'

'Oh, much more so than yours. Cecily wasn't exactly the most down-to-earth young woman. She and your grandfather loved their house in London, their parties and their friends. They certainly weren't the types to move to the sticks and have the local vicar round for tea. Everyone assumed it would go to her brother. He always lived here, went to Harrow and then Oxford, and then came back here. He was away during the war, but otherwise he lived at Roxborough. I remember when I first came to work in the kitchen, everyone who worked here was in love with him. He was terribly handsome and an appalling flirt. And he was married to Lavinia – your great-aunt. They loved the village, and they were expecting a baby when their uncle died. Everyone was absolutely sure that he would have skipped his children, all of whom were in London drinking their money, therefore entirely unworthy of the house, and given the house to him.

'The funeral went off without a hitch, and then they had the dinner in the dining room – just as we did. And the letters went out, and then, well. All hell broke loose. Your great-uncle was distraught, his pregnant wife apparently fainted, though that might be time creeping into the story. But whatever happened, everyone was dreadfully upset. Your poor grandmother just sat in the middle of the whole thing looking bemused. Her letter said that she needed a better life and that if she moved to Roxborough she would find it. And I suppose she did. But everyone was furious, even people who didn't want the house. I think they could have accepted defeat if the house had gone to her brother, because he was so perfect for the place. But if it could go to flighty, beautiful Cecily, then why on earth not to any of them?'

'Did they get over it?'

Violet smiled. 'I'm not sure if they ever did.'

Willa's face fell.

'But they were a different family. Very different people. Not like yours.' She put her hand, veined and spotted with sunshine, on Willa's. 'I know you're finding this difficult, my love. But you don't need to feel guilty. This was what your grandmother wanted. She chose you. You were supposed to have this house.'

Willa tried to smile. 'Thank you,' she managed.

'I'm too hot,' Lizzie said, peeling her top off. 'Let's swim.'

It was inevitable, then. Actually, Jonty thought, it had been inevitable the moment they were called back to Roxborough. They'd always been like this. Like too inconveniently strong magnets, straining at each other from across whatever distance was placed between them. He watched as she undressed down to her underwear – knickers; Lizzie never seemed to wear a bra – and picked her way across the stony floor of the shallows until she was waist deep in the cool, clear water. Then, after she had shouted her complaints that he was being slow, he followed her, trying to look brave as the freezing water met his groin.

It wasn't really deep enough to swim here. Further down, there was a deeper bit, where as children they'd tied a tyre to a rope and made a swing to jump off, spending hours there while one of their parents 'supervised' by reading a book. His mother had done it, and then the summer after she had died, Lizzie's mother.

It was astonishing bad luck, everyone had said, to lose two mothers in one family. After Lizzie and Willa's mother died, they would come here alone. Cecily said they were old enough to be sensible, and they had mobile phones. She was only half right. He remembered Lizzie insisting on jumping from higher and higher points on the bank above the water, until she clipped her foot on the bank and twisted as she fell. He remembered Willa's face, hollow with horror, apparently sure she was about to see yet another member of her family disappear. Jonty had charged into the water to grab her, with no idea how he was supposed to help. Lizzie had surfaced from below the water, gasping for air, her wet hair matted over her eyes, grappling for something to hold on to, finding Jonty's body and wrapping her own around it. And then, as soon as she had recovered her composure, laughing, claiming she was fine, that they were all being stupidly dramatic.

'You're miles away,' Lizzie said, floating on her back.

'I was thinking about the time you jumped in and hit your leg.'

'That's how I got this,' she said, showing him the outside of her left leg. It was flecked with short, sharp blonde hairs. At the ankle there was a small tattoo of a crescent moon. She'd been enormously proud of it when she debuted it, aged fifteen, having convinced some tattoo parlour in Spain that she was old enough. He sensed that she was probably rather less proud of the tiny, blurred image now. Below the knee, there was a shell-pink scar. That was what he was supposed to be looking at.

'I was terrified,' Jonty said. 'I thought you were going to die.'

'So did I.'

'You pretended to be so cool about it.'

Lizzie smiled but said nothing.

'I want to kiss you.'

A pause. The noise of birds in the canopy above them. Crickets. Bees. The real version of the sorts of sounds Lizzie had heard Willa listening to on Spotify when she was attempting mindfulness. The water moved her towards him. Or perhaps she moved herself. But his hands were on her waist, her legs around his torso, their faces touching, his skin cool, her lips wet. He stood and carried her easily to the bank where they'd sat before, trying to be cousins to each other. But once again that same force, the one they'd told themselves was just being young, being teenagers, having hormones, flooded both of their bodies. Lizzie had slept with dozens of people and enjoyed at least half of it. But it was never like this with anyone else. His body was so hard against hers, so delicious. His tongue against hers, his hands so large, his arms so strong. He was a cliché, and she loved it.

Eventually, she was on top of him, grinding herself against him. His hand between her legs. He knew how to make her come as well as she knew it herself. They'd discovered all of this together, after all. She bit her lip as she climaxed, trying to keep some semblance of control. He moaned quietly, just as he always had. And then, just as it always did, the tidal wave of shame hit her. She lay next to him, their bodies as close as it was possible to be without touching. The sun wasn't shining any more, the canopy that had been bright green, the sun highlighting every line of every leaf, was darker now. They'd been out almost the entire day. People would have noticed. Willa would have noticed. Lizzie reached for her top, pulling it on, suddenly very aware of her nakedness.

'We should get back,' Jonty said, putting his clothes back on.

He had only said exactly what Lizzie was thinking. So how did his words manage to feel hurtful?

'Yes,' she said. 'We should.'

1981

The holidays used to be fun. Elspeth would get back from school and turn the music up as loud as she could in her bedroom, and then pour herself a huge gin and tonic, smoke one of Cecily's cigarettes and have an hour-long bath. Then, she and Grant and David would hole up in the library to watch whatever programmes had been *verboten* at school, which Violet would have diligently recorded for them. But now, David was off at university and Grant was always staying with friends.

She'd arrived for the summer holidays, dumped her stuff in her bedroom and realized that she had absolutely no idea how she was going to fill the next six weeks. Though, she thought, once she'd told her mother her news, she didn't imagine there would be much in terms of shopping trips and mother–daughter lunches. She shoved her clean clothes in her chest of drawers and everything else in the laundry basket for someone else to deal with. Then she went downstairs.

'Can I help with supper?' she asked.

Cecily looked surprised. 'It's just the two of us this evening. Violet is visiting a friend and your father is still in London. I thought we'd just have some fish and a salad.'

The word 'fish' made Elspeth feel a bit queasy, but anything from Roxborough would be better than the plates of grey misery she'd been eating at school for the last term. Elspeth finely chopped half a red onion on a wooden board, sitting at the kitchen table. She watched as her mother poured a glass of wine. 'Do you want one?'

Elspeth shook her head. They worked in silence for a while. Elspeth wondered whether she could put the radio on or whether that would make things feel more awkward.

'How's school?' her mother asked after a while.

Elspeth made a face. 'I hate it.'

'No, you don't.'

'I actually really do.'

'Well, I'm sure you won't always hate it. You've only got two and a bit more years and then you can do whatever you like.'

'Actually, Mum,' Elspeth said, putting down the knife that she'd been using to chop tomatoes. 'I don't think I'm going to go back after the holidays.'

Cecily half smiled. 'Oh no? Why not?'

'Because I'm pregnant.'

Cecily considered her daughter for a moment, trying to work out whether this was just another test to see what her reaction would be, like the piercings and the tattoos, the aggressive atheism and the announcement that she didn't believe in marriage. 'I see,' Cecily said.

Elspeth had expected Cecily to be angry. 'So, I'm going to have a baby.'

Cecily went to the larder to get some more peppercorns to refill the pepper grinder. She said nothing.

'Mum,' Elspeth repeated. 'Are you listening?'

'The salt needs refilling too – could you fetch it?'

'Mum. I'm pregnant.'

'Yes, you said.'

'Can we talk about this?'

'What is there to talk about?'

'About what's going to happen next? I thought you'd be interested, that you'd want to know who the father is, how it happened. I thought you'd want to say things about how you feel about being a grandmother?'

Cecily gave a small half-laugh. 'I'm not going to be a grandmother.'

'What?'

'Elspeth, you're sixteen. You've only just taken your O levels. You're not having a baby.'

'You can't stop me.'

'How will you be paying for this baby?'

'I'll get a job.'

'And who will look after the baby while you're at work?'

Elspeth gave this some thought. 'I'll put it in a crèche.'

'And you'll have a job that pays enough for a crèche and all the other things the baby needs?'

'Well, the father can help.'

'Dare I ask who this man is?'

'He goes to St Edwards.'

'I imagine his parents will be supportive of him also abandoning his education to be a parent at sixteen. They'll be delighted.'

'Why are you being so horrible? I'm perfectly capable of doing this.'

Cecily refilled her wine glass. 'Darling, I don't mean to be cruel, but you are not capable of doing this. You can't do your own washing, let alone look after a child. We'll go to the doctor tomorrow and they'll sort it all out.'

Elspeth looked horrified. 'You want me to have a termination?'

'Of course I do. Don't be so silly. Now let's finish the salad and we can have supper. Do you mind if I put *The Archers* on?'

Cecily had been careful not to allow Elspeth to see much of a reaction. Elspeth loved to get a rise out of absolutely anyone, but especially her parents. Not giving her a reaction was the best possible way to make sure that it never happened again. But once she got into bed, she couldn't sleep. She was still sitting upright looking out of the dark window when Violet came home.

'What's wrong?' Violet asked before she'd taken her shoes off.

'Elspeth's got herself pregnant.'

'That was clever of her.'

'Well, fine, some boy got her pregnant. But she's pregnant.'

Violet said nothing but began to change into her nightdress.

'She can't have the baby,' Cecily said.

'No,' Violet agreed. 'I don't imagine she could.'

'But she says she won't have an abortion. I don't even know how far along she is. She doesn't look pregnant. That's got to be a good sign, hasn't it?'

Violet considered Cecily. She knew that once she said what she was about to say there would be no going back. But then there was already no going back. Elspeth would make the wrong choice; her life would be ruined. She was too young, too impulsive, too unhappy to think straight. 'There's a place she could go. Just north of London. A sort of centre. They'll do it, even if it's very late on. And if she resists, they'll tell her there's something wrong with the baby and that it's kinder this way.'

'How will we get her there?'

'We'll say it's just a normal appointment.'

'How do you know about this?'

Violet shrugged. 'When I was first training as a lady's maid it was still illegal. They told us about the places you could have things like that done, lest we were ever called on to sort it out. A friend's daughter went there last year. But Cecily, it's not pleasant. She won't feel at all well afterwards. And she'll be upset.'

Cecily shrugged. 'It's far better this way.'

★

Violet booked the appointment with a heavy heart, which grew even heavier the morning they were supposed to make the drive to Bedford. Violet and Cecily sat at the kitchen table, watching Elspeth toy with a bowl of Weetabix. 'Darling,' Cecily said. 'I don't want to be cruel. But I really do think you must have the operation.'

Elspeth ignored her.

'If you don't have the operation, I'm afraid Daddy and I won't be able to support you. There'll be no money. No Roxborough. Nothing. You'll be entirely on your own.'

Elspeth put her spoon down and looked at the clock. 'We should go to the scan.'

'I'm not coming,' Cecily said. She felt desperately guilty. But she couldn't do it. The idea of her little girl lying on a stretcher like a butterfly while some man put something sharp inside her – it was all too much. 'Violet will take you. But please, think about what I said. It's not too late to have it—' She stopped.

'Let's go, Violet,' Elspeth said, looking pale and crushed. 'I'll see the doctor. But I'm not doing anything to hurt it.'

Cecily watched the car move away and then went to the stables. She tacked up Esmond's horse, Thunder. He was too big for her, and too strong, but she needed something to distract her. She thundered over the fields, losing herself in the motion of the horse's huge body, looking at the flat grey sky, forcing herself not to think about where her daughter was, about what would be happening to her.

It was the right choice. Even if she didn't see that now, she would have to see it eventually. She couldn't be an adult now. And all the things she was supposed to do would be lost. Getting married, having a proper family, perhaps a career. None of that would be possible if she became a mother at sixteen. And this boy, whoever he was, his life would be changed too. This was neater for everyone. Fairer. Elspeth would realize that one day. Cecily had to be the bad one for today so that Elspeth could be happy eventually.

Much later, when it was dark and Cecily had drunk most of a bottle of wine and smoked half a packet of cigarettes, the dogs started to bark. Cecily didn't move. She stayed rooted to her seat, trying not to react. It seemed to take an age, but eventually Violet came into the kitchen.

'Where is she?'

Violet looked grim. 'She wanted to go straight to bed.'

'I'll go and see her—'

'No, darling. Leave her to sleep.'

Violet poured herself a drink and sat down.

'Is it done?'

'Yes.'

The clock seemed enormously loud. 'Was it awful?'

'Yes.'

Cecily considered for a moment whether she could bear to know, and then decided that, as she was largely responsible, she should ask, even though she would rather not know, like a sort of penance. 'What happened?'

'We arrived. It stank of bleach, but it looked like a sub-
urban house. Detached, on a leafy avenue. The waiting
room was like someone's living room. Then we went
upstairs and it looked more like a doctor's surgery. Some
oily man in a white coat told her off for not being careful
and then told her to get undressed. She said she was
excited about the baby, that it wasn't a mistake. He cot-
toned on, acted like it was a normal scan. Then he told
her the baby wasn't well. She didn't believe him. He told
her it was only very small, and this was the kindest thing,
then he asked how she was going to support a baby alone,
whether her parents would support her. And she asked if
the baby really was ill. I think she knew he was lying, but
she wanted to hear it again. He gave her some half-
hearted lie, and she let him do it. Cecily, I could hear her.
I don't think they gave her anywhere near as much pain
relief as she should have had. But he said it won't be on
her medical records and she should be perfectly able to
have another child when she's older. If she starts to lose
too much blood, we must take her to hospital and tell
them what's happened.'

Cecily nodded. 'Thank you for taking her.'

Violet squeezed Cecily's hand. They finished the wine
in silence.

Later, when Violet was asleep, Cecily slipped from their
bedroom and down the hall to Elspeth's room. She
watched her daughter sleeping, her face sweet and round,
still so childlike. She was pale and there were traces of

mascara underneath her eyes. Cecily put a pillow on the floor and lay down, taking a blanket from the end of the bed. She lay, half waking, half sleeping, watching her daughter until the sun came up. Then she slipped back to her bedroom, making sure that Elspeth would never know that she had been there.

9

'Well, that was something of a surprise,' said Bryony, opening her laptop. She had taken several days off work out of respect for David's grief, but the idea of spending yet more time here rather than back at school, where she was needed, was increasingly unappealing.

'Yes,' said David. He was sitting on the end of his bed, looking out of the windows at the lawns below. It was odd, Bryony thought, that this had been his childhood bedroom. It was such an adult space. Nothing like the nursery they'd decorated for Lucca, with black-and-white walls designed to stimulate his development as a baby, and then with murals of inspirational figures for him to wonder about as he fell asleep.

'But lovely for Willa,' she ventured. David could be so protective about his daughters. Especially Willa, who was so breakable. He wasn't entirely wrong there. After nearly three decades working in girls' schools, she knew girls like Willa. And she knew how often their lives ended prematurely. And his protectiveness towards Willa seemed to roll over to Lizzie. So, Bryony had to tread carefully when she tried to make completely reasonable suggestions like not giving Lizzie any money when she should be perfectly able to earn a living in her twenties, or not needing to now buy a house where each of the girls would have their own bedroom, given that neither of them had lived at home for half a decade.

'Yes,' David said again. He really did look dreadful. Grey.

She closed the laptop and went to sit next to David. 'Are you all right?'

'I . . .' He looked at her. 'I'm afraid I thought it would be me.'

'It should have been.'

'Really? Do you think so?'

'Of course, it should have been. Willa is barely out of her twenties, she's got her whole life ahead of her. How is she going to meet anyone or date living here? It's an extraordinary thing to give to a young single woman. And what about everything you did for your mother? We spent almost every weekend driving up here to make sure she was all right.'

'I don't think it was almost every weekend—'

'All right, but it was a lot of them. You were the closest to her. You're the oldest son. You had every right to expect that it was going to be you.'

David turned to her, studying the neat, pretty lines of her face. He felt so grateful for her that it almost hurt. 'Perhaps she wasn't as fond of me as I thought she was.'

Bryony felt a surprising surge of anger towards her late mother-in-law, and towards her stepdaughter. How dare Cecily pass over her most diligent, hard-working child? David had spent his entire life doing what he was supposed to do. Working in a dull job in the city, marrying the first woman he had a relationship with, visiting Cecily constantly. He was a perfect son. And yet Cecily had talked constantly about Grant. She'd smiled over Grant's failed business attempts, laughed at what a 'scamp' he was because he had been unable to hold down any semblance of a relationship after his wife died. Grant was clearly, unashamedly, the favourite.

Bryony had had a horrible feeling ever since Cecily's death that Grant would be left the house. But she could never have dreamed that it would go to Willa. And from the reactions downstairs, it seemed that no one else could have either. She drank in the profile of David's face, his skin pale, his hair almost the same grey as his neck. Something had to be done. This couldn't be allowed to go on.

'Darling,' she said, very gently, her hand on his leg.

'Yes?'

'If I ask you a question, will you promise not to be angry with me?'

David turned, looking concerned. 'My love, after everything I've had to tell you this week, I wouldn't have a leg to stand on.'

Bryony gave him a reassuring smile. 'We will sort it all out. But before that, I think we need to talk about Willa's letter.'

David looked confused. 'Willa's letter?'

It was difficult to know exactly how to manage this conversation. It had to be done delicately, otherwise David would flip. There could be no suggestion that Willa might be deliberately at fault. Bryony took a deep breath. 'I just wonder about all that confusion with the letters on the night of the funeral – and then the new letters just turning up like that, with all the chaos, people coming in and out of the house. There has been such a lot going on. And you said it yourself – it came as quite a surprise to everyone that the house went to Willa. Is it possible that might not actually have been what your mother wanted at all?' She paused, waiting to see whether she had handled it as delicately as she needed to, whether David was going to explode and accuse her of trying to come between him and his daughters – yet again – or tell her that she didn't understand how fragile Willa was. She had sometimes been tempted to ask him how he thought Willa ended up that way.

He got to his feet. 'I suppose,' he said slowly, 'it's possible. You might be right.' He sighed. 'But even if you were – there's nothing that can be done about it now. This is how things have worked since the 1700s. It would just look like sour grapes.'

Bryony reached up and softly stroked his face. 'Just leave it with me, my love,' she said. 'Let me see what I can do.'

David looked at the clock. 'We should get changed, I suppose.'

Bryony decided to do something she would never normally condone. 'Shall I get you a whiskey? A little stiffener before you go downstairs?'

David cracked a half-smile. 'You really must be worried about me.'

'I love you,' she said. 'I'll be back in a moment.'

The drawing room, where the drinks were kept on an enormous wooden table, was to the left of the stairs. But Bryony paused when she reached it, hearing noises coming from the little sitting room.

'What's going on?' she asked. Violet and Angelique were standing close together, huddled over something.

'Nothing,' Angelique said. 'That's a pretty blouse.'

Bryony had worked in boarding schools since she was in her mid-twenties. She knew exactly what it looked like when someone was trying to distract her so that they could get away with something. 'What's going on?' she asked again.

Violet handed her a photo frame. It was one of the many silver frames that stood on the mantelpiece of the small sitting room. This one had held a picture of Willa, Jonty and Lizzie, all sitting on the croquet lawn. Willa was sitting on the swing that used to hang from the apple tree in the far corner. Lizzie was climbing up the tree, one foot on Jonty's shoulder. They were young, about thirteen. The glass was broken, and the photograph had been removed and replaced clumsily. She was about to shrug it off, to tell Violet that accidents happen, when she noticed the eyes. All three of the children's eyes had been scratched out with something sharp.

'What on earth?'

Violet held up three other frames. David and Grant beaming in the south of France in the late 1980s. She and David on their wedding day. And Lucca, aged two, sitting on the main staircase. She took the picture of Lucca in her hands. Her baby son, a photograph from the first time they'd stayed at Roxborough as parents, the first time Lucca had met his grandmother. It had also been the first time she had finally felt able to stand up properly, without sitting in the shadow of her angelic predecessor. Lucca's sweet, tiny face, with gashes where his eyes should be. She felt sick. 'Who would do this?'

Angelique shrugged. 'There's no way of knowing.'

'Where is everyone?'

Violet looked frustrated. 'Willa was with me in the kitchen helping to prepare supper. You and David have been together, Grant went into town to get supplies for tonight.'

'What about Elspeth?' Bryony asked. 'Everything seemed fine before she got here.'

Violet took a deep breath, trying not to let her frustration show. 'She's visiting friends who live nearby, I saw her leave this morning and her car has been gone all day. I don't think we need to hold a full investigation yet, it's probably just—'

'Where were you?' Bryony demanded of Angelique.

'Grant and I spent the morning in bed and then I had a bath, I had lunch and then slept,' she replied, her tone making it very clear that she was above being asked such questions. 'Why would I want to do this?'

'Where are Jonty and Lizzie?' This seemed like exactly the sort of thing that childish, angry Lizzie would do upon learning that she wasn't simply going to inherit a house, having never managed to hold down a job for more than a year at a time.

'They went out on bicycles earlier,' Angelique said. 'I saw them go down the drive.'

'What?' asked Violet. 'How long have they been gone?'

Angelique shrugged. 'I don't think we should tell anyone else about this.'

'Of course we should tell everyone. We need to work out who did this. This is a picture of my son.'

Violet took the broken frame from Bryony. 'I know,' she said. 'And I understand why you are upset. But Angelique is right. The last thing anyone needs after what has happened with the letters is more confusion. It will only upset them. I'll have the frames repaired and order replacements for the photographs.'

'Fine,' said Bryony.

But, she thought as she went back upstairs, David had every right to know what was happening under this roof – a roof which by all rights should be his.

Lizzie opened the side door, one that was hardly ever used, and was relieved to find it unlocked. The freckles had come out on her arms, she realized, and she had caught the sun. She'd be properly brown tomorrow. Stained by the beautiful day she had shared with Jonty, she thought. She pushed the door closed behind her and then, with a start, looked up to see Violet standing at the end of the passage. 'Hi!' she said brightly, realizing that her enthusiasm made her look and sound guilty. Her hands went to her damp hair.

'You've been swimming?'

'Yes, it was lovely. It's so hot outside, I just really wanted to cool down, and it did the job, really recommend it.'

'Did you go to the lake?'

Lizzie shook her head. 'No, no. We went to the river.'

'We?'

Violet knew perfectly well who Lizzie had been with, and that her efforts in talking to Lizzie like some kind of disapproving parent were entirely wasted. But she owed it to Cecily.

'Jonty and I – we took bikes.'

'That's nice.'

Violet picked up the basket of laundry she was carrying from the back kitchen to the kitchen garden, the only place Cecily would permit anyone to hang sheets. 'If you want to get your swimming costume dry, I'll leave space on the line.'

Lizzie very rarely blushed, but she felt the blood swell under her skin. 'Thanks,' she muttered. Then, unable to stand it any longer, she half ran upstairs to her room.

★

194

'Thank you,' David said, taking the glass of whiskey from his wife. It was a surprisingly generous measure for Bryony, who hated anyone to be drunk. 'Are you all right? You look upset.'

'I'm fine,' she said, looking away from him.

'I'll go and have a shower then,' said David, unbuttoning his shirt.

'Something strange happened downstairs.'

'Oh?'

'Angelique and Violet don't want you or Grant or the children to know.'

David felt that he would probably rather not know, and that no good would come from this conversation. 'Well, if they thought—'

'The photographs downstairs have all been smashed.'

'Was it the cat? I swear, I will never understand why Mother kept having them. They bring dead birds in, they piss, and they climb on to the mantelpieces and knock things over—'

'No,' Bryony interrupted. 'It wasn't the cat. It was deliberate.'

'Deliberate?'

'They weren't just broken. All the people in the pictures had their eyes scratched out.'

David looked utterly bemused. 'Which people?'

'You and Grant on holiday years ago. Our wedding. Lucca as a baby. Lizzie and Willa with Jonty.'

'Jesus.'

'There's no way of knowing who did it.'

'I suppose not.'

'But don't you think . . .'

David didn't know what she was hinting at, a tendency that he knew enraged her.

'Think?'

'Well, first the letters. The fire. Now this. It's odd, isn't it?'

David was looking past her. He knew she was right. And he wasn't stupid enough to be naïve about what she was saying. Bryony could be prosaic. Self-promoting. Ruthless in her ambition. It was one of the things he loved about her. She'd been born to addict parents and handed to social services because of their neglect before she'd cut her first tooth, spent her childhood in and out of care and yet had ended up running one of the grandest private schools for girls in the UK. Things like that didn't happen to people unless they had developed a fair amount of edge. There had never been any prospect of her taking it well if they weren't going to inherit the house.

But even considering all that, he had to admit she had a point. Willa's letter was astonishingly unlikely. The entailment hadn't gone the way it was supposed to. And now, apparently, someone was doing deliberately sinister things to family photographs. Perhaps it was possible that there was rather more taking place here than he wanted to admit.

Willa was having a hideous time trying to work out what to wear. She had packed a spartan suitcase, too blinded by grief to care what she looked like. A smart black dress for the funeral, and then various T-shirts, jeans and shorts.

The one dress she had brought with her was pink with thin straps and seemed too young and frivolous to wear tonight. She couldn't help the situation by highlighting how much younger she was than everyone else. The idea that they had to have a dinner at all felt wrong. She had told Violet that afternoon as they sat in the kitchen shelling broad beans and peeling vegetables, the windows open to catch what little breeze there was. 'It feels wrong,' she'd said, 'asking everyone to celebrate me.'

'You can borrow something,' said Lizzie. Willa whipped around. She hadn't realized that her sister had come in. Her hair was damp, and her freckles, so perfect that they looked as if they had been drawn on to the bridge of her nose, were a little darker than they had been this morning.

'It's fine,' Willa said. 'I'm sure I've got something, or there might be something in the wardrobe.'

Lizzie snorted. 'The wardrobe? Really?' The girls had been leaving items of clothing at Roxborough for years. Things they'd grown bored of or decided over the course of a summer were out of style. Things they couldn't fit into their bags when they left because their grandmother had taken them shopping or (far more excitingly) allowed them to help themselves to her vintage treasures. As such, the wardrobe in the nursery was filled with things that neither of them ever wanted to wear again but couldn't bring themselves to get rid of. An acid-green skater skirt, a couple of pink polo shirts, dresses with waist belts – things Lizzie had assumed her own children would dress up in one day. She took a navy-blue dress from her suitcase – left unzipped with its guts spilled open in the space between her bed and the wall. 'Wear this.'

Willa took it gratefully. 'Is it what you were going to wear?' She was surprised at herself for asking the question.

'Yes,' Lizzie said. 'So, you should.'

Willa stared at the navy fabric. 'I'm really sorry.'

'Why?'

'I know you wanted – I know you were hoping—'

'We were all hoping. Anyone who says they weren't is lying. But it's yours.'

'It'll be ours, really. You know you'll have your own room and you'll be able to come here whenever you want. We'll share it—'

'No. We won't. Don't look like that, I'm not being mean. I'm just being honest. If Granny had left it to me, then it would be mine. But she left it to you – so it's yours. I don't want you to share it. I hope you'll invite me, and I'll come whenever you suggest it. But it's not going to be shared. That's not how it works.' Lizzie was stripping her clothes off and winding herself in a large towel. 'I'm happy for you. Really, I am.' She dropped a kiss on her sister's forehead, realizing that it was perhaps at least a little bit true. She needed a new plan now. Living at Roxborough had always been it. But now she wasn't going to live here, perhaps she needn't feel so guilty about doing the one thing she had always told her grandmother she wouldn't. Being with Jonty.

10

'Lucca, could you please come inside and get changed?' Bryony called out of the bedroom window. Lucca pretended that he couldn't hear her and carried on kicking his football against the apple tree. In the very long, very boring days since they'd arrived at the house, he'd got good at making it land squarely in the middle of the tree. There was a bird's nest on one of the upper branches and he had thought about aiming for it, but he thought that was probably a bit too mean. It wasn't the bird's fault he was stuck here for yet another holiday where people kept telling him to 'go and enjoy the garden', despite the fact that there was nothing to do in the garden. Kai, his friend at school, had a climbing frame shaped like a pirate ship in his garden, and a zip wire. Why couldn't there be a zip wire here?

'Lucca, please, your lack of response is making Mummy feel like you're not interested in what she's saying,' Bryony said. 'That makes Mummy feel frustrated and sad.' Lucca looked up. If he kept ignoring her, she would keep talking.

'Fine!' he shouted. 'I'm coming.'

'I'm not sure how much Lucca is enjoying this,' Bryony told David, closing the window behind her. She caught sight of her face in the reflection of the old glass and was startled to see that the crow's feet under her eyes seemed to have got even worse. Was there anything that could be done about that? Or was it just Botox in the forehead and the rest of the face being allowed to wither?

'I'm not sure how much any of us are,' David replied. He was drinking the whiskey she had brought him and buttoning his shirt after a shower. The room smelled like him, his expensive, old-fashioned cologne mingled with the steam from the extra-hot shower. 'We are in mourning after all.'

'Yes. Of course. You're right. I'm sorry.' David didn't look as if he thought she was. 'It's just,' she added, 'I've never really had anyone to mourn for.'

He softened and held his hand out to her. She didn't feel guilty. Yes, she was milking her tragic childhood. But she'd never had any issue with doing that. Other people got happy childhoods and solid home lives. She'd grown up not knowing where her next meal was coming from or whether one of her mother's many 'boyfriends' was going to try to stick his hand up her knickers. She'd had it far harder than anyone else she knew, and she wasn't ever going to hold back from using it for everything it was worth.

And it wasn't as if she had said anything untrue, either. She found David's grief at the loss of his mother utterly inexplicable. Her own mother had died when Bryony was in her early twenties, leaving nothing but a pile of credit-card debt. Bryony had had to spend all her savings – a meagre sum at that point – on a half-hearted funeral, unable to afford any of the trimmings even if she had wanted them. Her mother's hideous friends had turned up, no doubt hoping there might be free food or, more importantly, free drinks. Bryony had taken great joy in exclusively serving coffee, tea and other non-alcoholic beverages.

Her father was almost certainly also dead, but she didn't know. There was a blank square on her birth certificate where his name should be, and there were two possibilities for what his name actually was. David had told her, just after Cecily died, that losing his last parent was so strange because it was the final vestige of his childhood ending. He was now the top generation of his family – it was like the roof had been taken off. Bryony had nodded nicely and made sympathetic noises, but internally she had wanted to scream. David was in his sixties. Of course his childhood was over. Hers had been over before she'd started her first period.

She sat down in front of the dressing table, looking through her jewellery organizer for the pair of earrings David had given her for their first wedding anniversary. 'I was thinking that I might speak to Grant?'

'Grant? What about?'

'The letters.'

David looked bemused. 'Letters?'

Honestly, it was as if he had forgotten everything about their earlier conversation. 'About Willa's letter.'

'Oh.'

'What do you think?'

'I hadn't given it any thought.' David put his jacket on. 'I don't think . . . I'm not sure it would be worth much. The last thing I want is for Willa to think I'm trying to take the house away from her or that I don't think she deserves it.'

'Of course not – no, that's the last thing any of us wants.'

'We should go down.'

'You know, I'm not suggesting for a second that Willa would have done anything wrong.'

'No, no, of course not.'

'More that there might be a genuine mix-up with the letters. Or that someone else might be interfering.'

'I don't think so. Are you ready? We should go down.'

Bryony pulled her mouth into a smile. Clearly there was far more to be done before David was going to see sense.

Grant was the first down to have a drink. He'd put on a loud floral shirt his mother had given him for Christmas. It had lived in the wardrobe in his bedroom because there was no way he was going to wear it in London, but he'd put it on out of some misguided sense of loyalty. As if Cecily would care whether he wore it or not. She wasn't precious about things like that.

He took a bottle of champagne from the ice bucket and held it, waiting for someone else to come in. He supposed that standing here, holding it, was the right sort of image to convey to whoever came down first. No one could question how happy he was for Willa if he was pouring drinks and wearing a ridiculous shirt. And he was happy for her. Or at least he kept repeating to himself that he was happy for her, which had to count for something.

Angelique had been surprisingly supportive. She was usually so impervious to anything going wrong, just shrugging her shoulders and telling him that 'what will be will be'. But this morning she had woken him with her hand down the front of his pyjamas and whispered how much she loved him and how they would find something else wonderful to do together. He suspected that she might be a little bit glad that she wasn't going to find herself living in Norfolk and being mistress of the enormous house. She loved her little flat in South Kensington. Grant didn't entirely understand why. She had (ironically) inherited it from her grandmother and it was postage-stamp tiny, right at the top of a huge Georgian building. No outside space, just a view of dozens of other pointy roofs and the constant noise of London. Grant had found it all comforting once but, as he'd got older, he somehow couldn't cope with the miscellany of everything that took place in cities. Constant movement and noise. The air was too dry and thick, the people too rude and rushing. It was only when he got his letter that he'd realized quite how much he had been banking on being able to move, rather than waking up each morning in Angelique's queen-sized bed, squeezed against the wall, able to see every room in the place the moment he opened his eyes.

But there would probably be a small amount of money left to him; his mother had mentioned that the house wasn't the extent of the estate she would leave. It might be enough to get a cottage somewhere nearby. Would it be utterly tragic to move here, anyway? He saw visions of himself walking through the lower fields, along by the river, with a dog. A surprisingly dull fantasy for a man who used to enjoy class-A drugs in warehouse raves. But then wasn't that what getting older meant?

'Are you going to open that?' asked Bryony. Grant looked up, realizing he had been frozen in his pose.

'Yes, sorry,' he said. 'Would you like some?'

'Yes,' Bryony said, surprising them both. She rarely drank and couldn't conceal her distaste for how much the Mordaunts were able to put away.

Grant poured her a glass and then handed it over. 'I suppose everyone else will be down in a moment.'

'Yes.'

They stood in an awkward silence, listening to a bumble bee headbutting the sash window.

'It's lovely for Willa,' Grant ventured.

'Yes,' said Bryony, raising her eyebrows. 'I suppose so.'

'You don't think so?'

Bryony sipped from her glass and then adopted the expression of concern she used when she was telling parents that their children weren't keeping up academically at school – when she needed them to remove their child so they didn't pull the A-level average down but wanted them to think it was because she liked the child and couldn't bear to see their self-esteem damaged. 'I just . . .' She shook her head. 'It's not my place.'

'Of course it is,' Grant said. 'You're family.'

It was an odd time for Grant to start considering her to be part of the family. Perhaps not getting his own way for the first time in his life had been good for him. 'I'm just a little worried,' she said. 'You know, about Willa's history, the eating disorder, all that time spent in that centre. Her doctors always said that stress and pressure were the worst things for her, and I can't help thinking that running a house like this might make her ill again.'

Grant looked at Bryony, trying to decide if she was being genuine. He decided probably not. Bryony had clearly been expecting to get her feet under the table and to be playing lady of the manor by the end of the week. But, despite the fact that it was clearly meant in the most selfish way possible, was it possible that she had a point? Willa was delicate. She always had been. And running Roxborough wasn't for the faint-hearted. Their mother had made it look easy, but she was more a force of nature than a woman.

'I just wonder . . .' Bryony added conspiratorially. 'All that business with the letters, everything being so . . .' She stopped.

'So what?'

She shook her head again. 'I'm sure I've just read too

many mystery novels. I just can't help worrying that perhaps it wasn't a complete accident that the letters were lost and then found. If there might be someone who would benefit from Willa inheriting the house – take advantage of her.'

'I'm gasping for a drink,' said Elspeth, interrupting. Grant grabbed for the bottle, feeling guilty, though he wasn't sure why. It wasn't as if he had said anything about Willa, or the house, or the letters. 'Little brother?'

Grant handed her a glass. She looked wrong here. She shouldn't have come. Bryony was right – something he had never thought before in his life. It was more than likely that someone had intervened. But who? He looked across at Angelique, who had arrived into the room with an air of palpable boredom. She loved their life in London so much and had made no effort to hide her lack of interest in living at Roxborough. Could she have switched the letters to make sure she never had to live here? He dismissed the thought. He was being stupid. He considered his sister. Since Elspeth had arrived, things had changed, and not for the better.

'What?' she asked. 'You're giving me a look.'

'I'm sorry.' Grant smiled. 'It's just extraordinary. Seeing you here.'

'Well, don't get used to it. I've got to sign some paperwork and then I'll be off.'

'Isn't it at least a little bit nice to be home?' Bryony asked.

'No,' Elspeth said. 'Because this isn't my home.'

★

The door opened again and this time it was Lucca. 'Mummy,' he said, 'Violet says I can have fish fingers and watch YouTube, but only if you say yes.'

'Why are you wearing that?'

Lucca had put on his long-sleeved football top. 'It's Ronaldo,' he said proudly.

'Yes, but we're having a formal supper. I put some shorts and a shirt on your bed.'

He pulled a face. 'I want to watch YouTube.'

Bryony smiled and knelt down so she was at Lucca's height. 'I know you do, darling, but we all very much want to spend time with you because we love you and we value you.'

Elspeth snorted from the corner, where she was rolling a cigarette.

'I'm sorry?' Bryony said in a warning tone.

'Nice to meet you,' Elspeth said to Lucca, ignoring her sister-in-law. 'I'd rather watch YouTube and eat fish fingers too.'

'This is Auntie Elspeth,' Bryony said.

'If you call me auntie, I'll throw myself off the roof.'

Lucca laughed, deciding that he liked this woman, who his mother obviously found very annoying. 'Can I sit next to you?'

'Sure.'

Lizzie and Jonty were down next. Lizzie had chosen a white dress which was pretty much see-through. Bryony considered asking why she couldn't dress more appropriately, given that she was with her family and obviously not on some kind of pulling mission, but decided against it. Then came David. There was an indentation on his left cheek where he had been holding his mobile phone, and a look of quiet desperation behind his eyes. Bryony's stomach twisted. Her facade of being relaxed about his financial issues was getting rather heavier to hold up. They would find a way out. Of course they would. She wouldn't let her little family crumble because poor David had been spoonfeeding his daughters ridiculous amounts of money.

Violet came next, throwing worried glances at Lizzie and Jonty, who were sitting next to each other on the sofa, fractionally too close.

Finally, Willa quietly opened the door. She hadn't meant to be the last down, and she blushed as soon as she realized that she was. It looked like she was showing off. Everyone turned to look at her as she slipped into the room, willing them not to say anything.

'I'd like to say a few words,' Grant said, raising his glass. Willa blushed even more and wished that she had some kind of superpower to leave her body sitting on the edge of the sofa smiling nicely while Grant talked so as not to have to experience the toe-curling embarrassment of whatever he was about to say about her.

'It's not an easy thing – the way this house passes down. And we all know, Willa, that you were surprised to find that your life was about to completely change. But my mother was a surprise when she inherited the house, and she's the reason that Roxborough is what it is today.

And Cecily knew what she was doing. She chose you for a reason, and I have no doubt that you'll do the house proud, and make all of us proud.' He lifted his glass and everyone else followed suit, Lizzie smiling, cross-legged on the sofa, Elspeth with an unreadable expression in the corner. 'To Willa,' Grant said.

'To Willa,' David echoed, realizing that he should probably have been the one to make the speech. 'The new owner of Roxborough.'

Everyone echoed him, and Willa stared at a middle point between her uncle and her father, counting in her head and waiting for the agonizing focus on her to be over.

'So, will we still be allowed to visit?' asked Lizzie, breaking the odd silence that fell after the toast.

'I thought we would do it just like we always have,' Willa said, looking at the floor. 'That everyone would come whenever they wanted to, and that we would have Easter and Christmas, maybe the August bank holiday . . .'

'See how terrified she looks?' Bryony murmured to David. 'Honestly, darling, do you really think your mother would have wanted this for her?'

A knock at the drawing-room door was followed by a small, smiling blonde girl entering the room. She looked to Violet. 'We're ready to serve the starter,' she said.

'Lovely,' Violet said. 'Shall we go through?'

Once again, the dining room had been made beautiful, though with rather less fuss than the night of the entailment, which came as a relief to Willa.

Each place had a name card on it. Willa's had been on the left side of the table, between Jonty and Lizzie, ever since she had been old enough to sit there. She had sat on that chair – mahogany wood with a rattan seat – since before her feet had been able to touch the floor, when she'd swing them under the table and beg to be allowed pudding even though she hadn't finished her vegetables. And later, when food was the most terrifying thing in the world, that chair had been one of the places she had just about managed to eat.

Her grandmother had understood. Her generation, notorious in their suffering of 'mental health issues', seemed to be full of women who viewed food as the enemy. Cecily herself had been careful to the point of obsession to make sure that her figure stayed the same into her forties, fifties, and beyond. She had once asked Willa for a list of things she could eat, and then, all through that first summer after Willa's mother had died, when she would run for three hours each morning and try to keep her calories under five hundred a day, Cecily had served her plates of fresh vegetables from the garden, never with any sauce, never with any dressing. She'd waited patiently while Willa worked her way through a plate, never acknowledging that Willa had different food to everyone else. Where her father had bargained, whee-dled, begged for her to eat, her grandmother had simply treated her as if she had an inconvenient allergy that must be worked around.

But that was no longer her place at the table. And that

wasn't her life any more. She pulled out the chair at the head of the table, where her grandmother used to sit facing Esmond, seated at the far end, and sat down.

It felt as if something seismic should happen, but nothing did. Everyone else sat down too. Wine was poured, salad brought out. Jonty asked Angelique whether she and Grant were going back to France this summer. Lucca asked Elspeth whether she had any tattoos, and then told her that, when he was eighteen, he was going to get Ronaldo's shirt number tattooed on his back, and a snake on his arm. Bryony asked Lucca what the most interesting fact was that he had learned that day. David looked out of the window and glanced intermittently at his Apple watch, which kept vibrating with text messages. Lizzie was quizzing Violet about what would be done with Cecily's vintage clothes. It all seemed almost normal.

'What's that noise?' Lizzie asked, as the salads were cleared away.

'I can't hear anything,' said Jonty.

'Shh, listen.'

Everyone fell silent and strained their ears. 'I can hear it!' said Lucca.

'Hear what?' asked Bryony.

'I think I can too,' Willa agreed. It was a sort of high-pitched whining, like static.

'Me too,' Elspeth said. 'What on earth is it? It sounds like a badly tuned radio.'

They all strained their ears, trying to work out what it was they were listening to. Lizzie got up, walking around the room like a sleepwalker, slowly listening at each corner.

'I'm sure it's nothing,' said Violet. 'If we go back to eating, it'll probably go away.'

'No,' Lizzie said. 'Listen, it's getting louder.' She walked towards the huge mahogany side table that dominated the left wall of the dining room. On the top, some of the most-used silver was displayed, and the candlesticks were kept there when not in use. Inside were the linens, various specific knives and forks for fish courses or eating things like artichokes. It had three wide drawers along the top then two huge, square ones. 'I think it's coming from in there.'

'What on earth could be coming from there? That's where Mum kept the tablecloths, isn't it?' Grant asked Violet.

'Yes,' Violet said. 'Perhaps we should leave it—'

But before she could finish her sentence Lizzie had jerked open one of the deep drawers and, within seconds – less than seconds – the noise had risen from a faint humming to a scream. No, it wasn't the same noise; it was Lizzie screaming – screaming because the room was now filled with hundreds and hundreds of wasps.

'Shut the drawer!' Grant shouted. David jumped to his feet and pushed Lizzie out of the way, slamming it closed. But it was far too late for that. The enraged wasps had escaped from the confinement they had clearly been so furious to be kept in, and shutting the nest back in had no effect at all. The air was black in places. David and Grant threw open every window in the dining room.

'When I say, everyone run out of the door, all right?' David instructed. He opened the final window as far as it would go, swatting wasps away from his eyes.

'Fuck!' shouted Angelique as one of them stabbed her arm with a sting.

Then everyone was on their feet, running for the dining-room door. Once they were all on the other side, David slammed it behind him, ten, maybe twenty, wasps following them. They retreated to the kitchen, hurrying and stumbling down the little flight of stairs in the back hallway. Finally, reaching the kitchen, doors and windows firmly shut, they stopped.

Lizzie had been stung all over her beautiful face. Willa was surprised by how much she wanted to cry, looking at her sister's beautiful eyes, swollen already, and her cheek-bones warped. Her arms were studded with stings. 'Are you all right?' Willa asked. 'Should we take you to hospital?'

'I'm fine,' said Lizzie, trying to smile. 'I just don't want to see myself in the mirror.'

'Are you all right?' Bryony asked, grasping Lucca. 'Have you been stung?'

Lucca nodded. 'Yes, but I'm OK, I promise.'

'I'm going to go to the back kitchen to tell the staff to leave and not to go via the front of the house,' Violet said. 'I think everyone else needs a stiff drink.'

Grant hunted and found a bottle of port in one of the kitchen cupboards. They drank it out of the water glasses from the kitchen cabinet, because anything more appropriate was now unreachable. Everyone drank down a shot of it, apart from Lucca, who had been given a packet of chocolate buttons from Violet's handbag. Then they poured another round and sat around the scrubbed wooden table, everyone wondering the same thing. Eventually, it was Elspeth who broke the silence.

'I know we're an unusual family,' she said, 'but filling the dining room with thousands of bugs isn't some strange part of the tradition, right?'

Violet half smiled. 'No. It's not.'

'So how did they get there?' asked Angelique.

'Could they have made a nest in the sideboard?' Lizzie asked Jonty, rolling her glass between two hands.

'It's not really my area,' Jonty said. 'People don't generally get the vet involved when they've got wasps. But I don't imagine so. It's usually the corners of rooms. They like it warm and dry, but mostly attics and barns.'

'So then how did it get there?' asked Willa.

No one said anything for a while.

'Does that mean someone put it there on purpose?' Willa said, after waiting to see if anyone would say anything.

'I'm sure they didn't,' Violet said. 'Why would someone do that?'

Willa dropped her gaze to her hands on the table. 'Maybe because of me getting the house.'

Violet put her hand on Willa's. 'Everyone is delighted for you, Willa. No one wants to quibble over you having the house and, even if they did, do you really think any of us is horrible enough to do something like that?'

'No,' Willa said, shaking her head. 'You're right. I'm sorry.'

'Is it impossible that it could have been there for a while, Jonty?' David asked, willing his nephew to give him the kind of response that would put his daughter's mind at rest.

'Not impossible,' Jonty said. *Almost impossible. Extremely unlikely*, he wanted to add. *Basically impossible*. But Willa's horrified expression and Lizzie's distorted face told him that there would be nothing to gain by throwing further suspicions into the group. They all knew, deep down, that the nest wasn't there by chance. It was getting late, and they were all covered in wasp stings. No one was hungry any more. It wouldn't be a benefit to make anyone feel any worse.

'Another round?' Grant asked, holding the port bottle.

David called an emergency pest-control company that quoted him an eye-watering sum and said they'd arrive by 7 a.m. the next day. He wondered if he should have asked Willa for her sign-off before saying yes. It was so deeply, deeply strange, the idea that he was now supposed to ask his daughter for permission in a house he had lived in since before there had been any idea of her. Jonty handed out antihistamines to everyone as they went to bed. 'We're all going to sleep like logs – better make sure the doors are locked properly.' One by one, they filed off to bed, taking the back stairs to avoid the front of the house, each silently wondering whose fault the horrors of the evening had been.

'You were very good tonight,' Angelique told Grant as she took off her make-up.

'Really?'

'Absolutely.'

'I don't think I did anything. David was far better with the wasps.'

'I didn't mean that. I meant the speech. The way you behaved towards Willa. You were very kind.'

Grant was surprised by how much he enjoyed the compliment. 'Bryony thinks there was foul play. That Willa wasn't supposed to have the house.'

Angelique looked surprisingly disinterested in this theory. 'Perhaps.'

'You think?'

'It's not impossible. The letters disappearing, it was all very strange.'

'But why would someone want Willa to have the house?'

Angelique shrugged and undid her bra, stepped out of her knickers and got into bed completely naked, as she always did.

'Bryony thought perhaps someone might want her to have it so that they could exploit her.'

She shrugged again. 'Perhaps. It's not impossible.'

'But if that were the case – we would have to do something.'

'Why?' She squirted hand cream on to her hands and

massaged them together. Luella used to do the same thing before she went to sleep. Grant felt that old twist of grief.

'Why what?'

'Why would you do something? You don't actually want to live here.'

'No, not really,' he said. It wasn't true, and Angelique knew that. But it was somehow less embarrassing to pretend than to admit to himself that he had wanted the house, that his mother had known that he wanted it, but that she had found him lacking and chosen someone else instead of him. He knew beyond all doubt that if Luella were still alive, the house would have been theirs.

'And Jonty didn't want it?'

'No. I don't think so.' It occurred to him that he had never actually asked Jonty if he wished to inherit. But he wouldn't have wanted it, would he? He was young and free, wealthy and successful. Why would he want to be lumbered with an enormous commitment like Roxborough?

'So, what would you gain by getting involved? What if they find out that the letters were fake and it turns out the house is yours? You would have to move here, I would have to come with you, it would change our whole lives.' She leaned over and kissed him. 'Bryony has a stick up her ass, and she wanted the house for David.' Then she turned her light out and within moments was breathing gently. How could anyone fall asleep so easily? Especially at a time like this? Why wasn't she more interested in the Agatha Christie novel unfolding in front of them?

*

Willa lay down and was asleep within seconds. Lizzie, however, couldn't get comfortable. No matter how she lay, her face hurt. Eventually, she got out of bed and padded along the corridor. She knocked gently on Jonty's door, telling herself that if he answered on the first knock she could go in but that she wouldn't knock again. She waited in the hallway, the silence of the house ringing in her ears. Then she broke her own resolve and knocked again. Jonty answered the door, topless and wearing a pair of cotton pyjama bottoms.

'I can't sleep,' she said.

'I'm not surprised.' He reached out and very gently stroked her face. 'Does it hurt?'

Lizzie nodded. 'Can I come in?'

Jonty thought about it for a moment. He knew he was going to say yes. Of course he was. But somehow, he needed to at least pretend he was thinking about it, that he had enough control over himself to tell her that no matter how much they wanted each other, this thing that had been going on since they were teenagers, stopping either of them from ever truly being able to love another, more appropriate person, had to stop. He pulled the door open and stepped aside. 'Of course you can,' he said.

They lay next to each other in his bed, still a single bed, a hangover from all the childhood years in this room, her body lying against his. Her skin was cool whereas his was warm. He ran his hand up her thigh. 'Do you want some painkillers?'

'I've had some.'

'I could get you an icepack.'

'No – please. Just lie with me.'

He wrapped his arm around her torso, his hand creeping underneath her T-shirt, listening to her breathe.

'I was thinking about what you said before,' he murmured into her hair.

'What did I say?'

'About us.' He felt her body stiffen. It was the first time he had ever acknowledged out loud that there was such a thing as an 'us'.

'What about us?' Lizzie replied, simultaneously desperate to hear what he was going to say next and terrified about what it might be.

'I think we should do it.'

Lizzie giggled. 'We've been doing it for more than a decade.'

Jonty squeezed her. 'Can you take anything seriously, you nightmare?'

'OK, OK.' She stopped laughing. 'You mean you think we should see each other.'

'Yes.'

Lizzie considered this. They'd known each other her entire life. But they'd never been out to dinner. They'd barely exchanged texts or spoken on the phone.

'You want us to date?'

'I do.'

'Like normal people?'

'Just like normal people.'

'What about everyone else?'

Jonty considered this. 'I think we see how it goes, and if we make it six months and we're happy, we tell them.'

'They'll be horrified.'

'I know. But we're not actually doing anything wrong. We're not related. Grant knows that better than anyone else.' He smiled, trying to soften the accidental bitterness in his voice.

'What if it doesn't work?' she asked.

'Then at least we'll know. Maybe that would be easier.' After nearly ten years of trying to resist each other, surely anything would be easier. He didn't exactly relish the idea of telling Grant, and the prospect of telling David was far worse. But they would hide their horror. It wasn't as if either of their fathers ever offered an opinion on their life choices. Eventually they would get over it.

They lay there, bodies breathing as one, for a long time. Then, just as he was starting to drift into sleep.

'Jonty?'

'Yes?'

'Are we disgusting?'

He pulled her more tightly to him, breathing in the scent of her hair. It was a question he had asked himself before, many times. 'No,' he said. 'Of course we aren't.'

A tear slipped down Lizzie's swollen cheek. 'I'm so tired of feeling guilty.'

He hadn't realized it before, but the moment she said it, the words seemed to settle on him in a way that felt right. 'Me too,' he said.

1990

Cecily wasn't silly about clothes. She spent money. A lot of money, in fact. But she was fastidious. She only bought things that she knew she would wear again and again, things that would keep their shape and their quality over the years. And when a piece went out of fashion, like the Christian Dior dresses she had adored in the late fifties, she would have them packaged away and eventually tailored into something more modern, or she would keep them as they were until they came back into style.

Of course, all of this required a certain amount of discipline. Everything she bought was tailored to her, so there wasn't space to gain or lose much more than a few pounds. During pregnancy, she had compromised with various tent-like dresses and had spent the majority of the last few months in the garden at Roxborough apologizing for her appearance to anyone who popped by. And after giving birth to each of her children, she had been fastidious about losing the weight, living off grapefruit, coffee and cigarettes. Esmond and Violet had both laughed at her, but she liked her body to be slim. She enjoyed feeling light and free, and she adored her clothes. Which was why, when she discovered that a black Givenchy cocktail dress, not unlike the one Audrey Hepburn had worn in *Breakfast at Tiffany's*, was too small for her, she was furious.

'Violet!' she called.

'I'm reading,' Violet called back from the bedroom, where she was sitting at the writing desk with a D. H. Lawrence novel.

'I need you!' Cecily shouted.

She put the book face down on the desk. 'What could you possibly need?'

Cecily was standing in the dressing room between the bedroom and the bathroom, a small room open at each end and flanked by wardrobes. She wore a dress half zipped up at the back and looked pinker in the cheeks than she usually did. Cecily had unusually olive skin for a British woman and rarely looked pink or out of breath. But the warmth of the room and her frustration about the dress was taking a toll. 'I can't get the zip up,' she said. 'Can you do it?'

Violet attempted to give the zip a good tug and, in the process, it came off its runner. Cecily exploded. 'What am I going to wear now? What's wrong with me?' She pulled open a wardrobe door and inspected herself in profile. 'I've put on weight. Haven't I?'

'A little,' Violet said. 'I think it rather suits you.'

'Suits me? How can getting fat suit me?'

Violet privately thought that Cecily had become too

thin over recent years and had preferred the slight soft-
ness she'd had when they first met.

'It's the fucking menopause!' Cecily shouted. 'I know it.'

'That might explain the mood swings.' Violet smiled.
Cecily threw a shoe at her, missing deliberately. 'You are
a child,' Violet said. 'And I'm not giving this any more cre-
dence. Wear the brown-and-white spotted dress, it's in
the left-hand wardrobe and it was too big for you when
you bought it.'

Cecily stormed back into the wardrobe and pulled it
out. She yanked it over her body and went to show Violet. 'This?'

'Yes, it's lovely.'

'It's tight in the chest.'

'Then all of Esmond's colleagues will enjoy it.'

Cecily managed a snort. 'I do think it's the menopause,
you know. I haven't had the curse in months.'

Violet put the Givenchy dress back on the hanger.
'You're sure it's that?'

'What else could it be? God, I hope it's not some hideous cancer.'

'Of course it's not cancer.' Violet tutted. Cecily was an
odd sort of hypochondriac. Always assuming the worst
possible outcome but devoted to drinking and smoking
and taking exercise only when she walked the dogs. 'I
suppose it would be remiss not to ask you whether or not
you might be pregnant.'

Cecily's hand slipped as she was putting a gold earring
through her lobe. 'Don't be ridiculous. I'm far too old.'

'Are you?'

'I'm fifty-two. People don't have babies when they're fifty-two.'

Violet raised her eyebrows. 'Is it possible?'

Gravel crunched in the driveway downstairs, signalling the arrival of a taxi. Cecily picked up her handbag. She kissed Violet on the lips and smoothed her hair. 'I'll be home later, darling. Have a lovely evening.'

Violet watched as Cecily got into the car and it sped off. Years ago, when she first came to Roxborough, she used to burn with jealousy when Cecily went off to a party. She wondered how she was supposed to spend her whole life watching her beloved leave to sparkle in a room full of people who had no idea Violet even existed. But it had become easier year by year, and easier still when Esmond had made the transition to London full-time. These days, she was delighted to stay here alone. She would watch *University Challenge* on the television, videotaped because Cecily found it dull. Supper on a tray, with the dogs and the cat. A walk around the garden, picking anything that needed to be picked. Perhaps a gin and tonic in the bath. It was more luxury than she could ever have hoped for.

And when Cecily came home, she would wake Violet and tell her about the party, just as she had done when they were young women. They would lie with their limbs tangled and Violet would think about how enormously lucky she was.

This evening, though, Violet couldn't settle. The zip in

the dress. The fact she hadn't had the curse. Was Cecily right? Was it impossible for a woman in her fifties to have a baby? She wished she could find out, but even in the Roxborough library it seemed unlikely that there would be a book about such a thing. She tried to put the idea from her mind, to focus on the television and her embroidery.

Cecily wasn't enjoying the party. The room was crowded with well-dressed people and the bar was stocked with cocktails. The teenage daughters of the hosts circulated, holding plates of food. They had long hair and long legs and they made Cecily feel strangely sad. She had only agreed to come because the party was being given by one of Esmond's great friends, and part of their arrangement was that she would still put on a good show. Not that she usually minded. She and Esmond were quite the team when it came to entertainment, finishing each other's sentences and always knowing exactly how dry a joke should be to amuse but never offend. 'You look lovely,' Esmond said, winding his arm around her waist.

'You bloody liar,' she said, taking a Martini. 'I look dreadful. I've got fat.'

Esmond laughed at her. 'You're mad. You were miles too thin before. Much better now.'

She took a long drink from her Martini and tried to silence the voice at the back of her head that had been softly spoken before this evening. It had to be the menopause. Everyone said that your body went haywire when you went through the change. And of course it felt like pregnancy; it was the same process but in reverse.

She lit another cigarette and smiled at Esmond. 'How's London?'

'Quiet.'

'You like the quiet.'

'I miss you.'

'Don't be silly.'

'I'm not. I want you to come back.'

'Well, I can't, you know that.'

'I thought perhaps after what happened last time—'

'You know perfectly well that was an accident. It won't happen again. We agreed. I'm staying at Roxborough with Violet, and you're staying at Cheyne Walk with whatever undergraduate you have on rotation.'

Esmond recovered his composure. 'Of course. You're quite right.'

'You should really find someone else. A grown-up, someone you can settle down with.'

Esmond shook his head. 'I'm afraid, after you, my darling, there really isn't any chance of that.'

Cecily smiled, though his compliment had made her feel terribly sad. 'Now,' she said, 'who do we need to talk to?'

Violet woke in the middle of the night to the sound of Cecily being sick in the bathroom. Violet considered getting up, taking her a glass of water, stroking her back. But somehow, she couldn't bring herself to do it. So instead, she pulled the blankets over her shoulders and squeezed her eyes shut.

The next morning, Cecily woke up early and went downstairs to make them both tea. This was almost unheard of. Violet had known when she heard Cecily vomiting in the night, but this gesture of kindness served only to confirm it. 'Was it Esmond?' Violet asked.

'Yes.'

'Why?'

'He asked me nicely.'

Violet gave Cecily a cold look. 'We needn't talk about this if you aren't going to take it seriously.'

'I'm sorry,' Cecily said, looking at her hands.

'So. Why?'

'He was terribly sad. I had told him to stay in London because you and I were going to be together and he was so upset. He wanted to say goodbye. All those silly sorts of things people do in films.'

'And now you're pregnant.'

Cecily looked down at her stomach. 'I think so.'

'What are you going to do?'

She shrugged. 'I've an appointment with Dr Greenway.'

'You'll terminate it?'

'I think that's best. Don't you?'

Violet thought about it. She was only six years Cecily's junior. She had always assumed that she would marry and have her own children. But at some point, she had realized that, after so long in Cecily's orbit, it wasn't to be. 'You needn't do that on my account,' she said.

'Really?'

'No, of course not.'

'How extraordinary. I thought you'd be furious. I would be furious.'

'I know you would.' Violet smiled.

'Even so,' Cecily said, getting to her feet. 'I think it much neater for all of us if I go and see Dr G. I'm getting the train to London later, Harley Street before lunch.'

'I can come with you—'

'Don't be silly. The dogs, the house, the horses – you're needed here.' She kissed Violet. 'You are wonderful.'

Dr Greenway had always been the family physician. There was a local man for emergencies, but anything that needed consideration meant Harley Street. His office had a thick green carpet and a reassuring smell of chemicals and bleach. 'What can I do for you, Mrs Mordaunt?' he asked.

'I'm afraid I think I'm pregnant.' The doctor laughed, showing his extremely straight white teeth. Cecily prickled. 'Is that amusing?'

'I'm sorry, Mrs Mordaunt, please forgive me. It's just, very often when women in middle age think that they are pregnant, they are actually experiencing the menopause, or "the change", as it is sometimes known.'

Cecily got to her feet, hung her coat on a coat hanger, stepped out of her shoes, unzipped her skirt and folded it over the back of the chair. Then she lay down on the examination couch.

'What are you doing?' Dr Greenway asked.

'Examine me.'

So, despite being entirely sure his patient was going to be embarrassed and sent home with a prescription for HRT, he washed his hands and gently pressed on her abdomen. Then, unwilling to believe his own conclusion, he continued his investigation. 'Please take a seat,' he said, when he was finished. They sat across from each other at the desk. 'I'm sorry,' he told her. 'You were quite right. You are pregnant.'

'Yes,' Cecily said. 'I know. I want an abortion.'

The doctor looked horrified. 'You want what?'

'An abortion. Termination. Whatever you want to call it.'

'What does Esmond think about this?'

'That's really none of your business.'

Dr Greenway sighed. 'When was your last period?'

Cecily counted backwards in her head. 'A few months ago.'

'In which case, you are almost certainly too late for an abortion. Mrs Mordaunt, you are a married woman in a comfortable position. You should regard this baby as a privilege, not an inconvenience. I'll write a prescription for various medications that are important for geriatric mothers.'

Cecily didn't really approve of crying. She kept her tears back for as long as she was in the taxi, crossing the

station, and finally until she had driven back to Roxborough. She quietly slipped upstairs, and then, in the
privacy of her bedroom, allowed herself tears. Violet left
her to cry, having learned after many years together that
Cecily needed to be alone before she could be com-
forted. Then, after an hour or so, she went up to their
bedroom.

'How was it?' she asked.

'He said I mustn't have a termination.'

Violet tried to ignore her own feelings on the matter.
'Why?'

'Too far gone, too old, I don't know. He said I'd have to
have it.'

'All right.'

'I don't want another one.'

'I know.'

'I really can't have another one. I had three. I spent my
entire life feeling guilty and torn in different directions
and as if I was a bad mother every time I left the house. I
cannot do the sports days and parents' evenings and hours
standing around watching them play rugby. Truly I can't.
I won't.'

Violet considered her for a moment. 'I suppose there's
adoption.'

Cecily got to her feet and started to hang her coat up.
'But what if it ended up with someone awful who beat it
and starved it? I'd spend the rest of my life thinking about
what I'd done and how awful a person I am.'

Violet couldn't decide whether what she was about to

suggest was enormously sensible or utterly evil. 'Grant and Luella,' she said.

'What about them?'

'Luella can't have children.'

'What?'

'Grant told me.'

'Why would he tell you? Why wouldn't he tell me? And why on earth would he marry someone who couldn't give him children?'

'I think he probably didn't tell you about it because he thought you'd say something horrible like that.'

'But Grant wants a family.'

'Well, perhaps this is a solution.'

Cecily looked horrified. 'You're suggesting I have it, and then I give it to Grant and Luella to raise?'

'Why not? Plenty of people did the same thing in reverse – daughters got themselves in trouble and parents raised the baby as their own.'

'I suppose they did.'

'You could ask them.'

'What about Esmond?'

Violet shrugged. She couldn't tell Cecily to keep the baby a secret from her husband.

'I suppose I might be able to avoid telling him.'

'I think you could.'

'We could tell everyone that we're away. That I need some sun, and we're taking an extended trip.'

'We could.'

Cecily was starting to feel the heavy foot on her chest

lift. 'And then we would be able to go back to having life just as normal, just like we did before.'

'Exactly.'

Cecily had finished changing into her pyjamas. She rubbed cream into her hands and face and then got into bed. 'All right,' she said. 'That's what we'll do.'

Violet turned the lights off and lay in the darkness, listening to Cecily fall asleep, trying not to think about the fact that there was a third person in the bed with them now, or that Cecily had been with Esmond again, or that she didn't entirely believe their lovemaking would have been a one-off. But all of that was for tomorrow. For tonight she had found a solution, one that would make everyone happier. She had, she thought to herself, cleaned up yet another Mordaunt family mess.

11

The next morning, Bryony woke to find David fully dressed, furiously typing at his laptop. He still hadn't quite mastered the art of typing like a modern man; instead he used two fingers, searching for each letter individually. Someone had once asked her if it annoyed her, but she actually found it rather endearing. Alas, not everyone seemed to find his old-fashioned nature appealing. It seemed increasingly that people didn't want to keep their money with someone like David, the kind of financial adviser who kept a slow, gentle trickle of money coming in. They wanted younger, more impressive whizz kids who understood cryptocurrency. She had tried time and time again to assure David that he wasn't too old for the world of finance, that he was an impressive, weighty figure with experience. But as his clients had left one by one, even Bryony had to admit that perhaps there was something in David's theory that people thought he was past it.

That was the strange thing about an age gap. When

they had met, it had seemed like nothing. What was eight years, really? But as he got older, fractionally slower on their morning runs, marginally less enthusiastic to stay up late at night talking about the future, those years seemed to swell up between them. She tried to push the feeling away but, occasionally, when he needed to take a moment to catch his breath or wanted to turn down a dinner party to stay at home and watch television, she couldn't shake the sense that she might have shackled herself to someone who might eventually become more of a burden than an equal.

'You're up early,' she said, swinging her legs out of bed and popping her supplements out of her pill tray. She still took folic acid every morning, just in case she were to fall pregnant again. Unlikely, she realized. But she'd heard rumours of women getting pregnant just before they reached menopause, and the idea of another baby – especially if it could happen without all the indignity and expense of IVF – would be the most perfect thing that could ever happen. It seemed somehow unfair that David had three children, while she had only one. 'Are you all right?' she asked.

David looked grim. 'Not really. One of my clients wants to withdraw his investment.'

'And you don't have it?'

He shook his head. 'I will, in a couple of weeks.'

'How much is it?'

'Fifty.'

Bryony did some maths in her head. They had seventy

thousand in their shared account. And there was the thirty grand in a secret account that David would never have any knowledge of. She'd seen first hand what could happen when you tied your money to a man, even a good man like David. She wasn't going to run the risks she'd seen her mother and her friends take, ending up with nothing because someone who seemed like Prince Charming ended up bleeding you dry.

'You're sure?'

'Yes, it's a dividend payment, it's set.'

'You can borrow it from our account then.'

David's shoulders dropped at least an inch. 'Oh God, Bryony, you're an angel.'

She smiled. 'I know.'

'And I swear, I'm going to have all of this sorted out in a few weeks. It's all fixable. I just needed a quick boost.'

'Of course.' He looked so happy she hated that she was going to have to use this moment against him. But she knew that if she didn't, his guilt (entirely unfounded, given that he had always been an astonishingly good father) about Willa would swallow his good sense. 'I think we need to talk to Grant and Elspeth about Willa.'

David sat down on the side of the bed. Four, maybe five minutes of reprieve and now he was right back in the pits of it again. Bryony was probably right, he knew that. If he were advising anyone else, he would agree. There was something suspect about the letters, and the fact that Willa had been given the house was, arguably, hard to believe. Grant was the golden boy of their generation and Lizzie the golden girl of hers. Willa, much like him, was the plodder. The one who earned a proper salary, put her head down and got on with it. There was no celebration for that kind of considered, consistent behaviour. Cecily had never been the kind of person who celebrated reliability.

But how on earth was he supposed to support Bryony in this crusade against Willa? If it turned out that they were wrong, that the letter was real, then Willa would never forgive him for trying to take her inheritance away from her and taking Bryony's side. If it transpired that Bryony was right and something had been done to the letters to change the outcome, he would have stripped Willa of a whole new life, one that would have been easier for her to live than the one she had in London.

They were supposed to be going home tomorrow. Their real life wasn't so bad. Once the finances were sorted out – especially if Bryony could be prevailed upon to lend a little bit more to fill the gaps – things would be far smoother. Their house was pretty, their friends were entertaining, they had plenty to enjoy. Did they really need to fight for this place?

Bryony put her hand on his leg. 'My darling, I know this is difficult. But if the house was intended for you – and, knowing your mother, I think it probably was – then it's only delaying things. You could leave it to Willa when you pass on. Or have it shared between all your children. It's not about taking Willa's side or standing against her.

It's about finding out what your mother actually wanted and then making sure that it gets done. Come on – the fire, the letters, the wasps – there is very clearly something weird going on here.'

David looked out of the window. It was grey today. Still warm, but humid. His least favourite kind of weather, the type that made everyone sticky and frustrated. He sighed. 'I'll talk to Elspeth and Grant. If they think that we should have the letter verified, we'll ask the lawyers. We need a majority of the group to agree to have it done, so if they don't, then there's no point in raising this. And if they don't, then we leave it. All right?'

Bryony gave him the sad half-smile she'd developed for situations where she got her own way but didn't want to seem triumphant about it. 'I think that's very sensible, my love. Thank you for being so brave.'

David got to his feet, filled with dread at what he was about to do.

Elspeth was packing in her bedroom when David knocked. 'What?' she called. David opened the door and put his head around. It was odd, seeing the same face that had appeared in that space so many times across the years of her life, but suddenly so much older. She laughed.

'What?'

She smiled. 'Nothing. It's just weird. You look the same, but old.'

'Thank you. Can I come in?'

'Of course you can.'

He sat on the desk chair, surveying the room. 'You're leaving?'

'Yes, I think so. I've signed what needs to be signed. She left me some money, enough to make coming here tempting, presumably because she wanted to be deliberately difficult. I feel suitably mercenary for coming to get it, so she's had one last one over on me from beyond the grave. I'll give a chunk of it to Marie Stopes to get her back.' She gave him a knowing look. David got the sense that he was supposed to understand the subtext of what she was saying, but absolutely didn't. Elspeth shook her head. 'Don't worry. But yes, I've got a car coming tomorrow morning, and then I'm flying back to America. Far too long here, as far as I'm concerned.'

'Elspeth?'

'Yes?'

David looked at the floor. 'Did you know about Mum and Violet?'

Elspeth smirked. 'You didn't?'

'She kept it from me.'

'Did she?'

David considered the question. She and Violet had never been tactile in front of him. She had never told him that she was in a relationship with someone who wasn't his father. But, he supposed, Violet had been his mother's constant companion. He had assumed that it was simply that Violet was loyal to his mother, having worked for her for years. But Elspeth's question was a good one. Had his mother ever actually tried to hide her relationship with

Violet from him? 'God, you're right,' David said. 'How long has Grant known?'

'I'm not sure. I think he pretended not to for a while. You know he adored Dad. And no one wants to think of their mom having a romantic relationship.' She said 'mum' like an American, David noticed. She had been away for so long. Perhaps it was unsurprising.

'No,' he agreed. 'No one wants that.'

'But Violet was good to her, I imagine. She should probably have left this place to her.'

'I wonder why she didn't.'

'Don't ask me to fathom how that woman thought.'

'You're not disappointed, then? That it wasn't you?'

She laughed. 'No. Are you?'

'I'm not sure.' He dropped his gaze. 'Bryony seems to think that there might be more to all of this than meets the eye.'

'I'm sure she does.'

David ignored the snide note in his sister's voice. 'I know she can seem a little . . . intense. But she's a good person. You'd like her if you spent more time with her.'

'Planes fly both directions.'

'Yes. I know. I've been pretty useless. I'm sorry for that.'

Elspeth shrugged. 'It's a strange family.'

David nodded. Then, realizing that there was no point in beating around the bush, he stood up. 'I want to have Willa's letter verified by the lawyers.'

Elspeth looked faintly horrified. 'You want to try and get her letter invalidated?'

'No. I don't want that at all. In fact, I'm very much hoping that they'll find that it's real.'

'If you want her to have the house, why do this? Surely she's going to be hurt?'

'Yes,' he said. 'But we've both heard stories about people who've had their letters questioned, how it dogged them the entire time they had the house. I don't want that for her.'

'Is that really what this is?'

David shrugged again. 'Bryony wants it done. I think Grant might too. I don't want whispers behind her back. I don't want Lizzie questioning it after we're all dead and gone. It seems the safest way to ensure that everything goes smoothly.'

'Smoothly once you've broken that poor girl's heart.'

'Yes,' he said. 'Yes.'

Elspeth stopped folding and sat on the bed. How many generations of people was this family going to macerate before it stopped? Her conscience pricked her in a completely surprising way, and she heard herself say: 'I'll say I want it verified.'

'What?'

'I'll say it's me. She barely knows me. She won't care if I'm suggesting it might not be real. If you do it, she'll know it was you. She doesn't have a mother. She's got that absolute monster of a stepmother.' She held up her hand. 'I'm sorry, but she is. She's clearly got raging anorexia. I saw Willa when she got that letter. She's happy.

She wanted this. I can't watch her find out her father is trying to take it away from her—'

'I'm not trying to take it away from her—'

'That's how it will feel. You know that.'

She was right. David stood up. There was no point in trying to be noble about this; he was already being spineless. He might as well let his sister take the fall for him, if it would protect Willa. And protect him. He didn't want his daughters to hate him. He wasn't sure when he had become weak, but there was no question that it had happened. 'Thank you,' he said.

Elspeth smiled at him. 'You're welcome.'

She had only come to get the money, and to see whether the house might be sold. And now she was embroiling herself in Mordaunt business. *This family*, she thought. *It's extraordinary. How do they manage to get their nails into your flesh so quickly? So effectively?*

'Come for a walk with me?' Lizzie asked.

Willa looked up and saw her sister standing in the doorway of their room. She hadn't slept in the nursery with Willa last night, nor had she made any kind of excuse about it. Willa got up. She'd been reviewing some documents that her firm had asked her to look over. They seemed shocked that she had actually taken the bereavement and annual leave she was entitled to, sending her reminder after reminder when she ignored an email, despite the fact that her calendar clearly said she wasn't in the office.

She closed the lid of her laptop. 'OK,' she said. Lizzie looked surprised but currently guessed that making any comment about the surprise, even if it was praising her sister for finally discovering the smallest semblance of a work–life balance, wouldn't go down well.

They walked through the house, paused on autopilot by the side door and each pulled on a pair of wellies from the rack. No one had their own boots here, per se. But there was a sense of knowing which ancient pair of Hunters belonged to whom. One of their grandmother's favourite complaints had been that the company who made them had been sold off and the quality had plummeted. The girls had silently rather liked their boots, which made them look like they were at Glastonbury.

Then, they walked through the garden, into the field, through the field into the woods. All the while saying nothing. Eventually they reached where the river cut through the Roxborough land.

'It's so pretty,' Willa said benignly.

'Yes.'

'The river's so shallow. Remember that Christmas when it flooded?'

'I'm in love with Jonty.'

Willa almost laughed. 'That was abrupt.'

'I wanted to tell you.'

Willa started walking again, a gentle pace along the dry path, usually sodden with mud but now crispy from the heat. 'I know you are.'

'I think I always have been.'

Willa nodded. 'I think so too.'

'We've had feelings for each other for a long time.'

Again, Willa tried not to laugh. 'I've spent pretty much every summer of my life at Roxborough with you two. I know that you're—'

Lizzie cut across her. 'We've been sleeping together since we were teenagers—'

'Fuck.'

'Well, quite,' Lizzie quipped.

'Well, I guess he's not actually our cousin.'

'Exactly.'

'And people sleep with their childhood friends all the time without it being weird.'

'That's what I said!'

'And if you have feelings for each other, then I guess that's . . . good?' Willa tried to sublimate the faint sense of repulsion that came from the idea of Lizzie being intimate with Jonty. She'd seen his body naked in the bath as children, seen him running around in the garden, jumping in and out of the lake. He was almost as much her flesh and blood as Lizzie was. But she sensed that there would be nothing to gain by saying that. 'I mean, how many of us ever meet someone we feel that strongly about?' she said.

'Exactly!' Lizzie was elated by how well this was going. If Willa – judgemental Willa, who always had a pros and cons list – could see that this was a good thing, then maybe the rest of the family would be able to come round to it. At least, this way, they stayed close as a family.

No hideous in-laws. No arguments about where to spend Christmas. 'So, do you think they'll be OK with it?'

Willa stopped. 'They who?'

'Dad. Grant. The rest of the family.'

'You're going to tell them?'

'Yes . . . I thought it was probably better we told them than just let them find out.'

'Why would they find out?'

'Because we want to be together. Properly together.'

Willa couldn't hide her surprise now. 'I didn't realize . . . I thought you were saying you'd had a thing. I didn't realize you were talking about being serious.'

Lizzie could feel her face getting hot. 'Well, we are. That's what "in love" means. I know this isn't really your area, but it does.' She knew her words would sting her sister, who was incredibly reclusive about dating, if there was anything to be reclusive about. She sometimes worried that, between her job and her obsessive hatred of her body, there was a chance that Willa might not actually have had sex with anybody yet.

'I think you're going to have to break it to them gently,' Willa said, choosing to ignore her sister's bitchy comment. 'Maybe work them up to the idea slowly.'

'Yeah,' Lizzie said. 'That's a good idea.'

'And they might not be madly keen to start with.'

They walked on a little farther, looking at the ground. Eventually, Lizzie decided that the unburdening wasn't complete, that she somehow needed to purge all of it. 'Granny found us.'

'Jesus, Lizzie, bombshell after bombshell here.'

'I know.'

'She found you what? With Jonty?'

Lizzie nodded. 'The last time we came to stay before she died. We hadn't done it for years, we'd been so good. And then we had too much to drink and we got carried away, and she came downstairs and she saw us. She was so angry. I didn't think she'd mind. You know, she was always so open-minded and non-judgemental, always talking about who had a mistress and who was having an affair.' Lizzie gulped air. 'But she was so angry, she made it very clear she thought what we were doing was wrong.' She stopped walking. 'You know, I never saw her again after that trip. We said goodbye the next morning. And I was so embarrassed I barely spoke to her, just got in the car and went. And then we exchanged a couple of letters, but we barely said anything, and then she was dead. Do you think that's why she didn't tell us she was ill?'

Willa shook her head. 'No. She didn't tell us because she was private and she hated the idea of us sitting around worrying about her. She wanted to go out without making a fuss. You know her. That's what she was like.'

Lizzie nodded gratefully. 'I don't know how I could have thought she would give me the house after that. She thought I was disgusting. She thought Jonty was too. She hated us.' Lizzie was crying now, proper hot sobs, not the pretty delicate cry she put on when she wanted to be beautiful and sad. Her face was bright red and her nose was streaming. Willa wrapped her arms around her

245

sister, even though having someone else's body close to hers always felt like being shut into a small, dark space.

'She didn't hate you,' she said, stroking Lizzie's hair.

'What would Mum have said?' Lizzie asked after a while, her head buried in Willa's shoulder. What was Willa supposed to say to that? The two years more of their mother that Willa had on Lizzie didn't equip her to speak for her late mother, much as Lizzie always seemed to assume it did. But, Willa reasoned, there would be nothing to gain by refusing to answer the question. So, she told her little sister what she wanted to hear.

'I think she would have said that she loves you and that she supports you in anything you want to do.'

Lizzie wiped under her eyes. 'I've got snot all over your T-shirt.'

Willa laughed. 'Your snot is my snot.'

'That's disgusting.'

'Come on, let's head back. We don't want to miss tea.'

12

There was always tea on a Sunday at Roxborough. Once upon a time, there had been tea every day, but eventually, as the generations ran on and full-time staff became more and more scarce, the routine of laying it out and serving it to increasingly fewer people every day became sillier and sillier. So, after Grant left home, Cecily announced that it would be Sunday only. Jonty, Lizzie and Willa had loved Sundays. There would be lunch at one o'clock, after which they were left to watch as much television as they wanted. Then, at half past four, the dining room would be filled with warm scones, bowls of ruby-red jam and pots of clotted cream. Two types of cake, little sandwiches, toast if they wanted it. Their grandmother would sit on the sofa with a cup of tea and nudge a piece of cake around a plate while the children ate until they were almost sick.

All three of them remembered lying in bed while Willa and Lizzie's mother read *Peter Pan* and their eyes became so heavy they didn't mind falling asleep while it was still light outside. Even when food became terrifying, Willa almost liked tea. Not the food, of course. But the warm room, the fire and sitting around with the feeling that the weekend was almost over, but not quite. She would allow herself a cup of tea with a teaspoon of milk and watch as her sister ate toast with butter fingers and laughed with her mouth full of scone and jam. Jonty would eat three, four, five slices of cake as a teenager, seeming to grow taller every single day.

Elspeth had no idea quite how sacred tea was in this household – no idea what she was about to desecrate. When she was thirteen, she had been sent away to boarding school. Most Sundays she was at school, and if she did have the brief respite of an exeat, the driver would take her back to school before four. The cosy teatime routine that the Mordaunt grandchildren treasured had been invented many years later, allowing the family to pretend that they had always been so close, that they hadn't sent their own children away to school the moment that they had turned thirteen.

She wasn't entirely sure why she had offered to help David. It wasn't as if he had done anything for her in the last few decades. It was strange how the blood they shared seemed to bond them together even when they had done absolutely nothing to attempt to preserve the relationship. She saw their father in him. Unsurprising, obviously. But it wasn't just the long, straight nose or the pointed chin. It was his nervousness, his lack of ease in the world around him. It was hard to see how David and Grant could have come from the same parents, Grant lounging on the sofa with his sleeves rolled up, laughing, with one arm around his beautiful girlfriend's waist; David sitting on the edge of an armchair, gripping his glass.

David clearly knew that Elspeth was about to drop the bomb and wanted to be clear of it. She put her cup and saucer down on the little table in the middle of the drawing room and cleared her throat.

Elspeth was surprised by quite how difficult she was finding the job she had agreed to do. By how much she didn't want to hurt Willa. But, she reminded herself, this was the least hurtful outcome. Far better than her own father doing it. 'I need to say something,' she said. 'I've made a decision.' Everyone stared at her. 'I am concerned about the validity of the entail.'

No one said anything. A log on the fire made a loud crack and everyone flinched, and then returned to staring at Elspeth.

'What?' asked Willa quietly.

'I'm sorry,' Elspeth said. 'It's not personal. But I know how this family works, and if there's a hint of doubt about whether your letter is real, it'll get into the cracks and it will split you apart.'

Willa shook her head. 'Why would anyone think it wasn't real?'

Still, no one said anything. Elspeth held out her hand. 'It's not personal, Willa. It's just about being sure. The whole system is totally bizarre. It shouldn't be allowed.'

'Can you do that?' she asked. 'If it's only you who doesn't believe me—'

'I'm not saying that I don't believe you—'

'If you're the only one, then, can you do that?'

Another long pause. 'No,' Elspeth said. 'It has to be at least half of us. So, we would have to vote.'

Bryony was surprised by how uncomfortable this whole thing was turning out to be. She hadn't ever felt much sympathy for Willa. Yes, she had lost her mother, and yes, that was hard. But she had more family than most people, and she had been given almost everything on a plate. Ironic, given her total refusal to eat most of the time. But the way her chin was shaking, betraying the fact that she was clearly trying desperately not to cry, was making Bryony feel an unfamiliar maternal stirring towards her stepdaughter. But she couldn't allow that to take over. She had asked David to do this for a reason, because she and David needed their family home. They needed a future. 'I think Elspeth may have a point,' she said gently.

Willa turned to face her. 'What?'

'Well, the letters were missing for a good few hours, and there was all that funny business with the fire. Strange things have been happening – the wasps' nest. And Violet and Angelique and I found some photographs with the eyes of the people in them scratched out—'

'What?' asked Lizzie. 'What photographs?'

'It's not important,' Violet said, looking daggers at Bryony.

'What does everyone else think?' Bryony asked. 'David?'

David couldn't look his daughter in the eye. 'Perhaps it would be better to be sure. So that this conversation can be put to bed.'

'This is ridiculous,' said Grant, looking at Willa's pale, horrified face. 'The letter said that the house was Willa's. What are you all talking about?'

'I agree,' Jonty said. 'Do we really want to go through this whole thing again? And make Willa think Granny didn't really want her to have the house?'

Another painful silence. 'You should vote,' Willa said. 'Violet. Will you count?'

Violet had been standing by the door. Moments ago, she had been feeling a sort of peace she hadn't experienced since Cecily died, watching all the children she had helped to raise finally under one roof sharing a meal. Now she felt as if her chest was falling in on itself. 'Yes,' she said to Willa. 'I will.' She looked at them all. 'Will those who do not wish to have the entail investigated please raise their hands?' Grant and Jonty raised theirs. Willa looked at them, half grateful, half ashamed.

'Now, will those people who wish to have it investigated please raise their hands?'

Bryony, Elspeth and David raised their hands.

'Lizzie?' Violet asked. 'You will need to vote.'

Lizzie couldn't look up; the idea of seeing Violet's face or her sister's made her want to be sick. 'I don't want to.'

'It's fine,' Willa said quietly. 'Just vote to have it investigated.'

'Wouldn't you rather know, Willa?' Lizzie asked. 'Wouldn't you rather be sure?'

Willa said nothing and Lizzie slowly raised her hand. Violet wished that she could freeze the moment to leave the room and weep.

'Of course,' Willa said. She fixed her face into a neutral expression. 'I don't want anything that isn't mine.'

'That's settled then,' Violet said. 'Tomorrow we will go to see the lawyers, and we will have the letters verified.'

Elspeth looked at Willa's white face from across the room and wished she could tell her the truth about what she had just done, and why she had done it.

13

Willa had never been good at waiting. Any moment spent static was hard for her to bear. She wandered up the stairs, unsure where she was going, or what she was supposed to do. No one knew what to say to her, least of all Lizzie. So, she must keep out of the way. But there was no one to message on her phone, no work to finish. Nothing. She pushed open the library door, wondering if perhaps this might at least give her the illusion of having something to do.

It had been the easiest part of her mother being ill, the fact that there was always something to do. People had praised her for being so diligent, such a wonderful nurse, and she had wanted to tell them that it was entirely self-ish, that she had desperately wanted something to do with herself. But no matter how much she rejected their praise, everyone was convinced she was some kind of saint. People even came up to her at the funeral and smiled at her while saying, 'You're doing such a lovely job caring for your dad,' and 'I'm sure you're taking wonderful care of him.' *I shouldn't have to*, she'd wanted to say. *You shouldn't be praising me for this. Something is very wrong here.* But, of course, it had become her job. Cooking, tidying, reminding him to return phone calls and thank people for the flowers and lasagnes they constantly dropped off. And she'd buried herself in it.

She always stayed in constant motion throughout the day. And at night she had a long, complicated process leading up to sleep. Meditation, music, reading, black-out blinds – they all came into play so that she could go to sleep at eleven and wake up at five, run for an hour, shower and be at her desk by eight at the latest. Here, she didn't do any of that, and on every previous visit it hadn't mattered. The one place she had always been able to sleep was in the nursery at Roxborough.

The only night her insomnia had managed to find her at Roxborough was the night of the entail.

Willa had never considered herself a thief. No playful shoplifting from Claire's Accessories on a dare as a teenager. She hadn't even lifted clothes from Lizzie's room (though Lizzie had taken plenty of hers). The desire to take something that wasn't hers just didn't exist inside her. Or at least it hadn't. But the night of the entail, something had shifted in her.

When everyone else had admitted defeat and gone to bed, she had stared at the ceiling, imagining Roxborough being sold. Everything packed into boxes. And then what would happen to it? It was too big to be sold as a house.

It would be a hotel, perhaps. Or flats. Maybe she could sell her London flat and buy one, live in a slice of the house. But it would be filled with other people, people who wanted to paint over and bleach out her family. And there would be no more Roxborough Easters or Christmases or summer holidays. No more meals around the dining table, no more walking in the woods. Everyone who worked there would lose their jobs. Violet would have to leave. This whole magical little bubble of a world would be gone. And as she thought about it, she swung her feet out of the bed and on to the surprisingly cool floor. She went downstairs and decided that she would look for the letters from one corner of the house to another, without the distraction of the distraught family pulling her in all directions.

Her heart had pounded almost painfully as she went down the stairs. But she wasn't doing anything wrong. At least not yet. If anyone bumped into her, she decided she would claim that she was sleepwalking. After all, she was the kind of overachieving type-A person who was believable as a sleepwalker. She might as well milk it. She found herself at the top of the stairs and watched as her feet stepped down in front of her. They made a gentle sticking noise on the flagstones of the hallway. Eventually, she reached the dining room, turned the door handle and stood, looking at the table.

It had been re-dressed and was now just as it had been at the start of the evening. The flowers were perfect again, the table re-laid, the glasses clean and gleaming. The only change was that the candles were unlit. Unsure whether she believed it, Willa turned on the overhead light, dissolving the shadows instantly. With a sickening, exciting twist in her stomach she realized that at each of their place settings, there were letters. How was that possible? They hadn't been there earlier. And what was she supposed to do now? She had intended to look for them, that was true. But she hadn't actually expected to find them.

Willa was famously indecisive. She made pros and cons lists for everything. She read reviews before she bought a beauty product and read the British government advice before she booked holidays. But her hands were on her letter before she had considered it. The seal wasn't stuck down so she lifted the flap, drew the paper from the envelope and made a noise between a laugh and a sob when she saw that it wasn't blank.

Darling Willa,

It is extraordinary to think of you reading this when I am dead. Not that I mind the idea of being dead much – I've had a wonderful and extraordinary life and I'm quite tired now. More because it is odd to think I won't know what you are doing or where you end up.

I haven't given Roxborough to you because I don't think that you need it. You're such a wonderful success and you've already achieved so much. I wouldn't want you to give up on trying to build a life for yourself in London and hide here for the rest of your days.

*You are brave and kind and responsible and I hope that
you will surround yourself with people who appreciate those
qualities without taking advantage of them.*

All my love,
C.

She couldn't read the final lines very well; they swam in
the saltwater filling her eyes. It wasn't a surprise, of course.
She couldn't reasonably have expected to be left the house,
not when everyone thought she had this brilliant, glittering life in London. And she supposed that, tomorrow, they
would each open the letters and then she would know
who had inherited the house. She hoped it was Lizzie, so
she would be able to visit and spend her summer holidays
here. She also desperately hoped it wasn't Lizzie, because
that would mean that their grandmother, who had always
been fastidiously fair, down to sending Willa money
whenever she gave Lizzie a bump because she was broke
at university, had chosen her sister over her.

Neatly, she folded her letter back into the envelope and
looked at herself in the mirror that hung on the wall on
the other side of the table. She practised a surprised but
disappointed face. Not that it mattered much. No one
would be looking at her; they would all be far too consumed by their own letters.

Out of interest, she picked up Lizzie's letter, assuming
that it would be sealed. But it wasn't. She slipped the
paper out of the envelope, her heart beating even more

quickly now. This was stupid – was she really such a child that she couldn't wait until tomorrow morning to find out? And it was invasive. This was the last letter her grandmother had ever written to Lizzie, and here she was, opening it before she could read it.

> *Lovely Lizzie,*
>
> *I was reminded today, when Violet and I managed to make it down to the bottom of the garden, of the time when you visited me and we picked all the blackberries. You must have been fifteen or sixteen, and you insisted on making some ghastly blackberry vodka. You were certainly sick, and I have a feeling Violet might have been too. You were always such a joy to have here – so full of life and so entirely yourself.*
>
> *I have not left you Roxborough. I know this will be a disappointment to you, and you (unlike anyone else in the family) have been so clear about loving the place and wanting to live here. But I'm afraid I just couldn't do it in good conscience. I don't have a moment's doubt that you will make something extraordinary of yourself, but having this house would mean that you didn't need to do anything else with your life, and that just wouldn't be right.*
>
> *I hope that you're not cross with me. I love you very much.*
>
> *All my love,*
> *C.*

Willa put the letter back into the envelope with perfect precision. She paused for a fraction of a second, pretending to herself that she wasn't about to do what she knew without any doubt she was going to do. She opened Jonty's letter. A long, moving reflection on how he was part of the family and how she was so proud of the life he had created. And: *I have not left you Roxborough because I am not sure that you really want it, and I couldn't take that risk. It's as much of a burden as it is a joy, and I think that perhaps you will be happier without it.*

Bryony's letter was only a few lines long: *I don't think you would have expected anything, you are far too sensible for that. Please look after David.*

Hands shaking, Willa looked at the envelopes addressed to David and Grant. So, it was either her father's, or her uncle's. If it was Grant's house, then that meant she had lost any chance of having it. She would never inherit; he would pass it to Jonty or any of the children he shared with future girlfriends. But if it was her father's, it would really be Bryony's and would almost certainly end up with Lucca. She couldn't decide which was worse.

She opened Grant's first and skimmed it, willing her eyes to work faster, until she found the words *I am sorry* and *I am not leaving you Roxborough.* Then she grabbed her father's letter, almost forgetting to handle the paper as if it were breakable. So, this must be it.

Dearest David, her father's letter read. *I am sorriest to you of everyone to whom I did not leave Roxborough, because I fear it will hurt you the most.*

Willa dropped the letter and sat, silently, on the floor. Was she being stupid? She counted the letters again. No.

That was everyone. Everyone, she realized, apart from Violet. So, her grandmother had left the house to Violet. Willa tried to reason with herself. Violet had loved Cecily almost her entire adult life. They had been in love with each other. Violet had been like another grandparent to Willa, Lizzie and Jonty. And this was the only home she had ever known. It made perfect sense that she would inherit it. It was right.

But something told her that she had to check.

Cold water down her spine, the skin on her skull contracting, she scrabbled for Violet's letter and pulled it out of the envelope. *V – more a formality than anything else. You don't want it, so I haven't left it to you. Adore you now, adore you always. C.*

Cecily hadn't left the house to anyone.

The first, most obvious, question was why? Why would Cecily want to break the line of inheritance that went back several hundred years? And if she really did want the house divided among her children, then why wouldn't she have made that clear? Could Bryony have been right? Might her grandmother have been confused at the end of her life? Cecily had loved Roxborough more than almost anything. Surely she couldn't have wanted it smashed up and divided into open-plan flats?

It was wrong. It had never previously occurred to Willa that her grandmother could be wrong, but she was. And there was only one thing that could be done about it.

She'd gone into Cecily's office, a neat room at the back

of the house that faced over the river. It was always cold in there, even in the warmest summer. She'd pulled the typewriter from a shelf, googled how to use it, then cleared her search history. She took a deep breath. '*Darling Willa*', she typed.

When the letter was finished, she'd felt rather sick. But she wiped the typewriter down. How hard did you have to wipe to get rid of a fingerprint? She gave it another wipe. That was the best she could do. She grabbed a handful of papers from the recycling bin – mostly bills. Then she moved almost silently down the stairs until she reached the little sitting room. She crumpled the bills into balls and put them in the fireplace. Then she gently removed her real letter and replaced it with the fake, and placed the real one in the fireplace, determined to burn it so compressively that even the ashes would be mixed with other papers. She struck a match, shuddering at the noise, and then brushed the flame against the paper. It caught quickly, the air warm and orange in front of her face. She dropped the match in, then froze as she heard a noise on the stairs. It was almost certainly the cat, but Willa was spooked. She went to the dining room as fast as she could move, placed her letter in the middle of the pile, worried for a moment about fingerprints, and then decided she had done all she could do.

It had felt at first like she might get away with it. She had felt guilty, obviously. Desperately guilty some of the time. But, underneath, there had been a feeling of calm, as if she knew that what she had done was ultimately right, that she wouldn't have to spend her entire life looking over her shoulder, waiting to be caught. But then, all those smashed photographs with their eyes scratched out, it had felt like a warning. And the wasps. She had told herself hundreds of times already that it was an accident, that the wasps' nest had grown there, but she knew it wasn't true. It was a warning. Someone in this house knew what she had done, and they were letting her know that she wasn't going to be allowed to get away with it. And now there was going to be an investigation, and the absolute best-case scenario was that they would believe it hadn't been her, that someone else had tampered with the letters and left the house to her. But why? Could she come up with a convincing reason for anyone to do that? And when they discovered that her letter was a fake, would they just overturn it and sell the house? Or would they have to find out who had faked the letter and why?

She pulled a book off the shelf and tried to settle herself in an armchair. She forced her eyes over each line of each page, committed to the pretence of reading, and as she did so, she ran through it all in her head, trying to work out what mistakes she had made and where she was going to get caught.

14

Everyone gathered in the kitchen at six thirty, the point at which, when Cecily and Esmond were alive, someone would say, 'I think the bar should open,' and Esmond would make everyone a gin and tonic so strong you could stand a spoon in it. Sunday supper was always a relaxed affair, everyone too full from tea to want much. Just an excuse for a drink, really.

No one was really sure whether they should go downstairs, but one by one, so used to the rhythms of the house, they found themselves drawn to the kitchen. The only person who hadn't joined them was Willa.

'She wasn't in our room,' Lizzie said. 'She might be in the library. She goes there sometimes when she wants to be quiet. I could go up?'

Elspeth shook her head. 'I'll go. I started all of this. And I don't want you to fall out – she'll be upset.' Everyone privately thought that this was a foolish idea, but no one wanted to go and look Willa in the eye after what they'd done. So instead, they watched Elspeth leave the

263

room, and then tried to find conversation to make about the weather while Grant made the drinks and Angelique made a salad.

Lizzie had been right. Willa was in the library. The library wasn't quite as grand as it sounded. Less a full-scale library, more a large room on one of the upper floors where Cecily and David had installed shelf after shelf to house the enormous number of books that previous Mordaunts had managed to amass. Willa had revised for her A levels and GCSEs in here, sitting on the floor with her back against the cool wall, going over and over her meticulous notes with their highlighted sections and brightly coloured bullet points. Sound was deadened in here, absorbed by the thousands of volumes. Elspeth knocked gently on the door, her bare feet padding along the polished wooden floor. Willa looked up, getting to her feet. Yet again, Elspeth was struck by how frail her body was.

'We wondered if you wanted to come down to supper.'

'No, thanks,' Willa said. 'I'm still full from tea.'

'You didn't eat anything at tea.'

Willa couldn't help looking shocked. When was the last time anyone had mentioned her eating? Once upon a time, it had been decided that no one would. She liked it that way. She had forgotten it was even possible for them to be aware of what she was eating. Or rather what she wasn't eating. To her horror, her eyes filled with tears. She dropped her head, trying to hide behind her hair. 'I'm

fine, really. You go down. It's your last night, I don't want
to ruin it.'

Elspeth sat down in one of the uncomfortable, largely
decorative armchairs her mother had installed in this
room. She vaguely remembered it all being redone when
she was a child and asking if they could have a ladder
along the bookshelves like in the sweetshop in Willy
Wonka. 'I really am sorry,' Elspeth said.

'It's fine.'

'It's not fine. You've got every right to be upset.'

Willa pulled herself up to her full height. 'I'm a lawyer,' she said. 'I understand why this is important. I would
recommend anyone else take this exact action. It makes
perfect sense.'

'It's your family,' Elspeth said gently.

'This was your idea. Why are you trying to talk about
it like it's got nothing to do with you?' Willa snapped.
'Sorry,' she added. 'It's been a long day. A long week.'

Elspeth nodded. 'This house has a way of making time
slow down.'

'Not for me. Being here was when time went fast-
est. We used to come here at the start of every holiday
and we'd be going home five minutes later.'

'Different experiences,' Elspeth said, trying to be charitable. She had to remind herself that Willa's kindly
grandmother was the same cold, controlling woman
who had been her mother. 'It must be hard,' Elspeth said,
'not knowing whether the house is going to be yours
or not.'

'It's not that,' Willa replied quickly.

'What is it, then?'

Willa looked up at the ceiling. There was no overhead light because her grandmother had hated them, just a ceiling rose in the middle, inlaid with stars. 'Everyone in this family has someone.'

Elspeth said nothing. She'd had enough therapy to know that the best way to get someone to talk was silence. Willa went on. 'Dad has Bryony. Grant has whoever he's seeing at the time. Lizzie and Jonty have each other, even though they shouldn't—'

'What?' Elspeth interrupted.

'Lizzie and Jonty. They're – you know. Into each other.' She looked at Elspeth's horrified face. 'Oh no, it's OK,' she said, wondering how much Elspeth had missed. 'He's not really our cousin. I mean, he is our cousin, but he's adopted. So, it's not incest or anything. Grant and Luella couldn't have children, so they adopted him when they were in their twenties. I guess that was after you left.'

Elspeth got to her feet. 'They're involved?'

'I don't know. They have been. I think I sort of assumed eventually they would be. It's just sort of obvious when they're together – at least it is to me. And Violet. Dad and Grant haven't noticed, but then they never notice anything. They won't be pleased, but Lizzie and Jonty, they're like magnets. So, I suppose we're all just going to have to be all right with it.'

'Did Cecily ever try to stop them?'

Willa nodded. 'She caught them, the last time we all

THE WILL

stayed. She was upset. Lizzie tried to explain that it wasn't wrong, but she wouldn't listen. I think Lizzie thinks it's why Granny didn't leave her the house. What's wrong?'

Elspeth was pacing back and forward. 'And David and Grant don't know about this?'

'No, I don't think so. They weren't here in the summers. Grant was always travelling and Dad had to work.'

Finally, Elspeth sat down, clawing her long fingers through her hair. 'That stupid, stupid woman.'

'Why are you so upset? I told you, they don't share any blood.'

Elspeth thought about it for a moment, her expression that of someone who was about to jump into a very cold swimming pool. But there was nothing else to be done. Her resolve to come, take the money and leave was gone. She had involved herself. And now she was going to have to involve herself even more.

'Yes, they do,' she said.

1991

If she were really honest with herself, Elspeth had known from the start that Ralph was bad news. He had all the classic trappings of a man she should avoid. They'd met in their last year of university; she'd been reading History of Art and he was reading Politics. He had suited being a student. He smoked roll-ups, talked about socialism, shared long anecdotes about how he had met politicians and given them advice about how to change the world for the better. After university, the shine had started to wear off for Elspeth. Ralph seemed very cheerful about taking money from his parents and seemed to believe that getting a job was for stupid people. He drove a motorbike because he thought that cars were 'prisons' but didn't like to explain any of his opinions when questioned. It was obvious to everyone who knew Elspeth, including Elspeth herself, that she should leave him. But she couldn't ever quite bring herself to do it and, more confusingly, she wasn't ever really sure why not.

He was good-looking, unquestionably. Tall, solid,

younger than he looked. And he could be sweet. But he also smelled wrong. Not bad, just wrong. And when he got into a temper, he scared Elspeth. He was the first person she could ever really remember being frightened of.

Ralph had proposed while very drunk a couple of months ago and Elspeth had said yes because she wasn't sure how to say no, and because she was excited by the idea of being his wife, and a little bit because she knew that it would absolutely horrify her mother.

They had agreed that they would get married at the King's Road registry office and then have a reception at the pub. Nothing over the top or stuffy like her brothers' weddings, with the big white dresses, the poached salmon, the weeping aunties. Not that she resented her sisters-in-law for it. Cordelia and Luella had been saints. The daughters that Cecily had always wanted and never had. But everything Elspeth did was a disappointment or a shock in comparison to her siblings, so there really wasn't any point in trying. Far better to do things her own way. Unfortunately, it had transpired that her parents were right on this specific topic. Ralph was every bit as bad as they'd assumed. Which is how she had found herself on a bus from London to Norfolk, carrying a small suitcase of clothes and her guitar case.

She had come home to find Ralph missing, and then, to her total horror, found a spoon in the sink with a bend in its neck and a burned underside. She knew perfectly well what that meant. Either Ralph had taken heroin in their flat, or his friends had been and taken it, which meant it was only a matter of time until Ralph joined them, and then it was only a matter of time until he was a full-blown addict. He didn't seem to have the same will to survive that she did. The instincts that told her to wear a helmet on the bike or stop drinking at 3 a.m. didn't exist for him.

So, she started to pack. Halfway through, after she'd realized that she only had one tiny nylon suitcase, which wouldn't take all of her clothes, she heard the door open. She'd kicked the suitcase under the bed and tried to play it cool, but hadn't managed it. Ralph had realized what she was doing and held her up against the wall. 'I love you,' he had half cried, half shouted. 'You can't leave.' She'd tried to explain that she needed some space, a little bit of a break, that she would be back (which was a lie). But he didn't buy it, and when she refused to stay, he punched her, first in the face, straight across the cheekbone, and then in the stomach. He'd looked rather horrified with himself afterwards, as if he couldn't believe what he'd done. He'd apologized over and over again as she put the rest of her things in a carrier bag, but Elspeth actually felt rather grateful. She had felt guilty about leaving, and like a coward for going without telling him. But as soon as he'd hit her, he had moved the goalposts. Now she could make a run for it.

There was only one place to go. She didn't have much money, and her friends were either nice girls from school who were now married with young babies in Clapham townhouses or wasters who would tell Ralph where she was and let him come over so they could 'clear their karma' or whatever bollocks they'd started repeating from America. So, it had to be Roxborough. And she had decided that it would be better not to call ahead. If she called, her mother would have time to make an excuse. She still kept up the strange facade that Esmond lived there full-time, that their marriage was entirely normal. But if Cecily told her to wait twenty-four hours so she could bring Esmond home before her arrival, Elspeth wasn't entirely sure what she would do or where she would go. So, she used the last money she had, bought a bus ticket and headed towards home.

The countryside outside the bus window was gloriously wide and open. In London, she'd never been able to see more than a few metres without obstruction. Here, she could see for miles. What was she doing? She was twenty-six. Not a kid any more. Running home to her parents wasn't a silly teenage thing. It was proof that she wasn't able to make it alone. She hoped that her mother wouldn't ask about work, that she wouldn't have to explain that she had been let go from her job at the gallery because Ralph had got drunk at an exhibition and knocked two paintings off the wall.

The bus dropped her outside Norwich, and she waited half an hour for the number forty-nine bus, shivering and wishing that she'd brought a proper winter coat instead of her leather jacket. Eventually, the bus arrived, and she wedged herself into a seat, warming her feet on the little heater on the floor. She'd taken this bus into town almost every day in the school holidays, to go to the record shops and read magazines without buying them. She knew every movement and every bump of the journey.

It stopped at the top of the lane where Roxborough sat, hidden by the trees. She tramped down the drive, trying to convince herself that it would all be fine, that no one would mind her turning up unannounced with a bruised face.

Elspeth had never had a house key to Roxborough. Whenever she came back for weekends or the school holidays, there would be a half-dozen staff inside the house, and Violet was almost always here. She'd occasionally had to sit on the steps waiting for someone to come home and let her in, but that was rare.

Now, she reached the front door and considered whether she should ring the doorbell. But that might make rather more of her arrival than needed to be made. So, she pushed the door open and put her stuff down quietly in the hall. Then she kicked her shoes off and went to the bathroom to adjust her make-up. She looked a state, she was completely aware of that. But maybe that was better. Her mother might be more understanding about her arrival if she realized quite how desperate Elspeth was.

Either way, all that mattered was that she was home. There would be something to eat, and then Elspeth could have a long, hot bath and try to wash every last vestige of Ralph off her body. Tomorrow, she could wash her clothes and call some friends and find somewhere to stay, call the temping agency and see if they could get her a slot on reception for some poncy company who would overpay her because she had a nice accent. It wouldn't be perfect, but it would be better than what she had had before. It would be a start.

'Hello,' she said quietly, pushing the kitchen door open. It smelled warm and there was a jug of winter roses on the scrubbed wooden table. The cats were sleeping in baskets in front of the Aga and a dog was curled up on the armchair under the window.

Violet looked up from where she was chopping an onion and dropped her knife. 'Elspeth,' she said. 'What on earth are you doing here?'

'I needed to get out of London,' she said.

'What happened to your face?' Violet wiped her hands on her apron and then came to inspect the damage, reaching into a drawer for some arnica. 'What happened?'

'Ralph.'

Violet said nothing, but her expression made her opinion very clear.

'I've left him,' Elspeth said. It felt strange to say it out loud.

'Good. Listen, why don't you go upstairs and lie down, and I'll bring you some supper?'

'It's fine, I can help. I'll stay down here. Can I have a drink? It's been a long day. Where's Mum?'

'I think she might prefer it if you popped upstairs and she came to see you later. She's had a long day herself and—'

Violet's uncharacteristically quick chatter was interrupted when the kitchen door swung open and in walked

Cecily. Elspeth looked at her mother, whose hair had grown rather longer and whose cheeks were pink. 'I tried to pick the rosemary but everything's dead. I think it'll be spring before we get any herbs—' She stopped. 'Elspeth?'

Elspeth panned her vision down her mother's body, trying to understand what she was seeing. Below the pink cheeks, in the middle of her body, was an enormous protrusion. A swelling. Something that looked extraordinarily like a baby bump. Cecily put her basket down on the kitchen table and then went to sit down. 'Oh dear,' she said mildly. 'It looks like the cat's rather out of the bag.'

They sat at the table. Elspeth drank a bottle of red wine, smoked her way through a packet of Marlboro Red and asked question after question. Who was the father? How did this happen? And then, eventually: 'Why didn't you tell me?'

Cecily sighed. 'Because I'm not keeping the baby.'

'What?'

'I'm not keeping it. I didn't want it. I can't do all of that again. I wasn't much good at it in the first place – you remember. And if I wasn't any good in my twenties, just imagine how much worse I'll be now. I've got no patience. No, far better that someone else raises the baby.'

'Someone else? You're giving it away?'

'To Luella and Grant. She can't have children, you see. It all works out rather well, actually. They're delighted.

And we won't tell the child. It'll just grow up thinking it's a nice, normal adopted baby.'

Elspeth shook her head and looked at her mother. 'If you weren't going to have it, why didn't you have an abortion?'

Her mother did at least have the good grace to look embarrassed. 'I tried to, darling, but it wasn't very early, and once I found someone who would go through with it, I just couldn't. I didn't feel it was right.'

Getting to her feet, Elspeth searched for the right words. 'I didn't feel it was "right" either, Mum. I wanted mine.'

'Well,' Cecily said, also getting to her feet, though with rather more trouble thanks to her enormous bump. 'Not enough to give up all of this.'

Elspeth fixed her mother with a hard stare. 'What?'

'Oh, darling, let's be reasonable. If you had wanted the baby, you would have had it. It was all very well to pretend back then, but you're an adult now. We made the right choice. You needed someone to blame, and I was very happy for that to be me, but let's not pretend you didn't know what was really happening. Now, do you want Violet and me to make you some extra soup, or are you going straight to bed?'

Elspeth got to her feet. 'No,' she said. 'Actually, I'm leaving.'

'Leaving? Don't be ridiculous.'

'I'm not.' She picked up her bags. 'This place is awful. You're awful. What you're doing with that baby is awful. I don't want anything to do with any of it. I'm gone.'

15

'Jonty isn't our cousin.'

'No.'

'And he's not adopted.'

Elspeth looked grim. 'Well. He is adopted. He just wasn't adopted from some teenage girl who got into trouble, or whatever my mother claimed the story was.'

Willa tried to process all of the information, but it wasn't settling on her brain. She could usually digest information with incredible speed; it made her brilliant at her job. And yet now, she sat dumbly on the floor of the library, moving her head from side to side, trying to understand what was happening.

'Granny is Jonty's mother.'

'Was.'

'And Grant and Luella . . .'

'Adopted him.'

'So, he's my uncle. Not my adopted cousin.'

'Yes.'

'And he's Lizzie's uncle too.'

'Yes.'

'Does my dad know?'

'No. At least, I don't think so. Mum wouldn't have wanted him to know. She didn't want me to know. Though that was probably for other reasons.'

'What other reasons?'

Elspeth looked up at the ceiling. This was exactly why she hadn't wanted to come home. She couldn't have imagined that her niece would turn out to be sleeping with her uncle. But she had known that no good would come of being back in this place. It had held no happiness for her as a child and it held none now. She sighed. 'I got pregnant when I was sixteen. I had a boyfriend at school; we were serious about each other. I was going to drop out of school and get a job, take my A levels part-time, all of that. And then I told Cecily. She told me I was having an abortion whether I wanted one or not.'

'Surely she couldn't make you?'

'She said there would be no money, no university – nothing – if I didn't do it. And I know what you're thinking – I should have done it on my own if I really wanted to, but you don't know what Cecily was like with her own children. She wasn't the sweet little granny the three of you remember. She had a way of making you feel like everything you said and did was wrong. She told me I couldn't do it on my own without her money, and I believed her. So, she made me an appointment. Or rather, Violet made the appointment. My mother didn't like getting her hands dirty. They told me it was just a scan, and when I got there the doctor lied, he told me that the baby was ill, that I had to have an abortion. They didn't use anaesthetic at the place she sent me. I was screaming. And then Violet drove me home, and Cecily put me on the pill and told me not to be so silly in the future.'

Willa looked at the floor, trying to decide what to say to such an agonizingly personal story from someone she shared twenty-five per cent of her DNA with but who she knew almost not at all.

'I'm so sorry,' she said. 'So, you ran away?'

'No,' Elspeth said. 'I was too much of a coward for that. I stayed. And eventually I left university and got shacked up, and then that went to shit. So I came home because I had nowhere else to go. And when I got here, I found Cecily. Massively pregnant.'

'Where was Grandpa?'

Elspeth looked sympathetic. 'Oh, my love, they had been separated for years. He would come home for Easter and Christmas and that sort of thing, any time we were at home. But he lived in London and had affairs with various Russian teenagers. And Mum lived here.'

'With Violet? I thought that was only after Grandpa died?'

Elspeth laughed. 'Mum never waited for anything. She wanted Violet and Dad. So, she had her cake and ate it too, for years.'

Willa got up. 'We have to tell everyone.'

Elspeth shrugged. 'You can try. Violet will try to stop you. She'll probably lie about it.'

'Why?'

'That woman is a vault. Whenever my mother wanted something kept secret, Violet made sure it happened.'

'Violet's not like that.'

'Isn't she? Did she know about Lizzie and Jonty?'

'I think so.'

'Then she watched your sister sleep with her uncle for half her life and she didn't clue her in. Doesn't that tell you exactly who she cared about and who she didn't?'

'She's not like that, she just loved Granny, she wanted to make sure that no one found out anything that hurt them . . . I at least have to tell Lizzie. She thinks she and Jonty can be together. She's talking about telling the family, about moving in together and making a proper go of it. I can't let her do that.'

'No,' Elspeth agreed. 'You can't. You'll have to stop her. And I suppose Jonty has a right to know who his parents are. Just promise me you'll watch out for Violet.'

Willa got to her feet. 'OK. Jesus. What a fucking mess this family is.'

'The entail was supposed to make things fairer and better. But all it's ever done is make this family more complicated. Trust me, the best thing you could do, if they verify your letter, is get rid of the whole stupid, sick tradition.'

Violet put a Le Creuset dish on to the table. She had made quiche for the last night everyone would be staying.

Or, at least in theory, the last night they would all be staying.

'This smells lovely, Violet,' Angelique said.

'And that's from a fussy French woman.' Grant laughed.

'There is no such thing as an unfussy French woman,' Angelique retorted.

Everyone piled their plates with salad. 'I should probably explain,' Violet said, 'that the legal team have been in touch about what will happen tomorrow.'

Everyone seemed to shift slightly in their seats, trying to look casual and as if this conversation was of little to no interest to them. Violet went on. 'They will bring a team to the house tomorrow morning. Rihan gave them all the information we had, and they have assessed all the paperwork that they currently have. Next, they will read the letters, and perhaps take them away to glean further evidence. They will wish to talk to you, Willa, and they may wish to talk to some of the others. They said they will want to speak to me. Then, if things are clear enough, they will make a ruling. Otherwise, they will recommend that the will is officially contested. Does that make sense?'

Everyone nodded and agreed that it did indeed make sense, and then there was much discussion about who wanted more wine and if everyone had been served the vegetables. Willa looked across the table to where Jonty and Lizzie sat next to each other. It looked as if his hand might be brushing her leg under the table. Her heart buckled under the weight of knowing what she was going to have to do. She had stolen the one thing her sister had ever wanted, and now she was going to break her heart. But she had no choice. Just as Elspeth had said, Jonty had a right to know. And while adopted cousin might have been just enough to ignore, blood uncle certainly wasn't. She couldn't allow them to go through the pain of telling the family about their relationship, only for Grant to have to tell the man he raised as his son why he couldn't be with Lizzie.

Much later, after they had talked and laughed and drunk enough wine to forget what was going to happen the next day, Lizzie and Willa headed to bed. Willa washed her face in the nursery sink, moisturized, took out her contact lenses and brushed her hair. Lizzie brushed her teeth and then threw herself into her bed, which was still unmade from that morning. They turned out the lights and lay in the darkness, both looking up at the fuzzy blue ceiling.

'I've been thinking about what you said today,' Willa said.

'I said lots of things today.'

Willa threw a cushion across the room to where her sister's bed stood. 'You're so annoying.'

'I know.' Lizzie laughed.

'Seriously.'

'Do we have to be serious?'

'Yes.'

'OK, fine. What?'

'I think you should wait a while to tell the others.'

She could almost hear her sister thinking. 'Why?'

'The house, the letters – who knows what's going to happen tomorrow.'

'They'll find that yours is real, and you'll keep the house.'

Willa thought this was a bit rich coming from Lizzie, given that Lizzie hadn't been able to resist voting to have the letters validated. But this wasn't the time to start an argument with her sister. 'We don't know that. Someone might have switched the letters.' Her heart ran a little faster as she said it. 'All that other weird stuff happened. Like Bryony said.'

'If you quote Bryony, I'm going to push you out of the window.'

'Fair enough.'

'So, you think we should wait until all the house stuff is sorted?'

'Yes.'

Lizzie considered it. It wasn't as if she had been relishing the prospect of telling her father and Jonty's father that she and Jonty were sleeping together. And Jonty had suggested they wait a while before they bit the bullet anyway. 'OK,' she said. 'That makes sense. I'm glad you know, though.'

'Me too,' Willa lied.

Lizzie got to her feet and crossed the room. 'See you in the morning.'

'Don't go,' Willa said.

'What?'

'Stay.'

'Why?'

Willa searched for a reason. 'I just want you to.'

The silence told Willa that Lizzie was torn. 'I never ask you for anything,' Willa said. Which was entirely true. She listened with relief as Lizzie got back into her own bed.

'What bedroom are you going to have when it's your house?' Lizzie said.

'That's a good question,' Willa replied, awash with relief that she had managed to prevent her sister from going next door to unknowingly bed their uncle.

16

Jonty woke the next morning feeling a mixture of sadness and relief. He had enjoyed waking up with Lizzie's sweet-scented hair strewn over his face, her tanned limbs taking up most of the bed. His body ached for her, but there was something mixed with the ache. A note of relief that for once he wasn't going to spend the day trying to rid himself of the guilt that always came from a night spent with Lizzie, a sense that, while he was doing something that he wanted desperately, and that she wanted equally, he was doing something wrong.

He put his trainers on and went quietly downstairs, hoping not to have to speak to anyone. To his relief, he found his way to the drive without having to speak to another soul and began to pound his feet against the pavement, breathing in the scent of the early-morning air and relishing the movement in his muscles and the burn in his lungs. He had neglected his exercise while he had been at Roxborough, drinking too much and occasionally stealing one of Lizzie's cigarettes.

He wondered how long it would take Willa to escape the idea that Roxborough was a place for a holiday, a place where the rules didn't apply and it was perfectly reasonable to live from whim to whim. He had always told himself that Lizzie was just like the alcohol and cigarettes he consumed there as an adult, like the endless TV and sweets they were allowed when they stayed as children. The trappings of a wonderful holiday, but not real life.

But then, from what Lizzie had said recently, it seemed that she no longer wanted things to be confined to the walls of Roxborough. And, of course, he didn't want them to be either. She was the most brilliant, funny, alive person he had ever known. If he'd met her in a pub, he would have married her on the spot. But despite everything he had said to her before, he couldn't help asking himself the questions that Lizzie refused to answer. What would they tell their friends about how they met? Their colleagues? Would their family ever be able to see them as a real couple? What if they had children of their own? Could a relationship forged in secrecy and cultivated in the shadows ever really work? Could he and Lizzie really make each other happy when they were lying on the sofa watching television, instead of finding each other's bodies in the darkened bedrooms of a stately home?

And if they did try, if they told their friends and their families and they really attempted to make it work, and it failed, would it be worth it? Would there be an indelible stain on their personalities? Would he be for ever known as the friend of a friend who tried to sleep with, move in with, marry his cousin? Was it really worth the risk?

A large black people carrier sped down the road, almost knocking him over. He jumped backwards into the hedge, shouting at the car and then sticking his middle finger up at its rear window as it sped away.

Violet was nervous. She had got dressed that morning realizing that soon this would no longer be her bedroom. She had woken up to the same view every morning since . . . she couldn't put a date on it. She had fallen asleep here once with Cecily and then the next night it had seemed sensible to do it again. Occasionally, Esmond would come back from London and she would go back to her own pretty and chintzy room at the top of the house. Technically, it was in the servants' quarters, but it was large and comfortable with a television and an en suite, so nothing to complain about. But then, Violet never complained.

Cecily had remarked upon it once, before Esmond had disappeared to London for ever, when Violet still had to pack up her things ahead of his arrival and move back to her bedroom. 'What's it like to be so good?' Cecily had asked. Violet had considered it. She wasn't good. No more so than anyone else. What she was was satisfied. She could never have imagined that her life would mean living in a house like Roxborough and spending her days taking care of someone she adored. She had always assumed that the way she felt about other women was the kind of secret she would take to the grave so as to avoid giving any kind of offence or ending up in prison (she knew now that people didn't go to prison for wanting to kiss women, but as a child she had heard things about Oscar Wilde and wondered).

She hadn't told Cecily any of this. It wouldn't do to seem soppy or, even worse, grateful. Cecily was a funny thing. Flighty. Like an easily spooked horse. Violet knew that Cecily loved the easy, comfortable relationship they had, the way they woke up together every morning and went to bed together every night, watched the same programmes on television, worked on the garden and did the crossword. But it had happened very slowly, like water coming up to the boil. And if Cecily were reminded quite how cosy and domesticated their life had become, she would pull away from it. That was, Violet thought now, as she wiped down the dining table with a polishing cloth, probably how Jonty had come to exist.

Cecily and Esmond had had another enormous row, and it had been decided that he would go away for a few weeks so they would cool off before they discussed what to do next. Divorce was out of the question, but separation was almost certain. One evening, Cecily and Violet had eaten salmon from the local fishmonger's and minted new potatoes grown in the garden. There was a jug of sweet peas on the kitchen table and the buzz of the radio in the background. Everything was better than Violet could have dreamed.

'It will be like this always if you and Esmond separate,'

287

she had said, without thinking. Cecily had said nothing, but the next day she had announced that she needed to go to London. She had packed for herself, which was most unlike her and probably meant that everything was crumpled. And then she had stayed in London, without sending a phone number or a forwarding address, for six weeks.

Violet had tried to tell herself that this was Cecily. She had to pull away if Cecily was going to come back. But however hard she tried to pretend otherwise, she was hurt. Deeply, painfully hurt. When Cecily had come back, she had been pregnant, not that either of them had known it. The pregnancy had come with its problems – problems she was still wrestling with now. But it had changed Cecily. Or perhaps it was being away; it was hard to tell. Whatever the reason, she was different after that. Less afraid of it all. Able to enjoy the idea of things being calm and quiet and stable. Able to wake up next to Violet each morning and smile.

The doorbell startled Violet. No one had rung it for days. None of the family ever rang it, and the post was left at the bottom of the drive in a special locker. The legal team must have arrived.

The Mordaunts' legal team had been with the same London firm for six hundred years. Of course, the name, office and everything about it had changed, but in their vaults were every single important piece of Mordaunt paper. They knew the family inside out, the responsibility for all things Mordaunt resting with one person for their entire career. The Mordaunts liked consistency. They did not approve of change.

Violet opened the door as various family members began to emerge from corners of the house: Bryony, in a neat grey dress, from the living room; Lizzie, always curious, from the back stairs; Grant and Angelique from upstairs; and finally, presumably from the nursery, Willa.

'Please,' Violet said to the man standing on the doorstep. 'Come in.'

Charles Davenport was about sixty, and Violet had spoken to him twice before. Once for an insurance claim and once more when Cecily had found out that she was ill and decided to put her feelings about the house into letters. He was tall and had probably been handsome once upon a time. His shoes were clean and his suit neat, and just as in the previous times she had met him, Violet was reassured by him. He was followed by two younger men and a woman in her twenties. 'Please come through to the dining room,' Violet said.

They settled themselves there, taking out all of the papers and their laptops and mobile phones. Asked for the Wi-Fi code, accepted the offer of coffee and then asked that they speak to each member of the family individually.

'All of them?' Violet asked.

'Yes.'

'We have one child, Lucca. I presume you won't want to speak to him?'

'I think it's better that we do, actually.'

Violet was surprised.

'With a parent in attendance, of course,' Charles added. 'But it is best to leave no stone unturned.'

It was going to be a grim day, Lizzie realized. Everyone was in a sort of about-to-get-my-A-level-results mood. The weather had turned, too. It was still hot, but the wrong kind of hot. Grey and humid and oppressive, like they were all sealed into some enormous Tupperware box.

The lawyers were calling people into the room, one by one. Her father was first, then Grant. There had been some discussion about Elspeth not being there. She'd left that morning as planned, telling everyone that she didn't want the house and the lawyers could phone her if they really had to. The lawyer man didn't seem pleased, but he had carried on anyway. After the parents, they had Angelique in, but only for a few moments, and Bryony was there for an even shorter time. Bryony seemed cross when she came out, which Lizzie very much enjoyed. 'And you're really sure that's everything you needed to ask?' Lizzie heard her stepmother ask. 'I'm not sure how comprehensive that conversation was.'

'If we have any further questions, we'll ask you to come back,' the woman lawyer was saying. 'We really appreciate your help.'

Eventually it was Lizzie's turn. She felt hideously nervous, though she wasn't sure why. She closed the dining-room door behind her then took a seat on the opposite side of the table. She caught sight of herself in the mirrored candle holders on the wall. Her face wasn't quite so taut and hideous as it had been, but there were still blotches from the stings. She missed looking like herself.

'Thank you for speaking to us,' Charles said.

'No problem.'

'Were you disappointed not to be left the house?'

'Oh, wow, OK. Not wasting time. That's cool,' Lizzie stammered. 'Um. Yeah. I suppose I was.'

'I've heard that you had wanted to move here?'

'Who said that?'

'That's not important.'

'OK, well, it feels kind of important because it's basically grassing on me. But sure. Yes. I did want to live here.'

'Why?'

Lizzie looked around. 'It's a nice house.' Charles said nothing. 'It's my home, I guess. I grew up here more than anywhere else. My parents moved around a bit, my dad worked, I spent all my holidays here. I was close to my grandmother.'

'So, were you surprised when you weren't left the house?'

'No,' Lizzie said.

'Why not?'

She sighed and decided that she might as well tell the truth. 'Because a bit before she died, she walked in on me having sex with my adopted cousin and she wasn't happy about it.'

Charles choked slightly on his coffee. 'That's very help-ful,' he said. 'Thank you.'

Willa was last. She wasn't sure if that was for any signifi-cant reason. She watched Lizzie leave from her position sitting on the stairs, where she had been counting the posts of the banisters and willing time to either speed up or slow down. 'Willa?' the female lawyer said. 'We're ready for you.'

They're not the police, she repeated in her head. *This isn't an interrogation. They're just lawyers. You're a lawyer. You're like them. They're like you. There is nothing to be nervous about.* Only, of course there was something to be nervous about.

She took a seat. It was still warm from her sister's body before hers. 'Hi,' she said, trying to sound calm. 'Thank you for doing this.'

Charles didn't seem especially interested in niceties. 'Were you surprised to be left the house?' he asked.

'Um. Yes.'

'Why?'

'Because my grandmother had a lot of people she could leave it to, including my dad. I didn't think it would be me because it would have been kind of presumptuous to assume it would be.'

'But you're glad that it was you?'

'Yes. Of course.'

'Why do you think she chose you?'

What a question. 'I don't know.'

'If you were to hazard a guess?'

Willa looked around the room. 'I think she knew I'm not really at ease with living in London, or—' She wanted to say her job. But they worked for a firm not dissimilar to hers, and the legal world was small. She didn't want someone repeating back to them that she couldn't hack it. That way, she might end up with no Roxborough and no job. 'She knew I liked a slower pace of life. She knew I loved the house. I think of it as home. I think she wanted someone who could settle here and maybe start a family.'

Charles raised his eyebrows but said nothing. 'And if the entail is found to be corrupt, what will you do?'

Willa felt herself getting annoyed, though she wasn't entirely sure why. 'I'm not sure that's relevant,' she said.

Charles said nothing but perused his notes. 'That's everything,' he said. 'Could you invite everyone in?'

Willa decided that she didn't like Charles Davenport. She went into the corridor and rang the enormous bell that sat on the hall table. It had been used for summoning the children in from the garden or bringing people for meals ever since the ornate gong had been broken in the 1920s during some party filled with Bright Young Things.

Again, everyone began to emerge from the creases of the house. They filed into the dining room. Someone from the legal team had half closed the curtains, presumably because they were casting a glare on to their computer screens. The room looked so different with protective mats on the table to shield it from scratches, all the beauty of the night of the funeral completely absent from this now purely functional space.

'Thank you all for your time today,' Charles said, getting to his feet. He wore glasses. Willa could see that they were impeccably clean. 'It was a useful first step. We will be taking all of the letters with us, and we have permission to open the lockbox in the late Mrs Mordaunt's safety deposit box, which is held with the firm. We anticipate being able to give you an answer in four to six weeks.'

'Weeks?' asked Lizzie.

'Does it have to take that long?' Grant asked.

'Surely it can't really take four weeks?' said David.

Charles waited for everyone to stop talking. Eventually, once the noise had died down, he said, 'I appreciate that this is a frustrating situation for all of you, and that you're probably most anxious to understand what is to happen next. But these things must follow a set process and we are unable to expedite them, much as we may wish to.'

Charles and his team filed out and got back into the enormous people carrier to which Jonty had given the finger earlier. The driver put his hat back on and woke up from the warm doze he had been enjoying, and the car slowly rolled away down the drive, crunching the gravel as it disappeared.

The Mordaunts all stood in the hallway watching the car go.

'What now?' Jonty asked, after a little while.

'Well,' Violet said. 'Everyone was going to leave today, I think. But you might as well stay for supper at least. And then I suppose everyone will go home, at least for the time being.'

'But we don't know what's happening with the house,' pointed out Bryony.

'No,' Violet said. 'But I don't imagine many of you would want to stay here for the next four to six weeks.'

'No,' Angelique agreed. 'That is true.'

'So, I suggest that when they reach their findings, I will contact each of you, we can all reconvene, and we'll share the news together.'

Everyone made muffled acknowledgements that this was a sensible course of action and they began to disperse, Grant and Angelique for one last swim in the lake, Bryony to find Lucca and help him pack, David to work on his laptop in the bedroom, Lizzie and Jonty to walk down to the woods. Only Willa hung back. 'I'm not sure what I should do,' she told Violet. 'I guess I'll go back to London.'

'Why?'

'Well. The house. The letters. If I stay here, I'll have to tell work that I'm not coming back, and if I do that, they'll be furious. So, really, if I'm not going to stay here for ever, I suppose I should get the train back tomorrow morning.'

Violet looked grave. 'Try not to think about that. There's no reason to think that you won't get the house.'

Willa shook her head. 'I don't know. I—'

Violet interrupted her. 'You would have had to go back to London at some point anyway. Why don't you and Lizzie get the train tomorrow, and you can start to pack up your flat and think about your next moves?'

Willa nodded. It was good advice. At least in theory.

'Lucca?' Bryony called. She found her son lying on the sofa in the snug, looking at his iPad. Yet again, guilt twisted in her abdomen. Lucca had had so much screen time since they had been here. He had been largely ignored by the rest of the family, who seemed to show so little interest in hearing him play his musical instruments or sing for them, let alone hearing about what astonishing grades he was achieving at school. 'Darling?'

He took his headphones off. 'What?' he asked.

'I'd like you to come and pack,' she said.

'We're going home?' Lucca jumped to his feet. 'There's a whole two weeks left of the holidays. Does this mean I can go to karate camp?'

Bryony had originally said no out of fear of injuries, and then because they were going to be staying here. But, looking at his beaming face, she softened. 'All right,' she said. 'I'll call them and see if they have any spaces. I can't make any promises, but if they have room to let you in, you can go.'

Lucca whooped, running from the room. 'I'm packing!' he shouted as he went.

★

'I was thinking,' Angelique said to Grant as they peeled off their swimming costumes and got into the shower together. She worked a piece of soap into a sponge and ran it over his body. 'Perhaps we should go this evening.'

'Not wait for tomorrow morning?'

Angelique shrugged and then intimated that they should swap places so that her body was under the water. She tipped her hair back and soaked it so it hung like black ribbons, clinging to her skin in places. 'We don't have to go,' she said. 'I just thought, if we leave soon, we could make it for a late dinner at Bellanger.'

The idea of being alone with Angelique at a table for two after the last five days of shared dinners with the entire family did not lack appeal. It was only a few hours on the motorway. They could park at her place, walk to the restaurant. If they arrived late, there would almost certainly be a table on the terrace. A bottle of Sancerre, Dover sole, the noise of cars and the smell of pollution. The more he thought about it, the more magical it all sounded. 'How quickly could you be packed?' he asked Angelique, kissing her shoulder.

Grant decided that saying goodbye to everyone was an unnecessary disruption. Instead, he found Violet in the back kitchen, hulling strawberries. 'V, darling, I think Ang and I are going to leave now.'

Violet looked neutral about the idea. 'Of course,' she said, giving him a hug, painfully aware that Cecily should be here, should be chiding her son for not giving enough notice, for not saying that there would be two fewer for supper in good time. The absence of Cecily felt larger than it ever had in that moment. Violet realized that, once all of the children were gone, there would be nothing else. No more funeral to work towards. No more visitors to prepare for. Just emptiness, until they discovered who would be living here. And then, quite possibly, that person would want to hire their own housekeeper. Why would they want their mother's companion lurking in the background like some Mrs Danvers figure?

'Have you said goodbye to Jonty?'

Grant pulled a face. 'I couldn't find him, and if I start doing goodbyes, I'll be here all evening.'

'Of course,' said Violet. 'Drive safe,' she said, kissing Grant's cheek and squeezing his hand.

Jonty was reading in his room when Willa knocked on the door. He opened it, expecting to see Lizzie's face, and was jarred to see one that was at once so similar to Lizzie's and yet so different. 'Hi,' he said. 'Everything OK?' Willa looked grey and grave.

'Can you come with me?' she asked.

Jonty put the bookmark in his book and followed his cousin next door to the nursery. He noted that the striped pink-and-white blankets on the beds were still the same ones they had always been. He wasn't usually a sentimental person. Perhaps because he spent much of his working life telling people that the animals they loved so much were going to have to die. But something about the blankets felt reassuring and strangely moving. Lizzie was sitting on one of the beds, looking worried. 'What's going on?' she asked Willa.

'Sit down, Jonty.'

Jonty did as Willa asked, taking a seat on the bed next to Lizzie. Lizzie reached for his hand and Jonty wasn't sure what to do. They'd always been fastidious about not showing affection for each other in public, but they had agreed that they were going to go public, and clearly Willa already knew. He guessed she had probably known for years.

'I've got to tell you something,' Willa said.

'If it's bad, I don't want to know,' said Lizzie, sounding like a child. Jonty felt for Willa. She looked tired, as if everything that had happened over the previous few days was weighing on her. He still didn't know whether he thought she might have had something to do with the letters, but increasingly he was realizing that he didn't really care. He had never wanted the house. He wanted to go back to his normal life, only this time he wanted to do it with Lizzie beside him, to finally be able to take her out for dinner or introduce her to his friends. All of the frightening things about it were still very, very real. But then, so was the way his blood seemed to prickle when he was near her.

'I don't know how to say this,' Willa went on. 'So, I'm just going to say it. Jonty isn't adopted.'

'What?' Jonty looked at Willa, trying to understand

why she would say something so bizarre. 'Yes, I am. Grant and Luella adopted me.'

'Sorry, I'm doing this wrong. It's not that you're not adopted.' She sighed. 'Granny was your mother.'

There was silence, and then the pipes that led to the sink in the corner began to gurgle, just as they did whenever anyone upstairs ran the hot water. 'What?' Jonty asked weakly.

Willa sighed, and then forced the words out. 'Granny got pregnant when she was in her fifties. She thought she'd had the menopause. But then she had you. And she didn't want another baby, so she wanted to have you adopted, but she didn't want anyone to know, and Grant and Luella couldn't have children, and it all seemed like a good idea. That's why Elspeth hated Granny. She left because she thought it was all so awful.'

'Who's my father?' Jonty asked quietly.

'Elspeth said it was Grandpa.'

Jonty shook his head, completely unable to say anything.

'Why would she say something like that?' Lizzie asked, her eyes filled with tears. 'And why should we believe her?'

Willa shrugged. 'Why would she lie? You can talk to her yourself. She seemed like she was telling the truth.'

'So, if she's not lying, then we're not cousins,' Lizzie said. She'd removed her hand from Jonty's and was worrying at the edge of the blanket, pulling at loose threads. 'You're my uncle.'

Willa wished Lizzie hadn't said it. They all knew it, but somehow it felt more awful to hear her sister say it. 'Yes,' Jonty said, looking into the middle distance. There was a rushing noise in his ears, like a waterfall. He looked out of the window, at the starlings darting through the sky. He hadn't ever felt anything like this before. Time was moving strangely fast and strangely slowly somehow. He wanted to say something, but he couldn't open his mouth. So, he sat, completely still, almost paralysed, looking out of the window.

Lizzie got up, graceful as she always was, walked to the corner of the room and then, without any warning, threw up in the sink.

Lizzie didn't come down for supper. She stayed in the nursery, claiming a headache. Then she packed her suitcase with uncharacteristic neatness. She needed to keep moving. If she stopped for even a moment, the noise in her head would become too loud. So, she tidied the room. And then, once everyone had gone to bed, she walked around the house. She'd once taken cocaine with a friend from school who claimed that their dealer was a 'sweetheart'. Only it had turned out to be more speed than cocaine and Lizzie hadn't been able to bear it. The energy had burned in her veins and she'd found herself running up and down the stairs trying to get rid of it. She felt the same way now, despite the fact she hadn't taken anything.

She was exhausted, but her body was completely alive.

All she wanted was to slip into Jonty's room. She knew without a doubt that if she lay next to him, his body would calm hers, her breath would follow his, and she would be able to sleep. But she couldn't. She wouldn't be able to ever again. The door hadn't just slammed shut, it had been painted and nailed shut. Bricked up. The one person she had ever really been in love with was effectively dead to her.

Jonty lay in bed, half dreading that Lizzie would come in, half hoping she would. He had gone down to supper because he knew how it would look if they both stayed upstairs. He'd claimed that he was worried about work and that was why his answers were monosyllabic. Bryony had monologued about Lucca's schoolwork and talent at singing and dancing, so no one had had to say much else. It was a testament to quite how desolate everyone felt that Bryony talking was a relief.

Eventually, after he'd had four glasses of red wine, Jonty had made his excuses. It was impossible for Roxborough to feel small, and yet he felt like he was being sealed in by the walls. He watched the hands ticking on the clock on his bedside table. The clock had belonged to his grandfather. Well. Actually, it had probably belonged to his father. How was it possible that knowing who his mother was, and who is father almost certainly had been, was actually more confusing than having no idea where he came from?

He tried to work out how long he needed to wait to be

sober enough to drive. Another five hours should do it. By 5 a.m., he could be gone. And once he had made the arrangements, he would book a flight to America to see Elspeth and ask her everything he needed to know. And then, he supposed, he would tell Grant. Or perhaps he wouldn't. How was he supposed to know what to do? Under the confusion, there was a sadness. He had already mourned the death of his mother once. Now he was doing it all over again. These stupid, selfish, wealthy people. How could you have every possible chance to be decent and still end up fucking it all up?

The next morning, David hugged Violet in a strange, uncomfortable way that told her he finally knew that she and Cecily had been more than simply employer and employee. 'See you soon,' she said, trying to make sure he knew that she meant it. Bryony was already in the passenger seat, phone and iPad out so that she could 'make use' of the journey time. Lucca was in the back, sitting in a booster seat. Violet wondered whether it was normal for children of nine to still be in booster seats. But then there was nothing normal about Lucca. He'd managed to do some extraordinary things in his time at Roxborough. She tried not to be angry with him about the photographs, or about the wasps' nest. On the latter point, she was almost impressed that he had managed to manoeuvre it into the house and hide his stings from his mother. And, she supposed, he had been lonely, and bored. He was desperate to go home, and perhaps the only Mordaunt who was hoping not to come back.

Jonty had left before sunrise. Like his father, he disliked long goodbyes and making a scene. He left a sweet note on the kitchen table thanking Violet for everything, and a patch of dry gravel where his car had been in the drive.

He knew it was cowardly not to offer to stay with Lizzie and talk it all through, that he should drive her back to London and stay with her while she came to terms with it all. But he couldn't. He didn't know how to love her in a way that was appropriate now. So, he wanted to run away. He drove back to his flat, the basement of a pretty townhouse in the centre of Norwich. He unlocked the door then stood in the middle of the living room, looking at everything there, thinking about how, the last time he had stood here, the last time he had touched each thing in this room, his entire world had been different.

It was impossible to know where to start. A large part of him wanted to drive to London and punch his father in thanks for the lifetime of deception. But, of course, that would be pointless. He could see now that his father hadn't wanted any of this. It would have been Cecily's idea. How could his mother, who everyone said had desperately wanted a child, have turned down an offer like that one? He began to unpack, shoving his clothes in the laundry basket, trying to keep moving enough that he could shake the thoughts out of his head, especially the question he kept asking himself. If Cecily really was his mother, why wouldn't she have left him some kind of explanation? And, to his own horror, he couldn't help but wonder: why hadn't she left him the house?

Violet drove Willa and Lizzie to the station. She was a good driver, far better than Cecily, who had pranged so many expensive cars she had eventually bought a second-hand Micra and driven that all around the county.

At the station, Violet gave them each a tight hug and then told herself not to be so silly. They looked so young standing on the station platform, just as they had when she and Cecily had dropped them off at the end of the holidays when they were teenagers. Violet tried to shake the memory of them in their denim skirts and school hoodies, all legs and enormous hair, wrists covered with dozens of bracelets. The clothes might have changed, but they were still the same lost little girls, waiting for a train to take them somewhere that didn't really feel like home. She blinked back tears as she drove away. 'Stupid old woman,' she told herself crossly in the rear-view mirror. 'Foolish, sentimental old lady.'

The house was predictably silent when she got home. The dogs barked. One of the cats came to ingratiate itself in the hope that Violet might dole out a handful of Dreamies. But she could feel that everyone had gone. The house rang with its loneliness. This was not a house to be empty. It was a house for families, parties, people. And now she had to wait for the lawyers to ring, and to pretend to act surprised when the call came through.

★

Willa got her and Lizzie a cab from King's Cross. She insisted on dropping Lizzie off, even though it was out of her way. She watched Lizzie drag her huge bag up the steps of the house where she lived with a collection of similarly itinerant party girls, then tried to steady herself as the car headed towards her flat.

It looked the same, of course. No one had been here. There was nothing to change. Her cleaner had come to water the plants, but otherwise no one had come inside. She put the pile of post – all bills and flyers – on the kitchen table and opened the windows to let in some air.

She had liked her flat, once upon a time. She'd been proud of herself for buying it. Her father had given her the money for the stamp duty and the solicitor's fees, but other than that, she'd done it entirely by herself, saving ruthlessly and living in the cheapest shared house she could find until it was finally possible to own this. But, compared to Roxborough, it had no redeeming features. It was a modern new-build in the middle of a glossy block. The newness and the fact that it looked like a hotel had been part of the initial appeal. It was easy to heat, and all the appliances were brand new. It had been an extremely sensible choice. But Willa wasn't sure she wanted to keep making sensible choices.

She looked at her phone, yet again. They had said it would be four to six weeks until they reached a verdict, so why was she checking obsessively already? There would be plenty of time to panic about it once they discovered what she had done. She should try to enjoy the calm before the storm.

Willa wasn't entirely sure how much trouble she could get into. Her legal training hadn't covered anything this complex, unsurprisingly. The best-case scenario, she reasoned, was that they would realize that her letter was fake but would assume someone else had written it. Or that they would feel that discretion was the better part of valour and not seek to find out. The house would be split among the children, which would mean selling it. But no one would know what she had done.

And then there was the worst-case scenario. Which was that they easily uncovered what she had done. And it would be easy. She'd touched all the letters and their envelopes. She wasn't entirely sure – her memory of that night wasn't perfect – but she thought she might even have licked the envelopes to seal them, leaving her DNA all over everything. Though she had very similar DNA to most of the people there, and she didn't know how that would work in terms of tracing it. Obviously, she couldn't google it, in case someone took her phone. Maybe she could go to an internet café tomorrow, pay in cash and google it there. She could do some research while she was there, too. Try to find out if anyone had ever done something like this before. How much trouble they had got into when they were found out. She tried not to think about what her father would say. What Violet would say. Worst of all, what Lizzie would say.

Lizzie would blame her if Roxborough was sold, there

was no question about that. Lizzie didn't see in shades of grey when she was happy, let alone when she was sad. And between the news about Jonty and the house, she couldn't imagine Lizzie would ever really recover.

She took a deep breath, trying to convince herself that she had a few weeks until anyone found out what she had done, that it wasn't worth letting herself panic yet. Her phone started to buzz. She swiped at the screen, expecting it to be someone from work asking yet another question about where on the server she had filed a document.

'Willa?' It was Violet's voice. 'I think you had better come back to Roxborough.'

'Now?' she asked, willing herself to sound natural.

'Yes,' Violet said. 'Now.'

2002

The phone rang during drinks. Cecily had been playing the piano for Violet, sipping her gin and tonic at intervals. It was early spring, and too cold really to have the windows open. But Cecily and Violet were both so pleased to have finally come through the miserable winter that they were cheerfully chilly, breathing in the fresh spring air. 'I'll get it,' Cecily said, hurrying down the hall. There was a slight twinge in her left hip, which she supposed was all part of being in her sixties, but which she resented enormously.

'Hello?' she said, forgetting to take her earring off in the rush.

'Hello, old thing,' said a familiar voice on the other end of the line. 'How are you?'

'Esmond?'

'Yes,' he said. 'Is that all right?'

'Of course it is. How are you?'

'Well, that's rather why I'm phoning. I'm afraid I'm not well at all.'

'Oh.' Cecily sat down on the hall chair, looking into the middle distance. It was always cold in the hall, but she felt rather hot on the back of her neck. 'What sort of not well?'

'Cancer.'

'Oh, Esmond.'

'Yes. Rather a bugger.'

'Quite.'

'So, I thought I'd better let you know. Not sure what Debrett's advice is on dying, but I didn't want you to get *The Times* in a couple of months and see my name in the obits.'

'A couple of months?'

'It looks like it. Maybe a little more. Maybe a little less.'

'Come to Roxborough.'

Esmond laughed, and the laugh turned into a cough. He tried to stifle it with a glass of water. 'I couldn't possibly impose.'

'You wouldn't be imposing.'

'You've got no idea how much of an imposition it would be. Dying is a grizzly business. When my father went, it was an enormous disruption, threw the whole house into disarray.'

'I'm not asking,' Cecily said. 'I'm telling. If you don't get someone to drive you down tomorrow, then I'll come to Cheyne Walk. And you know how I hate spending more than two nights in a row in London, so I'll be miserable. Come here. We'll have nurses, I won't have to do a thing.'

Esmond felt he should say no. That would be the brave thing to do. But the idea of dying in the London house with only paid staff for company was rather more depressing than the idea of having cancer in the first place. 'All right,' he said. 'But if I'm a nuisance, you're to palm me off on the nearest hospital, or just get the local vet to come and put me down.'

Cecily laughed. 'Do the children know?'

'No.'

'I'm going to call them.'

Esmond sighed. 'Could I stop you?'

'Absolutely not.'

'What about a compromise? Don't call them yet. Wait until I'm really on the way out, so they can say goodbye but they don't feel obliged to give up their whole lives.'

'All right.'

The ice in Cecily's gin and tonic had melted when she got back.

'What's wrong?' asked Violet, reading Cecily's expression.

'It's Esmond,' she said. 'He's dying.'

Violet looked pained. 'I'm sorry.'

'He's only seventy-three. We're supposed to have longer than that.'

Violet made comforting noises, and Cecily looked up at her. 'I told him to come here.'

It was difficult to look as if she thought this was a good idea, but Violet did her absolute best. 'What a good idea,' she said, wiping a water mark left by Cecily's glass. 'Far better for him to be here, and then the children can come too.'

'I'm sorry,' Cecily said weakly, wiping her eyes. 'I don't know what's wrong with me.'

'You silly thing,' Violet said, dropping a kiss on Cecily's head. 'You love him.'

Esmond arrived two days later, wearing a jacket and tie. He slept all afternoon, exhausted by the journey. That evening, Cecily wheeled him around the garden in his wheelchair. He grumbled about being unable to walk, but she couldn't mistake the joy in his face as he breathed in the scent of the new flowers and the cool air. It was the first time he had seen Roxborough in over a decade. He didn't say it, presumably because he didn't want to sound presumptuous, but it was abundantly clear that he felt that he had come home.

For the first week, he managed to make it down to din-ner every evening, though he ate almost nothing. Cecily and Violet cooked light, gentle food that he could pick at and kept topics of conversation as far away from mortal-ity as they could manage. But after ten days or so, Esmond started asking for a tray in his bedroom. He was always in clean pyjamas, always chatting (flirting) with the nurses who tended him. But clearly fading.

One evening when Esmond was asleep Violet went in to refill his water jug and take in some peonies from the garden. Esmond stirred and started to sit up. Violet glanced at the door, wondering whether she could pretend she hadn't noticed, but she hesitated too long. She was acutely aware that she had stolen Cecily away from him, and that, as a dying man, he might have a few choice words for her. But, to her surprise, Esmond gave her an exhausted smile. 'I can't think of a worthier adversary,' he wheezed. 'You've done a wonderful job looking after her.'

Violet wondered if he knew quite what a comprehensive job she had done in looking after Cecily. If he knew that she had placed his son for adoption, or about the hideous place she had taken Elspeth to. But it was far too late for any of that. She smiled, like a servant. 'Thank you,' she said.

The children arrived as soon as they were told. Or rather, Grant and David did. Both of them were pale, unsure quite how to approach the death of a parent, but far too familiar with grief since the loss of Luella. Cordelia looked after the children all day, every day, watching films and playing endless board games so that the brothers could sit at their father's bedside. Occasionally on a trip downstairs to get a jug of water or to sneak outside to smoke, Grant would catch sight of Jonty and the girls and wonder how it could possibly be right that both he and Jonty were losing their father but that Jonty would never have any idea. And then he would banish the thought and go back upstairs to sit by his father's side, telling himself he wasn't depriving

Jonty of anything and that, anyway, he was far too young to understand.

They spent their hours reading to him, telling stories they'd all heard a hundred times before. Cecily moved from room to room, sometimes sitting with her boys, sometimes with the children and Cordelia, never really sure where to place herself in the strange world where almost everyone she had ever loved was underneath one roof and determined to play nicely together for Esmond's sake.

And Violet disappeared into the background, just as she had been trained to do as a girl. Food appeared on the table, nursing schedules were drawn up, medication fetched from the pharmacy. The house ran with perfect, unwavering efficiency. Cecily slept in Esmond's room by the end. She said it was for him, but everyone knew it was because she was terrified that he would die alone.

Esmond never asked about Elspeth. He knew that Cecily would have asked her and that, by not appearing, she had said no. What he didn't know was how many letters, phone calls and emails Cecily had sent, begging Elspeth to come home. Eventually she had received a response to her email.

Mum. Stop calling, stop writing, stop trying to get in touch. I told you that I would never come to Roxborough again, and I meant it. I presume you brought Dad back there, despite not having been together for more than a decade, to try to tempt

me back, or perhaps to make it impossible for me to see him
without seeing you. Either way, I will have nothing to do with
it. And, let's face it, you wouldn't want me around, running
the risk of telling him your secret, now would you? Dad
knows I love him. I've written to him. Please do us both a
favour and leave me alone. Tell the boys to stop calling me.
Whatever happens, I'm not coming back.

Cecily had gone into the larder and sobbed as quietly as she possibly could. Then, she had deleted it, wishing it were a proper letter so that she could shred it and burn it. That night when she went into Esmond's bedroom he was paler than before, and his breaths were long and slow. 'Elspeth wanted to come,' she whispered. 'She told me how much she loves you.'

Esmond half smiled. It was hard to know how much he was taking in because of all the morphine.

'They all love you,' Cecily said. 'You've been such a wonderful father.'

He squeezed her hand and blinked slowly. She knew what he was telling her: that neither of them had been perfect parents, but that they'd done their best. And that it had been quite a road they'd driven down together. That he didn't regret marrying her. That he regretted nothing.

Violet found them the next morning, Cecily lying on top of the covers, curled in their marital bed, Esmond's hand between hers. Cecily sleeping, Esmond dead.

17

It was strange, Willa thought, how it was possible for time to move so slowly and yet so fast. She'd picked up a rental car and been on the motorway within an hour of the call. She didn't want to go, obviously. But hanging around wasn't going to improve anything. She'd chosen to drive rather than take the train because she realized that once Violet knew what she had done, or rather, once she had faced up to what she had done, she would need to leave. The idea of standing around in the hallway waiting for a taxi was almost worse than the idea of Violet finding out what she had done.

So, now she was on the motorway, her suitcase in the back of the car, which smelled faintly of cigarette smoke and sugar, as if someone had spilled a bottle of Fanta on the back seat. She changed lane without indicating and then shouted her apology at someone who beeped at her. She wasn't concentrating. She leaned forward to change the radio station, unable to settle to anything. Classical music was too sharp, pop made her head hurt, but the silence of the road underneath her was worse.

She settled on some obscure station that played songs from musicals and tried very hard to focus on the road. Her mother had loved old musicals. She had looked a little like Grace Kelly and, sometimes, when she and David were in the best of their moods, they would dance together, and it would be as if one of her films had come to life. Willa remembered sitting on the floor of the telly room in their house, watching *The King and I* while her mother ironed, the scent of clean clothes and the feeling of ironed cotton. It was a lovely, safe memory.

She pulled off the motorway and on to the slip road, then after a while took the sharp left on to the quiet little lane, inexplicably labelled with a 60mph speed limit. Who on earth would go that fast down here?

She always craned her neck to see Roxborough as she got close, had done ever since she had been a small child in the back of her parents' car. There it was, in all its beautiful symmetry, calmly nestled between two hills. She thought that this might be the last time she was ever able to see the house, and then corrected herself. Even if the rest of the family were so angry that she wasn't welcome at the house any more, no one could stop her from coming up to this point and looking at the house. They could sell it, and she would still be able to do that.

She took another deep breath as she reached the drive and parked neatly at the far end, allowing for an easy getaway. Hopefully this would be quick. She hadn't ever been summoned to see the headmistress when she was at school. Not her style to get into trouble, and certainly not worth the humiliation of having to go into Bryony's office and be told off by a woman she'd seen in her pyjamas that morning. But she imagined that this must be the same feeling. It was like the one she used to get before they weighed her at the centre, when she knew she wasn't any heavier than the previous weigh-in, that the nurse was going to give her a mournful look and tell her she couldn't go home until she reached her target.

There was another big black car on the drive. Presumably that was how the lawyers had arrived. At least it wasn't the police.

Violet opened the front door. She pulled her cardigan around her, surprised by the cold. 'Hello, darling,' she said as Willa closed the car door behind her. 'You'd better come in.'

Willa didn't think to take her suitcase out of the back of the car. She knew she wasn't going to need it. Violet wondered if she should mention it but decided not to. 'Do you want a cup of tea?' Violet asked.

'No, thank you.'

'Water?'

Willa shook her head. She felt sick. Speaking was difficult.

'Shall we go through, then?' Violet asked.

Yes. No. Willa didn't know which it was. The sooner it was over, the better, she told herself. She watched the outline of Violet's body moving in front of her as she followed her down the hall to the dining room, where all of this had started. Not for the first time, Willa asked herself how and why she had done something so enormously stupid. What had she been thinking? What sort of a person did something like that?

'Hello,' she said, looking at Charles Davenport across the table. He put down a stack of papers and took off his glasses. There were coffee rings on some of the papers and the room felt fusty, as if people had been working in there all day without a break.

'Could you excuse us?' he said to his assistants. They took their leave. Violet stayed standing by the door. She had no intention of leaving, and if Charles had meant to suggest that she should, he certainly wasn't going to do so again.

'What's going on?' Willa asked, deciding she should at least try to look as if she didn't know what was happening.

'Rather a complex situation, this one,' said Charles. 'Perhaps you should give some consideration to whether you will be continuing the entail in the same way.'

'What?'

'The entail, how the house passes from person to person.'

'I know what the entail means. I'm confused about why you think I could change it.'

'Oh, it's not a condition of the ownership. No owner of Roxborough has ever been obliged to keep the entail working in the same way, it's only that all the previous owners have chosen to.'

'You're saying that I'm the owner?'

Charles looked surprised and shuffled his papers again. 'I am sorry,' he said. 'I should have been clear. Yes. It has been made clear that you are indeed the legal owner of the house.'

Willa tried very hard to control her face. 'My letter was validated?'

'Letter? No. Well, it's unclear. There was no need to get into the forensics of that. Your grandmother had left her own instructions, witnessed by a solicitor from the firm, saying that she had told Violet Mackenzie who the house had been left to, and that, if there were any confusion, she would be able to clarify. Once that letter was opened, we were able to speak to Mrs Mackenzie, who confirmed that your grandmother had left you the house. It was all surprisingly simple. I am only sorry that we weren't able to establish this before you went back to London. We might have spared you a journey. We did need you to come back, though. There is rather a lot of paperwork to sign.' He took out a folder of papers, littered with little paper tabs to indicate where they needed to be signed, and handed her a pen. 'If you would start by signing this one? Are you all right?'

'Yes,' Willa said weakly. 'It's just rather overwhelming.'

Charles averted his gaze, uncomfortable with this display of emotion. He was rather worried that the young lady might be about to cry, and then he really wouldn't know what to do with himself.

Eventually, all of the papers were signed, Charles packed his briefcase and the team left. On the dining-room table were laid out pages and pages of documents, all of which added up to one thing. The house was really, honestly, truly Willa's. But how? She traced her finger over each of the pages, willing herself to be happy, to believe that this was how it was supposed to be. She had the house. There was nothing anyone could do to change that. It was hers. So why did she feel even worse than she had when she thought she was about to get caught?

'I'm afraid there isn't anything terribly exciting for supper,' Violet said as Willa went into the kitchen. 'I wasn't expecting anyone tonight. Just a salad and some gazpacho, though I could probably—'

'How did that happen?' Willa stood by the kitchen window, looking out across the lawns, beyond the path to where the lake was, just out of sight. She drank in the view, but she knew now that she wasn't going to be able to pretend that everything was fine. She couldn't live with this tight, frightened feeling for the rest of her life. She couldn't spend the entire time she lived at Roxborough worrying about what was going to happen next, about whether someone might discover something that pointed to her being the most enormous fraud.

Violet sat down in Cecily's chair, the one with the prettiest view of the garden where she had always sat. 'I told them that you were supposed to have the house.'

'Why?'

'Because it's true.'

Willa swallowed. 'It's not.'

Violet looked at her for a moment. 'Why?'

'Because I faked my letter. I found the real letter, the one with my name on it, the one that said she wasn't leaving me the house. And then I destroyed it, and I went to her study and used her typewriter and forged a new one that said I got the house. I stole Roxborough. From my family.'

Violet got to her feet and went into the back kitchen where the fridge was. She returned with a bottle of wine. Not the type kept in the wine cellar, which came out covered in dust and in need of decanting. A nice screw-top from the local Waitrose. It happened to be the exact brand that she and Cecily had become so fond of in the latter years of her life, favouring the £7.99 Sauvignon over any of the complicated offerings from the cellar. She poured herself a glass and one for Willa, pushing it across the table. For once, Willa took an enormous gulp of it, apparently temporarily suspending her concerns about the calorie and sugar content.

Violet sat back down and considered Willa's worried, pinched face. 'You didn't steal Roxborough,' she said.

'What?'

'Or if you did, it wasn't your fault.'

'I don't understand.'

Violet sighed. She had been dreading this speech since the moment she had learned that she would have to give it. 'Your grandmother asked me to do various things across the course of our life together that I hated. I don't know exactly how much Elspeth told you, but I will never forgive myself for what happened with her. And I helped Cecily to break your grandfather's heart. And then, when she found out that she was dying, she asked something else of me. To help whoever wanted the house the most to take it.'

'I don't understand.'

'Cecily didn't leave the house to anyone. Instead, she had me set it up. She had me put the blank letters at your table settings for the entail, and then she told me to go down and put the real letters on the table after everyone had gone to bed. She said whoever wanted the house the most would carry on looking for them after everyone else had given up. She told me to make it so that anyone who wanted to take the house could do it. And then she left a letter for the lawyers claiming that I knew who the house was supposed to go to. She told me that someone – probably Bryony – would call it all into question if anyone other than David took the house and that it was my job to protect whoever wanted the house the most.'

'What if more than one of us had tried it?'

Violet gave a half-smile. 'I asked her the same thing. She said it wouldn't happen. I think – though she never said anything to this effect – I think she knew you would do it.'

Willa tried to digest the information. 'You knew that I was lying the entire time.'

'Yes, I did.'

'But you're not angry with me?'

Violet shook her head. 'That's what Cecily wanted.'

'Why on earth would she want that? Why would she want a member of her own family to try to steal this place?'

'Because that's how she got the house herself.'

1961

'Tell whoever it is that I hate them,' Cecily grumped as the phone rang. She was very, very pregnant with her first child and was not taking the experience well. She complained about practically everything and resented everyone who wasn't pregnant. She hated her enormous fingers and feet, the indignity of struggling to get up off the sofa, everything about the whole hideous experience. People kept telling her it would be worth it when the baby arrived, but she was very much unconvinced that they were right.

Esmond got up to answer the phone, but Violet was already standing in the hall holding the receiver. It was strange how she always seemed to beat him to everything.

'Who is it?' he asked.

'It's for Cecily.'

'She's lying down. I'll take it.'

'I think they want to speak to her.'

Esmond gave Violet a look, one that was supposed to tell her that she was fifteen years his junior and his employee, and that she should do what she was told. Of course, he knew that Cecily loved Violet like a best friend and a sister and that the house would fall apart without her, so any attempt at being critical towards her was entirely fruitless. 'Fine,' he said. 'I'll get her.'

Cecily complained from the moment she was on her feet to the moment she was handed the phone. And then she went very quiet. 'What?' she whispered. 'Are you sure?'

Esmond assumed it was a death, and he was correct. Cecily's uncle, who had been frail and miserable since he lost his wife, had died. 'I'm sorry, darling,' Esmond said. 'That's rotten news.'

'Yes,' Cecily agreed. 'We had better start packing.'

'Packing?'

'We've been called for the entail.'

Esmond was still a little fuzzy on the details. He knew that Cecily stood a chance of inheriting a house and piles of money, but that it was rather unlikely because her brother, who had an angel of a wife who was pregnant with his child, lived in the area and was making noises about being an MP, was a shoo-in. Their parents weren't interested, as they lived in India and had no intention of returning, and the cousins were all so utterly feckless that Cecily and her brother were the only real candidates.

A week later, they drove up to the house, Cecily still desperately pregnant but completely unwilling to miss the reading. 'If you miss it, then you don't get the house,' she told Violet. 'I'm not taking any risks with that proxy nonsense.'

Violet had told herself that she would break her news to Cecily before the car journey, but now, here they were, being bounced around in the back of the car, and Violet knew that she was going to have to say it. Esmond was in London and was following by train that evening. This was her window.

'Cecily,' Violet said.

'Yes?'

'I'm afraid I've got to tell you something.'

Cecily looked horrified. 'What? Oh God, not more bad news?'

Violet almost laughed at how impressively non-stoic her employer was. 'It is a little bit bad, I think.'

'You're leaving me?'

It was classic of Cecily to take the wind out of her sails like that. 'Yes,' she said. 'I'm afraid I am.'

Cecily's bottom lip was wobbling but she seemed determined not to give in to it. 'Why?' she asked in a small voice.

Violet had rehearsed her explanation many, many times. 'I just can't be in London any more. I know it's a bit wet, but it's just so loud and busy and I miss the open space and the fresh air. I'm from the country. I need to be back there.'

Cecily's tears disappeared. 'But that's fine! We're not going to be in London any more. We'll get Roxborough, we'll move.'

It was hard to know how to phrase the next question. 'But what if we don't? You. What if you don't?'

Cecily smiled. 'I will.'

They drove on for half an hour or so, neither saying anything. Then, as they reached the turn for Roxborough, Cecily took Violet's hand. 'Is it just about being in London?'

'Yes,' Violet lied.

'So, if we move, you'll stay?'

There was no possible answer to that question other than yes. 'Yes,' she said. 'Of course I will.'

The funeral was a nice one, standing room only at the back. It was reassuring to all the Mordaunts to see how loved their uncle had been. Cecily's parents sent a telegraph from India expressing their deep sadness at being unable to attend, and the rest of the family hosted a neat, unremarkable drinks reception at the house. Then, just as Cecily had always been told there would be, there was a dinner. Letters were handed out. She watched across the table as her brother opened his, his eyes filled with expectation. He almost managed to keep the exact same expression on his face as he skimmed the page and realized he hadn't inherited the house.

Each cousin announced that the house was not theirs until, eventually, Cecily, doing a perfect impression of someone who was surprised, said very quietly, 'It's me. He left it to me.'

Much later that night, when the papers had been signed and everyone had acted as if they thought it was a good thing that spoilt, childlike Cecily had been given the house while privately asking each other what her uncle could possibly have been thinking, Cecily sneaked along the corridor to Violet's room. She knelt on the floor and woke Violet up.

'Violet,' she half whispered.

Violet sat up, shocked to see Cecily in her bedroom, despite the fact she had woken Cecily herself every morning of her married life. She gathered the covers around herself and sat up. 'What?' she asked.

'We got the house!'

Violet smiled. 'How lovely,' she said. 'Your uncle didn't consider your brother the favourite in the end.'

Cecily laughed. 'Oh no, he absolutely did.'

'What?'

'He did. He left the house to him.'

Violet felt sick. 'What?'

'I found the letters when we first got here and I switched them. They hadn't even been personalized! All I had to do was swap the envelopes. No one will ever know.'

'You can't do that.'

'But I did it.'

'That's stealing. You're stealing a house.'

Cecily put her hands on her bump. 'It's for all of us. This way, you'll stay, the baby won't have to grow up in that horrid little house, and everything will be perfect. Why aren't you pleased? This is the best thing that could have happened. Now we can stay together.'

'You're right.' Violet smiled. 'Now I won't have to leave.'

She watched Cecily leave the room, surprisingly graceful for a woman so pregnant, and then tried to breathe in as much of the scent of her as possible. To her own horror, she found her hand between her legs, pressing at the part of her that seemed to cause so much of her trouble. She couldn't leave. Cecily wouldn't let her leave. And now Cecily had committed an enormous crime. That was how much Cecily wanted her to stay. And she couldn't deny Cecily anything. Let alone this. She would just have to live with this exquisite torture. To be grateful for the snatches of Cecily that she was allowed to enjoy.

TWENTY MONTHS LATER

There wasn't a season at Roxborough that Willa didn't love, but spring carried with it a very special type of magic. She woke early, sleeping with the curtains open, just as her grandmother had, so that she woke with the light and lay in her huge white bed, looking out across the valley, watching the mist roll in. The light was warm and yellow, dappled in places. The trees were soft again with blossom after a winter of hard spindles. There was nowhere else in the world that she wanted to be.

People often asked her if it felt strange to live at Roxborough alone. But she was so rarely alone she didn't know how to answer. There was always someone from the village there to discuss some issue, a tenant who wanted something, a local wanting to see around the inside of the big house. And she had started, very tentatively, to make friends. A couple about her age who had left London to open a shop on the high street. A friend of Jonty's who lived down the road and liked to occasionally share a bottle of wine. The farrier who came to shoe the horses twice a year. It wasn't finished, but she had started to build something here, something she loved very much.

And there was work, too. She had set herself up locally as a solicitor. Nothing taxing; mostly just land disputes and, ironically, wills. She probably did as much work in a month as she had done in a couple of days back in London. But she kept her prices low, and she liked helping people.

She had helped the others, too. Combing through the Roxborough records, she had realized that almost everyone who had inherited the house had felt guilty, because all of them had done things to appease the others, those who hadn't been given the house. In previous generations, it had been gifts of cottages in the grounds, or a living as the vicar at the local church. After weeks of reflection, and with help from Rihan, who seemed to know absolutely everything about property law and who spent rather more time with Willa than perhaps was strictly necessary, she had worked out what she thought would be best for everybody. Sometimes Rihan stayed into the evening and they shared a bottle of wine. Sometimes he even stayed the night.

She sold two large fields at the bottom of the estate, far away from anyone else, to property developers, who had signed dozens of pieces of paper committing to building affordable housing. The village needed more houses far more than Willa needed an additional ten acres on top of the two hundred she already owned. She gave the money from the sale to her father. She had half expected him to refuse it. It was only when he didn't that she realized quite how bad things must have become for him. He was grateful in a way that made her feel both guilty and sad. But she reminded herself that there had once been a possibility of Bryony ruling the roost at Roxborough, turning the dining room into a staff room and the nursery into a dormitory, and she managed not to feel quite so bad. Her only real concession to Bryony was that she had a state-of-the-art football goal put on the croquet lawn. She had Facetimed Lucca to show him and he had announced that 'maybe it won't be so boring now'.

She had given Grant permission to trial his glamping business in the woods during the summer. She wasn't entirely sure that he would get around to it, as he seemed to prefer to talk about ideas rather than actually put them into practice. But he seemed mollified, and if he did decide to go ahead with it, it might be rather exciting. He was currently rather busy, as Angelique had moved back to France without giving Grant a second look, and he was now embroiled with an even younger and even more beautiful Italian woman.

It had been hard to know what to offer Elspeth to make amends until she had found an enormous box in the attic filled with everything that she had left behind in her bedroom. Records, diaries, photographs and letters. She had shipped it to Elspeth without giving her a chance to refuse and, weeks later, Elspeth had sent a short email of thanks, clearly more touched than she knew how to explain. She had turned down Willa's invitation to come for Christmas but mentioned that she might come back to the UK the following year, and would perhaps want somewhere to stay. Jonty had stayed with her for a couple of weeks earlier in the year.

Jonty hadn't wanted anything. She'd offered him space to keep a horse there, saying there was plenty of money for a groom and that he wouldn't have to visit all that often. He'd been grateful but had turned her down. He had told Willa, very calmly, that he had decided to cut ties with the family for now. It was ironic, he had half laughed on the phone. All those years wishing he were a blood relative, feeling just a little outside of the family. And now he knew he was so completely related to all of them, all he wanted was to get away.

Lizzie had been the hardest person to appease. Willa had found it almost impossible to shake off the feeling that had settled when she saw Lizzie's face, broken by the news that she hadn't inherited the house. In the end, she had settled on a simple gift. She had given Lizzie her own set of keys to the front door. And without having to explain, it meant that the house was sort of Lizzie's too.

Willa's anorexia hadn't disappeared, because it never would. She still attended a weekly therapy session, in Norwich, and she had the knowledge that the centre was there if she needed it, as it probably always would be. But she had entrenched herself in the process of growing food at Roxborough, helping to pull little waxy potatoes from the earth or snip purple beans from their stems. Slowly, she was finding ways to feel a little more at ease within her body. She wasn't one of life's naturally happy people, she knew that. But for the first time in her life, she had found something just as valuable – a calm kind of contentment.

There was still guilt. Willa assumed there always would be. She had stolen something that should have been impossible to steal. But sometimes, when she wandered in the garden in the early evening, breathing in the scent of the flowers planted by her grandmother and the trees planted by her great-great-grandmother, she was able to find a sort of compromise within herself. Her grand-mother had left the house to whoever was most desperate for it. Whoever was willing to do something objectively terrible to make it theirs. Cecily had wanted the house to belong to the person who wanted it the most. And, in these quiet moments, Willa would admit to herself that that person was her. She was the only one who wouldn't have sold the house, or changed the way it was run. She was the only one who really cared enough to make sure that everyone who worked at Roxborough still had a job, that they ran it in the greenest, most efficient way they could manage, until it was time for her to pass on the house again. Which, in spite of everything she had learned, she knew she would do in the same way that generations before her had done.

Violet hadn't wanted to stay, in the end. She had watched quietly as Willa set everything up, offering advice when Willa asked for it but never interfering. And then, after about a year, she told Willa that she had bought a little cottage by the sea and that she was moving. No amount of argument from Willa could convince her otherwise. So instead, they had settled on Willa coming for tea once a week. They both liked it, because for both of them it was a chance to see a little bit of Cecily reflected back at them.

They rarely talked about what Willa had done, or what Violet had helped her to do. There was no sense in reliving it, and neither of them took any pride in what had taken place. But when Violet watched Willa, brown and smiling, her hair streaked with blonde from the sun, her limbs less hollow than they had been, walking away down the path to her house, getting into her little car and driving back to Roxborough, all the while surrounded by an aura of calm that had previously been a sad, nervous energy, she knew that Cecily had done the right thing.

ACKNOWLEDGEMENTS

The first port of call on thank yous for *The Will* has to go to Alice Rodgers, who inherited the book upon joining Transworld and who then had the unenviable task of untangling all of the dates and ages that I had confused throughout the book. I am beyond appreciative of her work. It transpires that I am a great deal better with words than I am with numbers.

The next must go to my agent Eve White, who is a continued source of support, wisdom and all general brilliance, as is her first agent Ludo Cinelli. Eve signed me up in my very early twenties, taught me how to write a book, and then taught me how to have a career. I am very lucky to have her in my corner.

I would also like to thank Transworld for publishing four of my novels, and for allowing me to write *The Will* with such complete freedom. I decided to write a book that I would love to read, and I'm very proud of how it turned out.

Lots of the settings in *The Will* (though thankfully not the awful bits) were lifted from my real-life family, especially my grandmother, who I still miss a great deal. While we're happily not as dysfunctional as the Mordaunts, and there certainly isn't a stately home to inherit, the Reids and the Sillars formed the basis of what it means to be a family who love each other, even in slightly complicated ways. So, thank you for that.

The obligatory list of thank yous: Tim, Charlotte, Lucy, George, Marcus, Steph, Felicity, Madeleine, the Oakfield girls, the Mayfield girls, the Metro girls, Chloe & the Reynolds, Emma, Jon all invaluable.

And the final thanks must go to someone who isn't quite a someone yet – my daughter, who is due to be born a little while before this book is published. While nothing is ever for sure in pregnancy, and I know all too well that you can't count your chickens until they are hatched, the book is dedicated to her and it would feel wrong not to acknowledge her part in its creation. Admittedly her main contribution was to make me too tired/ sick/emotional to want to write, but technically we did the latter part of the book together, and she has already changed my life. So thank you, Pom (not her real name – I promise). This one's for you.

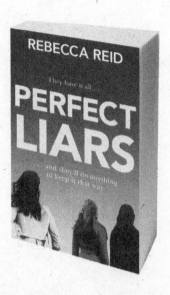

Sixteen years ago, best friends Nancy, Georgia and
Lila did something unspeakable. Their crime forged
an unbreakable bond between them, a bond of
silence. But now, one of them wants to talk.

One wrong word and everything could be ruined: their lives,
their careers, their relationships. It's up to Georgia to call a
crisis dinner. But things do not go as planned.

Three women walk in to the dinner, but only two will leave.

Murder isn't so difficult the second time around . . .

★★★★★

Available in paperback and ebook

What is more dangerous, a secret or a lie?

When Poppy meets Drew, she's at rock bottom: broke, jobless and with nowhere to live. So when he proposes after a whirlwind romance, she says yes – even though he has suggested they don't tell each other anything about their lives before they met.

It's unconventional, but it suits Poppy's needs perfectly. Because Poppy has a secret – and she isn't so sure Drew would still want to marry her if he knew the truth.

But, of course, this is a two-way deal – and Drew has secrets of his own. But surely they can't be worse than what Poppy's hiding . . .

*****

Available in paperback and ebook

How far would you go to correct your worst mistake?

When Chloe goes to university and meets wild, carefree
Zadie, she is utterly seduced by her and her lifestyle. It
doesn't take long for Chloe to ditch her studies in favour
of all-night parties at Zadie's huge house off campus.

But when something goes badly wrong one night and
Zadie disappears in the aftermath, Chloe knows she
should have done more to help her friend. It's
something she'll always regret.

Fifteen years later, Chloe finally gets the chance to
make it right. But in order to do so, she'll have to put
everything at stake . . .

★★★★★

Available in paperback and ebook

dead good

Looking for more gripping must-reads?

Head over to Dead Good –
the home of killer crime books,
TV and film.

Whether you're on the hunt for an intriguing
mystery, an action-packed thriller
or a creepy psychological drama,
we're here to keep you in the loop.

Get recommendations and reviews from
crime fans, grab discounted books at bargain
prices and enter exclusive giveaways
for the chance to read brand-new releases
before they hit the shelves.

Sign up for the free newsletter:
www.deadgoodbooks.co.uk/newsletter